Wiley Royce

LM Foster

This is a work of fiction. Names, characters, places and incidents are products of the author's imagination. Any resemblance to actual events, locales, organizations, or persons, either living or dead, is entirely coincidental.

9th Street Press
www.9thstreetpress.com

"And above all, watch with glittering eyes the whole world around you because the greatest secrets are always hidden in the most unlikely places." – Roald Dahl

NATE

"You shouldn't've said that about my sister, Chumley," Neal said, and shoved the dark-haired kid against the bricks. His backpack dropped to the ground.

"Ah, so you're gonna kick my ass now, Neal?" Wiley, whose name wasn't Chumley at all, grinned brilliantly. I thought that some of his nice white teeth were gonna wind up in the dirt before long. "Because your sister's a slut?"

"My sister's a slut because she turned you down?"

"You know the difference between a slut and a bitch, Neal?" Wiley asked, still grinning. Unafraid. I wondered if he was really as fearless as he pretended, or if he was just dumb. "A slut gives it to everybody. A bitch gives it to everybody but you."

"So now you're saying she's a bitch, too, Wiley? You're not the sharpest tool in the shed, are you?"

I had to agree with Neal. Wiley was about to get his ass handed to him, and for what?

"Better men than you have said so," Wiley agreed, still smiling.

I was standing a few feet behind them, observing. It wasn't really any of my business – I wasn't a crusader, out to save the downtrodden of our little high school from bullies, or anything like that. It was true that Neal was a bully, but Wiley wasn't a little wormy weakling about to lose his lunch money.

Neal was the star-center of our school's football team, destined for college immortality, and perhaps even NFL greatness. I used to be part of his crowd, used to be on the team with him. I'd been a wideout, not a star by any means, but I did well enough, had made my share of touchdowns. I almost always started.

Two days before practice was supposed to begin in August, I broke my hand. It was at a party at Neal's house, as a matter of fact. Some other stupid shit that wasn't my business either, any more than this was. Some other guy I didn't know, any more than I knew Wiley.

Everyone was standing around by the pool and this guy next to me suddenly slapped his girlfriend, out of the clear blue sky. I hadn't heard any arguing; just the rifle-shot sound of his palm hitting her cheek, and the splash as she went into the pool.

I said, "What the fuck?" in surprise, and the guy whirled on me.

"You want some, too?" he said. It would've been to his benefit if he would've waited for an answer, because like I say, I'm no crusader. I didn't know him or his girlfriend. Don't get me wrong, I would've stopped him if he tried to hit her again, but the damage from this one was already done, and she was safe enough in the pool for the moment.

But he didn't wait for me to say that I didn't want any. Instead he just swung. But he was drunk, and probably not much of a fighter anyway, since he liked to hit girls. I blocked his punch and nailed him in the chin. He went backwards into the pool, and he would've drowned had Neal not fished him out, because I'd knocked him out cold, and broke his jaw.

Unfortunately, I'd also broken my hand. The long, apparently delicate bone that ran from the knuckle of my ring finger to the wrist had snapped in half like a chop-stick, according to the x-ray. There was surgery, and a cast and a pin that stuck out of the end of my knuckle. They put a little green soft thing on the end of it, so I didn't snag it on anything; to protect it in case I accidently bumped it. I made sure not to bump it.

I went to football practice anyway. The coach shook his head and told me to sit on the bench in the heat with the other losers. Then when practice was over, he told me to come see him in his office.

"You're about a dumb ass, you know that, Osbourne?" Even though I hadn't told him how it happened, he knew anyway.

I nodded. "They say six or eight weeks, Coach. Then I'll be good as new."

Coach shook his head. "It's never gonna be good as new, son. Those kinda things never are." He paused, shuffled a few papers on his desk. "I'm gonna suggest something to you, and I want you to hear me out." I nodded, and he continued. "You know you're not any kind of scholarship material," he said gently. "You would've heard from them by now." I nodded again, because it was true. I hadn't even hoped for it.

"Maybe you can play ball in college, but . . ." He shrugged. "It's not gonna pay your way through. I know you know all this, and I'm sure you've thought of something else to do with your life besides athletics."

I hadn't thought a whole lot about what I was going to do with my life. But he was right. I knew it wasn't going to involve too much more football.

"So this is what I'm gonna suggest to you. I'm gonna suggest that you quit the team. Let that hand heal up completely, as much as it's ever going to. Forget about football for this year. You can always try out again when you start college. If you stay on the team now, you're just gonna ride the bench for the next three months, and by then you'll be rusty. Simpson is rarin' to take your place, and he actually has some potential."

"Are you cutting me, Coach?"

"No, not at all, Osbourne." He came around his desk and clapped me on the shoulder, and it vibrated down my arm and out through the pin in my hand, ending in a burst of pure electric pain that made me grit my teeth. "I'm just offering you my best advice."

"Can I think about it for a few days?"

"Of course."

And I thought about it, and I talked to my dad about it, and in the end I took Coach's advice. I quit the team, and after a few weeks, I discovered that I didn't miss playing football. Not one little bit. I'd been getting my bell rung since Pop Warner, and it was truly nice that it had finally stopped.

What I did miss, however, were all the little perks that come with a starter's life, even in high school. Wistful male teachers, thinking of their own glory days, now long past, ceased to slap me on the back and tell me I'd had a great game. Freshman hopefuls didn't look at me with awe. But worst of all, my girlfriend Judy dumped me. She was head cheerleader, and she surely couldn't be seen about town with a non-team cripple. Not three days after I quit the team, Judy was dry-eyed, annoyed, when she said, "I'm sorry, Nate." She wasn't sorry at all. "This just isn't working out." I didn't even get a consolation blow job.

While it was true that I didn't miss get tackled on the field by friends and enemies whose main aim was to hurt me, I did miss getting tackled by Judy, in her soft bed, when her parents weren't home. She aimed to hurt me too, but it was that good hurt. Judy was spectacular in the ways and means of such things, and all the hurts on the field were worth it, just because she took so much delight in kissing them all away.

3

The cast came off, and they took the pin out of my hand, and it seems like it really is good as new, although there is a little twinge of pain sometimes. I don't miss playing ball, but ever since school started in this, my senior year – that last year of high school, the one your parents are always so nostalgic about – I've found that I've gone from moderately Big Man on Campus to just another nobody. Judy dumped me, and Neal and all my other teammates don't give me the time of day any more. They go out of their way, as a matter of fact, to call me *fag* and *chickenshit* and *quitter* and *loser.* So much for the understanding of my peers.

Fuck 'em, I thought frequently. They're all assholes anyway. I'd never really liked any of them – you can't pick your teammates – and it was okay to be by myself. I wasn't missing anything but getting my head kicked. How many more times did I want to get knocked into the dirt, anyway? Like Coach said, there was only a thin chance that I'd even make a college team, and nothing after that. How many more drunken parties did I really need to attend? How many more times did I have to let Judy gnaw on me like a chew toy? Well . . . I did miss that. Being by myself was really okay, most of the time. But I did miss that.

Now I was again sticking my nose in where it didn't belong, about to watch Neal whip Wiley's ass. Like I say, Neal was a bully, but Wiley wasn't a little wormy guy, born to be a victim. Well, that wasn't entirely true. Wiley was kinda wormy – he was supposed to be some kind of electronics genius, and if that wasn't enough to make him bully-bait, he also had a mouth on him, and his derision was universal. He said smart-assed things about everyone, big, tall, and small. It didn't matter to Wiley. He never missed an opportunity to comment on the inadequacies and clumsinesses of our peers, while any insults to himself he took in stride with nothing but that constant grin. The rude shit he said about our lovely female friends would turn fathers – and in this case, brothers – into vengeful brutes, and make mothers blush in shame.

But Wiley was by no means a little guy – while maybe not as buff and ripped as Neal, who had a neck like a bull – he was just as tall, and leaner, and muscular enough. I imagined he'd be quite a sight quicker than Neal, if he knew how to fight at all, which I doubted.

But like I say, I wasn't there to save him. I didn't even know him. I'd just been on my way to lunch, and had cut across there behind the gym. I'd heard Neal threaten Wiley's life in Government

4

– the whole class had heard him, just like the whole class had heard Wiley's remark that Neal's sister Bev was like a shotgun – give her a cock and she was ready to blow. Everyone had roared at that one.

"You're gonna die, Wiley," Neal had growled when the laughter died down.

"Tell me something I don't already know, Fat Boy," Wiley had returned with a grin.

Mr. Jackson, who was a hard-ass in his own right, entered the classroom, and everybody turned to the front and pretended that they cared about what he was going to say today about the legislative, the judicial, and the executive. Neal gave the still smiling Wiley another threatening look, then did likewise.

So I wasn't really looking for them, there behind the gym. I was just minding my own business, cutting through to go on to the cafeteria for lunch. But I wasn't surprised to find them there, either, and as I'm always amused by a good fight, I paused to watch. But then my other old teammates, Ed and Lyle, sauntered up, and now it didn't look like it was gonna be such a good fight, after all. It was gonna be an assassination.

"Ah," Wiley said when he saw them, "I see you've invited your sister's boyfriends to the party."

Neal looked over his shoulder at his friends, who suddenly looked at their feet, then back at Wiley. "What the fuck are you talking about?"

"I've got pictures, Neal," Wiley said. "I was just about to send 'em out. From Hilda's party last weekend. You wanna see?"

"You weren't at Hilda's party," Lyle said, still looking guilty. "Nobody ever invites you to anything."

"I've got pictures, nonetheless," Wiley said.

"I'm gonna kill you," Neal reiterated.

"You talk too much, Neal," Ed said. He stepped forward and swung on Wiley. Wiley ducked the punch, but Lyle caught him and held him, while Neal punched him viciously in the mouth. Then Ed socked him in the gut, doubling him over, and Lyle dropped him to the ground.

Neal cocked back his foot, aiming to kick Wiley in the head, and I said, "Hey." I set my backpack down when they all looked at me. "It takes three of you tough guys to shut up one lippy asshole? I hear your sister takes 'em on three at a time, Neal, but seriously? You need two of her boyfriends to help you take care of this?" I grinned.

5

Neal roared in surprised outrage, and swung on me. I dodged like Wiley had done, but his punch still hit me squarely in the chest. I heard a crunch as he connected with my phone, which was in my pocket, and I said, "Goddamn, Neal, now you're attacking defenseless cellphones?"

I swung the ol' haymaker and it landed on his eyebrow, and yes, ladies and gentlemen, it hurt like a bitch, but he dropped to his knees. I just had time to shake my hand and look at the blood and flap of skin hanging from my knuckles, and hope to Christ I hadn't broken again, and over what? when Lyle shoved me. I staggered backwards, and he punched me in the chin. But it was a weak shot, and I didn't go down.

"I'd heard you'd gone homo since you quit the team," Lyle said. "Is this skinny kid your new boyfriend?"

"This isn't even your fight, Lyle," I said. I smiled, and nodded behind him. "I hear you got yours from Bev, just like Ed did."

"Now you're gonna get yours, Nate," he told me, and took a step forward.

"I don't think so, Lover-boy," I said, as Wiley deftly tripped him, and he went down, his face landing in a fresh pile of dirt thrown up by some gopher. Realizing he was outmatched, he stayed down.

While I'd been dealing with Neal and Lyle, Ed had been looking on, not paying attention to Wiley, doubled over on the ground. Wiley had taken advantage of his inattention, had in fact jumped up and dropped Ed's glass-jawed ass like a bad habit, then proceeded to trip Lyle before he could hit me again.

With all of them laid out, if only temporarily, Wiley picked up his backpack. He clapped me on the shoulder and said, "Thanks for saving my life, pal. What's your name again?" He held out his hand.

I introduced myself, and shook his hand.

"I'm —"

"I know who you are, Wiley," I said. "You're an asshole."

"Better men than you have said so." He grinned, and his teeth were pink with blood.

I picked up my own backpack, and we walked away toward the cafeteria, without a backward glance. "You had it coming, you know," I told him. "Why'd you say that about Bev?"

"It was just like Neal said," Wiley told me. "She turned me down. She was standing there with Deneen and Bobbi, and I said, 'Ladies! Was it love at first sight, or should I walk by again?'

"'And then you woke up, Chumley,' Bev said. I hadn't expected any of them to answer me. But hearing words come out Bev's talented mouth, directed at me, made me feel all froggy, so I decided to jump."

"How do you know she's got a talented mouth?" I asked. Although he wasn't a bad-looking guy, especially for an electronics geek, I hadn't heard of Wiley ever having a date. Not since he'd moved here. The girls didn't like him. He was just too insulting.

"Ah, I've got pictures," he told me. "Courtesy of Ed back there."

"Ed sent *you* pictures?"

Wiley grinned. "Something like that."

I wanted to hear the rest of this story, so I asked him, "You said Bev made you feel froggy?"

Wiley walked around some kid coming out of the cafeteria, who stared at the blood on his face for a second, then quickly scuttled away. He grinned at me again. "Yeah. So I jumped. I said, 'You can come a little closer to me, Beverly, my dearest, as long as you don't complain about the heat.'

"Deneen giggled, and Bev said, 'I wouldn't come closer to you if you were the last man on earth.'

"I said, 'Why don't you lie down then? I'll tell you I love you. I hear that's all it takes.' She stopped smiling then and stalked away. I said to Deneen, 'How am I doin' so far?' She blushed, and taking Bobbi by the arm, they started off down the hall. I called after them, 'You girls wanna fuck, or should I apologize?'"

"Jesus, Wiley," I said. "Why do you talk to them like that?"

He shrugged, still grinning. "Why not? It's what they all want, my son, and if you don't believe that, I've got some beachfront land in Fontana for you." Fontana is not on the coast. "They're not blushing innocents, Nate. They have appetites, just like we do. You should hear the things they say about us."

We found a table and dug around in our backpacks for our lunches in silence for a minute. Wiley set a brown bag on the table, then extracted a yellow handkerchief and held it to his bleeding mouth. I noticed that there was already dried blood on it. I said, "Not your first fight, Wiley?"

He looked at the handkerchief. "First this week," he replied. There were three almost perfectly round places over his knuckles where the skin was missing, caused by contact with Ed's delicate jaw. They were already starting to scab over.

I gingerly flexed my hand. It hurt like a mother, but it wasn't broken again. Wiley looked over at my shredded knuckles, then handed the handkerchief to me. I wrapped it around my hand, then unwrapped my sandwich, left handed, so I wouldn't get any blood on it. I took a bite and asked him, "What's your deal, anyway?"

Wiley grinned yet again, this time around a mouthful of his own sandwich. "You know those people that think they're smarter than everybody else? Those people that consider themselves worldly and wise? The ones that think they're above the petty intrigues of our wondrous high school life?" He gestured at the crowded tables around us. "Better than the jocks and tramps and dopers?" I nodded. He tossed his sandwich on the table. There was blood on the brown bread and between the seeds in the crust. "Well, I'm one of those guys."

I ate the rest of my sandwich, then asked, "But why is that, Wiley? What's so special about you? You haven't got a friend to your name that I can see – you're always by yourself. And there's not a girl that I know of that would go out with you –"

"These girls!" he said and picked up his bloody sandwich again. "They parade around here like they're all supermodels, like they've got something that we'd all give our front seat in hell for! Like they've got something that they don't give away every weekend to guys like Neal and Lyle and Ed for a beer or a line of coke!"

"You don't like girls, Wiley?" I asked.

His grin widened. "Don't you like girls, Nate? Is it true what Lyle said – have you gone homo since you quit the team? Is that why you're talking to me? Is that why you saved my ass? Think I'll be grateful, do you?" He wiggled his eyebrows at me.

"I like girls, Wiley," I said. "I surely treat 'em nicer than you do. And I only saved your ass because it wasn't gonna be a fair fight."

"The fair comes to town once a year, Nate," he said, and took another bite from his sandwich. "And don't think I'm not grateful to you for saving my ass. But I'm not gonna suck your dick for it."

I shook my head. "You're a piece of work, you know that?"

"What a piece of work is a man! How noble in reason! How infinite in faculty!" Wiley paused to see if I'd get the reference, and when I didn't, he shook his head.

"But why did you talk shit about Bev with Neal standing right there? Are you too dumb to know that he'd want to fight you behind it?"

"I just told you, Nate. I'm not dumb."

"But why would you want to get your ass beat over nothing?"

Wiley shrugged. "I wouldn't have gotten my ass beat. Neal's big, but he's slow. I'm in a lot better shape than him. It would've been fun. I need the exercise. The occasional fight keeps ya focused, alert, tip-top. Sometimes, ya gotta remind the sheep who the rancher is.

"Neal was pissed, like a big, dumb bear. You fight when you're pissed, you lose half your advantage, Nate. I would've held my own, if the odds hadn't suddenly changed."

"Seriously, Wiley," I said. "What makes you think you're better than the rest of us?"

"What makes you wanna hear my life story, Nate? You don't even know me."

I glanced across the cafeteria, and noted Neal, Lyle, and Ed, standing just inside the door, just as bloody and dusty as we were. They were talking to a few other guys from the team, one of which turned and glowered in our direction. I used to think these guys were my friends, but I didn't think so any more. They considered me a quitter, even before this fight. Now I'd given them another excuse to hate me.

I said, "I've just made some fairly bad-assed enemies on your behalf, Wiley. I'm gonna be looking over my shoulder for the rest of the year. Let's just say, I'd like to know a little more about the guy I've gotten myself into it all for."

Wiley looked at me in surprise, then followed my gaze across the cafeteria. He waved at Neal and his crew. They didn't wave back. Wiley said to me, "Don't worry about them. They lost."

"And because they lost, I don't think they'll forget about this shit all that quickly."

Again Wiley shrugged. "Fuck 'em if they can't take a joke. But if you're scared, I'll watch your back."

"I don't know if I want you watching my back, Wiley. You seem like the type that's always getting into this kind of stupid scrape. I think you enjoy it."

"I do."

"I think you're –"

"Mad, bad, and dangerous to know?" He grinned in delight, and again waited for me to get the reference. "Lord Bryon, Nate. The poet. That's what they said about him."

"You're no poet, Wiley." I said, still watching my fresh enemies across the room.

"You might be surprised."

I shook my head. "I doubt it. You're a son of a bitch."

"Ah, don't blame it on my mother, Nate," he said. "She's a grand ol' gal."

My phone rang, and I took it out of my pocket. The screen was starred, splintered, from where Neal's fist had connected with it. I tried to answer the call anyway, even though I couldn't tell who was calling. The touchscreen didn't respond. "Fuck," I said.

"Lemme see it," Wiley said. I handed the worthless phone to him.

He examined it for a moment. "How delicate these are," he commented. "Yet how we do depend on them."

"You're not supposed to let 'em get punched," I said. I looked inside my shirt, and discovered a square, iPhone-shaped bruise forming on my chest. *"Fuck!"* I said again.

"Come over to my house after school," Wiley said. Again he smiled, and I wondered how he could keep doing it, as his mouth was swollen and shredded on one side. "I'll fix this for you. Free of charge. It's the least I can do. I owe you."

"You can fix it?" I asked in disbelief, daring to hope. The damn phone was almost brand-new, it wasn't insured against getting punched, and I surely didn't have the money for another one.

Wiley closed one eye and squinted at me, what I'd discover passed for a wink with him. "I can fix damn near anything, Nate. Anything electronic, that is." The bell rang and he rose, and he told me where he lived. "Come on by. You'll be amazed, I promise you."

****

I was surprised to discover that Wiley lived only a few blocks from me. I walked over to his house, and seeing the beat-to-shit, ancient Prius he drove parked out front, I knew I had the right house. I walked up the three steeps, crossed the porch and knocked on the door.

"Entrez-vous," Wiley said, and I walked into a neat living room. Just like in everybody else's house, it was dominated by a big-screen television. But Wiley wasn't watching it, because it wasn't on. It was kinda odd to see the blank black screen, because the TV was almost always on at my house, and everywhere else. Wiley set a

10

thick book down on the table next to him, and leapt up from the recliner he was sitting in, gracefully, like a big, black cat. I noticed he was barefoot, though it was only April. "Come with me. I live in the garret, like Claudin."

"Who?" I asked.

Wiley opened a door off the living room, and started up a dark staircase.

"You're a Philistine, Nate, truly. Just like everybody else."

"A what?"

"All you people have the attention span of a housefly," he said. "No culture. No history. Like my dad says, *they're gonna take over this country without firing a shot.*" He opened the door at the top of the stairs and flipped on the lights. "Have you ever seen any black and white movies? Listened to any old music?"

"I'm not into that ancient shit, Wiley."

"What about books? Have you ever read anything? Anything at all?" I shrugged, and Wiley sighed. "Let's see that phone." I took it out of my pocket and handed it to him. He pointed to a chair and commanded, "Sit. Don't touch anything."

I sat, and looked around the room. It was painted a somewhat institutional shade of green. A fairly high ceiling sloped up to a peak, and had a skylight in it: we were directly under the roof. The two short walls were only about five feet tall, and there was a wide, four-rung stepladder leaning against one of them. The rest of the short walls were lined with bookshelves, overflowing with books.

Against the wall with the door in it was Wiley's rumpled bed, and next to that was an old wooden desk. Between them was a pile of dirty laundry. On top of the desk was an ancient desk top computer, and a closed laptop, and a busted tablet, and the innards and out-tards of uncountable cellphones. On the wall opposite hung a television, about a forty-incher. Beneath it was another desk, holding an open laptop and an intact tablet and several green circuit boards, and the guts of more cellphones and other electronics.

Wiley sat in a chair in front of the desk beneath the television. He set my phone down on it, then dug around in a drawer for a minute. Then he rolled over across the bare wooden floor to the other desk and found a selection of small screwdrivers. He rolled back across the room, and started working on my phone.

"So if it's not 'cause you suddenly couldn't help yourself in the locker room, why *did* you quit the team?" He unscrewed the two screws next to the charging port, then rooted around in a drawer again. He removed a plastic suction cup and a little plastic chisel-looking stylus thing, like an artist might use to sculpt clay with.

I looked at my freshly busted knuckles. Neal's eyebrow had neatly scraped the skin off of all four of them. I tugged at a tiny piece of hair stuck in the scab, and wondered if it was his or mine.

"I punched a guy at a party last summer."

Wiley's own eyebrows went up in surprise. He stuck the suction cup on the shattered front of my phone and began working the stylus back and forth along the edge, then gently lifted the top of the phone up. "Did he have it comin', like I did? Were you championing some other whore's honor?"

"Whores do it for money, Wiley. Bev doesn't even charge." He looked up and I grinned at him. "This guy hit his girlfriend. I don't know what the fight was about, but he smacked her and she fell in the pool. Then he felt frisky like a bunny, and like you said, he jumped, and I knocked *him* into the pool. I also knocked him out and broke his jaw." I grinned a little in satisfaction. This story got better every time I told it.

Wiley loosened the three screws that held the ribbon connector that ran between the top and the bottom of the phone.

"So they kicked you off the team for that? For punching some asshole that really did have it coming?" He took off a bracket, then popped the flex cables off with the plastic stylus, released my phone's shattered screen and set the bottom part down on the desk.

"No, Wiley. They didn't kick me off the team. I quit."

He tossed the screen into an open drawer, then rolled the chair back across the room to the other desk, and began searching through the various bits of electronic junk on top of it.

He shook his head. "And why was that again?"

I sighed. "When I punched this guy, I broke this bone, right here." I tapped at where it was under the skin, just below my scabbed over knuckles. "There was an operation. There was a pin. I was never going to be Heisman material anyway, so the coach recommended I quit, and let my hand heal up."

Wiley was still moving stuff around, looking under it and behind it. "When did you say this happened?"

"August."

"You broke your hand . . ." he counted on his fingers, ". . . eight months ago? And you just punched Neal? For me? You're a few colors short of a rainbow, aren't you?"

"Fuck you, Wiley," I told him. "I wasn't gonna stand there and let those three assholes kill you, even if you did have it coming."

"That was really nice of you, Nate." Wiley stopped rummaging and stared at me for the space of probably fifteen seconds. "I haven't noticed a lot of real kindness in this world – people are always out to see what they can get, it's always seemed to me. Just like Holden Caulfield, most people have always struck me as phonies. So when someone does something nice for me, I'm genuinely touched. You have my sincerest thanks."

"You have my sincerest welcome, Wiley, but I'm not gonna kiss you." I grinned at him. "Why haven't you got my phone fixed yet?"

He went back to pawing through the stuff on the desk. "Shit," he said after a minute. "I don't have a screen for this." I looked in horror at my phone, busted before, but now busted and in two pieces, one across the room from the other. I was about to object, whine that he said he could fix it, when he held up a finger. "Hold on a second. I know a guy."

Wiley took his own phone out of his pocket, pushed a button. "Bradley, my nearest and dearest! Would you happen to have any –" and he told Bradley the model of my iPhone. "Excellent. Say, twenty minutes? I'm gonna bring my friend Nate with me, if that's all right with you." Wiley paused and squinted at me. "No, he's cool. I'll vouch for him." He hung up and said, "He's got one. Let's go."

As Wiley drove, he said, "Know any drug dealers, do you, Nate?"

I did not, but since he was doing me a favor, I thought I could talk to some people at school who might know some other people, and so on, so I said, "What're you looking for, Wiley?"

"Ever heard of mephedrone?" I shook my head. "How about Meow?"

I'd heard of Meow, the way you hear about heroin: that it was deadly, the very Devil. They warned us about it in Health class – it was supposed to be some kind of hideous, horrible compound that turned you into a raving, homicidal, delusional, sometimes cannibalistic psychopath, if you didn't die from a heart attack first. Like all warnings from Health class, I considered the descriptions to be overblown. Why would anyone risk all these side effects, just for some kind of temporary high? But then I wasn't a druggie; or even much of a drinker, past the occasional beer at a party.

"You do Meow, Wiley?" I asked in surprise.

13

"Me?" He mirrored my surprise. "Not me, Nate. I'm a drug virgin. I've never even smoked pot. I don't want to dull my senses in any way."

I shrugged. "They say that Meow enhances your senses."

"That's what they say about all that shit, and the first time's always free. Have you done it?"

I shook my head. "I've smoked a little pot, once upon a time. There was this girl –"

"There always is."

"And I got high with her a few times. But that's about it." I looked at him curiously. "If you're not looking for it, then why do you ask if I know any dealers?"

"My good friend Bradley deals Meow. He's also dabbles in stolen goods." Wiley grinned at my no doubt shocked expression. "I met Bradley at *Radio Shack,* of all innocuous places, not long after we moved back here. You know the recliner in the living room?" I nodded. "My dad closed it on the charger to his brand new tablet. Shredded the insulation on the cord all to shit. I would've just put some tape on it, but Dad's not the type to go around with a taped-up anything, so he asked me to stop by the *Shack* and pick him up a new charger.

"I saw Bradley in there, looking as out of place in an electronics store as a redheaded stepchild at a family reunion. You'll see what I mean when you meet him. He was looking at security cameras, and asking the salesman dumb questions. I listened to the guy's line, which was going right over Bradley's head. When he stepped into the back to retrieve some overpriced piece of shit, I said to Bradley, 'This guy's cheating you.'

"Bradley turned around and frowned menacingly at me. *I am sincerely a bad-ass,* his look said. He asked me, 'Do I know you?'

"What did I care if he was a bad-ass? What was he going to do, cut me in the *Radio Shack?* I said, 'No, but you don't know him either, and you're gonna give him too much money for not much surveillance. And he's gonna need your name and your address to sell it to you, and he's gonna keep a record of what it is you paid too much for, on that fine little inventory-keeping cash register there. You obviously have something you want to protect – do you really want every minimum-wage geekball that works here knowing all your business?'

"'You don't know anything about my business,' he said.

14

"'True. Nor do I care. But I know a little bit about surveillance systems –' I really didn't, Nate. Not more than I'd read, but electronics is electronics, and anything I didn't know, I could figure out. 'And I work cheap,' I told him.

"'I don't even know you, kid,' he said, 'and I know you don't know me. And I'm suspicious as fuck of kindly strangers just walking up and offering to help me out. How do I know *you* won't rob me?'

"I told him that he didn't know that I wouldn't rob him, but I knew for sure that the *Radio Shack* guy was robbing him. 'I don't care what you're trying to protect,' I said. 'I don't even have to see it. But I know I can set you up better than this guy, and cheaper, and I'm not going to put your name and address into a database that has no security of its own.' I nodded at the cash register.

"'Why do you think I'd trust you?' he said.

"'Why're you gonna trust him?'

"'Okay,' he said. 'Let's step outside and talk about it.'

"I bought Dad's new charger and went outside with Bradley. He asked me a million questions – how old I was, where I went to school, where I lived, how I knew about surveillance and security, like it was some kind of fucking job application. He must've liked what I said, because he brought me to his house, and I set him up with a cool system. We paid for it all in cash. No one steps foot on Bradley's property without him knowing about it; no room in his house is too private for his watchful eye."

Wiley had taken us to Arlanza, to some nameless backstreet. I looked at the house: the place was in need of a paint job – it might've been blue once, but the color had faded to an oxidized white. The grass in the front yard was dead. There were bars on the windows.

"If your security is so good, why does he need bars?"

"Look around you, Nate. But I recommend you don't make eye contact with anybody sitting on their porch. This isn't the best neighborhood. The bars came with the place. And some people – law enforcement, perhaps – might insist on coming in someday, anyway. The bars are to allow Bradley time to be prepared in case of such an event. He also has a big dog, should the power fail, or if it should be cut by that same law enforcement." He got out of the car. "Bradley is not a very trusting person," he said to me over its roof. "I vouched for you, but . . . My advice is to not speak unless spoken to, and don't touch anything."

I wondered just what I was getting myself into, but I really needed to get my phone fixed, so I followed him up the cracked concrete walk to the Meow dealer's house. Wiley didn't knock, and there was no bell. There was a plastic garden gnome, molded in a sitting position, perched on the corner of the top of the door frame, and Wiley looked up at it, and snapped his fingers in front of its nose.

A moment later, a girl about our age opened the front door, then unlocked the security door. She smiled shyly at Wiley, and said hello. Then, with girlish concern, she said, "What happened to your mouth?"

"My mama slapped me," he said, then looked at me. "This is Kendra, Nate. She's very religious. She thinks I'm the answer to her prayers." Kendra's smile faltered. "Where's Bradley?"

"He's in the backyard."

"Thanks."

I followed Wiley across a stained carpet to a sliding glass door on the other side of the room. He opened the door, and a guy in his early thirties, sitting at a picnic table, looked at us. He was wearing a tank top, and his beefy arms were closely covered from knuckles to shoulders in tattoos. Apparently the brisk April afternoon didn't bother him, as he was barefoot, like Wiley had been earlier. Wiley was wearing flip flops now, like it was August. He took them off to drive.

Bradley threw a ball to a lean brown Doberman, who bounded off to fetch it like a puppy, then gleefully returned it.

"Hey, Wiley," he said.

"Hey, Bradley. This is my friend, Nate."

Bradley considered me, unsmiling, for a moment, then said, "Hey, Nate."

"Nice to meet you, Bradley," I said.

"That remains to be seen." He threw the ball for the Dobie again, then sighed. "You remember Casey, Wiley?"

He looked over his shoulder, and we saw a thin, long-haired guy of about twenty-five, talking rapidly on his phone, pacing back and forth on the other side of the concrete slab.

"You're a bitch, then!" he said and disconnected his call. "She won't give me any more money," he told Bradley.

"That's the saddest story I've heard all day, Case." The dealer patted the dog on its long, thin, ferocious-looking head, and threw

16

the ball again. "I'm afraid we can't do business, then. I told you last time. No more credit."

Casey looked at us for a second. I noticed he was grinding his teeth. He was pale and sweated, even though it couldn't have been more than seventy degrees. He looked back at Bradley. "You know I'm good for it. Rachel gets her check next week."

"You're already into me for Rachel's check," Bradley said. "Come back when you have cash American, Casey. This ain't the Midnight Mission."

"I can't, Bradley," he whined. He looked down at his phone, and as if seeing it for the first time, he said, "Here. Take it. It's gotta be worth a couple hundred bucks to you."

"What d'ya think I am, a fucking pawnbroker?"

"Come on, Bradley!"

Bradley looked at Wiley, and he said, "Lemme see it." Casey tossed the phone to him and Wiley looked it over, pushed a few buttons. He nodded at the tatted-up drug dealer.

"I'm not a fucking pawnbroker, Casey, so don't come back here asking for it. It's gone." Bradley stood up. "This is the last time. Next time you show up without any money, I'm gonna sic the dog on you. I'll be right back, Wiley." He entered the house, and Casey eagerly followed him.

"Fuck, Wiley!" I said, unable to believe what I'd just witnessed. The dog tilted his head curiously at me.

"Commerce and industry, Nate." Wiley was scrolling through Casey's phone and didn't look up. "Wow. Rachel's a busy girl."

"I don't know if I want a stolen cellphone, for Christ's sake, Wiley."

"There's no such thing as a stolen cellphone, my son. There's purchased cellphones and traded cellphones, lost ones and borrowed ones and gifted ones. But if you know how to disable the . . . Well, after that, their just components. We just need the screen." He continued to scroll. "Damn," he said.

Bradley reappeared. "Fucking junkies," he said and grinned at Wiley.

Wiley grinned back. "This'll work out perfectly. Have you seen the pictures of –"

"Yeah," Bradley said, "and I don't wanna see 'em again. Casey said something about her once, something about a trade . . ." He shook his head, shuddered. "Yikes. Fucking junkies." He nodded at the phone, which still captivated Wiley. "I had a different one for you, but if that one'll work, take it." The Dobie wagged its stubby tail and dropped the tennis ball at Bradley's feet. He picked it up and threw it.

"How much do I owe ya?"

Bradley shrugged. "Twenty bucks?"

"Pay the man, Nate."

I found two tens in my wallet and handed them to Bradley. "You don't say much, do ya?" he said to me.

"He's never seen the economics of drug addiction before," Wiley said, still not looking up. "Wow, what is *that* thing?"

"I told you, Wiley, I don't wanna see it," Bradley said and grinned at him again.

Wiley gestured at the roofline with the iPhone. "Everything working okay?"

"Everything's great." Bradley looked at me again. "I don't mean to run you guys outta here, but I got some people coming over."

Wiley immediately handed the phone to me. "All right. Call me if you need anything."

"And you call me." Bradley stood, and to my surprise, he hugged Wiley, and Wiley hugged him back. I wouldn't have pegged Bradley as the demonstrative-to-other-men type. Wiley either, for that matter.

The Meow dealer silently walked us to the front door. Kendra called goodbye to Wiley from the couch, and Bradley looked curiously over his shoulder at her, perhaps a little annoyed. Wiley ignored her.

****

We drove in silence for a while, then he looked over at me and said, "What?"

I shook my head. "I'm gonna have to re-evaluate you, Wiley. I didn't know you hung out with people like that. I didn't know you were a –"

"A criminal?" He offered me a toothy grin. "I'm not a criminal, Nate. And I most assuredly don't *hang out* with Bradley. Anyone you know that calls himself a dangerous man probably isn't. Bradley would never say that about himself. But some of the shit I saw go down there, while I was putting his cameras in . . . We just do business sometimes. I get rid of any handheld stuff he can't use, that

18

he takes in trade when he's feeling generous, and I fix anything that goes wrong with the security system I installed for him."

"What does he do for you?" I asked, thinking of young Kendra.

Wiley seemed to follow my train of thought and looked over at me in amused disgust. "Bradley saved my ass one time, Nate. From an entirely worse fate that you did today. It's because of Bradley that I'm *not* a criminal. He set me on the straight and narrow, you might say."

"Did he. This I've got to hear."

"Like I said, I met Bradley not long after we moved back here. He liked me, and he told me about his business, about the Meow, asked me if I might like to work for him, sell a little bit of it to our gullible school chums." Wiley wrinkled his nose in distaste. "Not my cup of tea. I had no desire to have a bunch of teenage Caseys following me around, sweating and grinding their teeth, offering to blow me for a drug.

"So when I asked him what else he might have for me, Bradley showed me a garage full of rather expensive electronic components, still in their boxes. Asked me if I thought I could move any of them. Without going into any details that could be used as evidence against him, or me, he told me where he'd acquired them, how much he'd paid for them, what we could sell them for, how much we were gonna make.

"I unloaded a few of them for him, and thought about what a sweet deal the whole thing was. Feeling entrepreneurial, I went down to the area where he said he'd picked up this shipment, diverted somewhere between our Asian friends that'd built it and our American friends that were gonna legitimately sell it. He'd mentioned that changes in itinerary like that happened all the time, and sure enough, after about a week of wandering around in a certain industrial park, I met a guy. Bertie, he said his name was.

"He showed me a small truck full of similar components, and said that I could have them all, and the truck, too, if I wanted it, for an incredibly reasonable price. I'd be able to sell them for almost half what Bradley was selling his for, and still make beau coup bank.

"But like I say, during the time that I was at his house installing his cameras, I'd observed some of Bradley's dealings – trust me when I tell you, Nate – he was *nice* to Casey today. So I figured that it wouldn't be a good idea to cross our tatted-up friend in any way. I was new to this game. So I went over there to see him, to tell him

19

about it. I did gloat about the fantastic deal I was about to make, though."

"Not you."

"Bradley listened to everything I told him about Bertie and the electronics, and the prices, and what a sweet deal it was. He didn't interrupt me once, didn't ask any questions. When I was done, he looked at me for a moment, then shook his head.

"'What d'ya think this is, Wiley, fucking *Walmart?*' he said at last. 'Do you think that just anybody can walk in off the street and jump into the stolen merchandise biz? I thought you watched old movies? Gangster flicks? Where ya had to be a made man and all that to do this stuff?'

"I blinked at him in surprise. This wasn't the reaction I'd been expecting. 'Good job, Wiley,' I'd expected him to say. 'How bout you cut me in?' Or something like that. But no. Bradley the drug dealer was telling me that I was a dumb-ass.

"'It's not as Italian as all that around here, my son,' he said. 'But it's not fucking *Walmart* either, where you walk around back alleys and shop for the best deals. It's not who you know or how you blow, it's how you blow who you know in the stolen goods biz, Wiley. And you're blowing the wrong guy.'

"'What're you talking about?' I said. 'You're just saying this 'cause I'm gonna get a better deal than you did. You paid too much.'

"'You're not as smart as you think you are, Wiley,' he told me. 'I see kids like you every day, showing up here in their expensive cars, all eager to shove that white powder up their noses. And I'm more than willing to oblige them, 'cause it sure beats working. At least you're smarter than that.

"'You're from a nice little white bread family. You're as rotten as they come, though – that's why I love you. Somehow Mom and Dad's upper middle-class morality missed you, so you're willing to break the golden rule, to fuck others just because they're dumb enough to let themselves get fucked. Stealing is okay to you, especially if you're not the one doing the actual stealing. You didn't hijack that truck; you just got the space to hide a few hundred components; you've got the cash to liquidate them for – what was his name?'

"'Bertie.'

"'Bertie who?'

"'He didn't say.'

20

"Bradley smiled at me. 'Of course he didn't. You're thinking, *Hot damn, this is great! Why the fuck doesn't everybody do this?* Because it's illegal, my son, that's why, and there are people whose entire boring lives are devoted to stopping you from turning a little dishonest profit.

"'But you're not thinking about the risk; all you can see is how easy it is, how much money you're gonna make. All you can see is what a great deal it is. Everybody wins: you, Bertie, your projected receivers of stolen goods. Everybody wins, except the guy that misplaced that truck in the first place. And he doesn't lose too badly, because you know that truck was insured. So really, the only person who loses is me, because you're gonna undercut my price and flood the market. So you're here to cut me in, 'cause you think we're friends, and more importantly, because you don't wanna piss me off. And in that thought, you're showing some smarts.' He winked at me. 'Is that about how you see it?'

"I nodded.

"'But you're not a criminal, Wiley, not by a long stretch. You're just an opportunist who thinks he's gonna make a fierce killing, by virtue of a quick criminal enterprise. You're trying to be something you're not. And by trying to be something you're not, you're about to fuck yourself, and big time.' He grinned at me.

"'Because of the nice, safe, comfortable life you've lived, you think everything is generally fair. You get what you pay for. People are what they represent themselves to be, even if they're representing themselves to be thieves. But nothing's fair in the real world, my son. Everybody is trying to fuck everybody else. Why should I pay for this, when I can only say that I'm gonna pay for it, then steal it from you? Doing that kind of shit gets you dead, but don't think it's not on everybody's mind. That's why everyone's got a piece. You got a piece, Wiley?'

"I shook my head.

"'I didn't think so. You're about to get fucked, my boy.'

"'What are you talking about?' I said. 'It's a great deal –'

"Bradley held up his hand. 'Like I say, we have a loosely knit network around here, but it's still a network. Everybody knows everybody, more or less; and you usually trust who you know. But someone new is universally suspected. An undercover cop can't just waltz in here and start doing business, any more than you can.'

"He put his arm around my shoulders, gave me a little squeeze. Bradley loves me, Nate, I'm telling you. He smiled at me and went

21

on. 'But that's exactly what you've done, isn't it? You didn't like my price, so you just walked around the shadier parts of town 'til you happened on a better deal, right? It just fell into your lap, because you're a lucky guy, a discerning individual. A fucking criminal mastermind is Wiley Royce!'

"When I didn't say anything, Bradley told me, 'Your new pal Bertie is a cop, Wiley, as surely as you're standing here. When they can't find a way in to established places, they settle for netting first-time dumb-asses like yourself, who don't know what they're doing, who believe exactly what they're told. *Sure, I'll sell you a truck full of stolen components, just because you walked down this alley and expressed an interest in them. Gee, you couldn't possibly be a cop, and I'm not one either. We're just regular guys who had the good fortune to run into each other while out engaging in grand theft.*

"'If that all makes sense to you, head on. But I'm telling you, if you take that money over there and give it to Bertie for that truck full of technology, you're going away for a long time, Wiley, my bad little boy. It wouldn't seem so long to someone who's already done time, but to someone like you, smart and pretty as you are, it'll seem like the rest of your life.

"'And then when you get out, the cops'll be watching you, and they'll throw you up against the wall when you're walking down the street and fuck with you, just because they can, because you're an ex-con, and they're the law. If prison doesn't mark you, and it will, boy, just 'cause you're so pretty – you think you're a bad-ass, but the real bad-asses in there *will turn you out* – you're still marked forever, because now you've got a record.

"And every time someone so much as shoplifts a charger from *Radio Shack,* your name's gonna come up on the list of usual suspects. Then they'll be knocking on your front door and showing their badges to your mom, and she'll have to relive all those months when she talked to you on a phone behind a plate of glass, and cried over your black eyes and your split lips.

"'Leave crime to the real criminals, Wiley. Pass on this deal. Stay in school, go to college, be a good boy.' Then he grinned and hugged me again."

Wiley looked over at me. "It was of no benefit whatsoever to Bradley to clue me to all this, Nate. If he didn't like me, it would've been funny as hell for him to watch smart-ass Wiley get busted because of my own ego and stupidity. But he does like me, so he let me know I was about to make the biggest mistake of my life. And it scared the shit out of me. Never again have I gotten anywhere near any trucks full of hot electronics. Like I say, I don't even hang out over there."

****

Wiley sat down at the desk in his room and began taking Casey's phone apart. "Besides my almost misstep into the criminal underworld, I'm still smarter than everybody else, Nate, just like I told you at school. You wanna know why?"

"I wanna know why you think you are."

"From the time I was ten years old until just last year, we lived on my grandparents' farm. All this stuff – the books, the desks – they're from the attic room of the farmhouse. It was my room – I've always liked attics." He grinned at me. "It was a great space – had its own little bathroom, and everything. I didn't much pay attention to all the books at first." He gestured at the library with the screwdriver.

"My mom's a nutritionist, and she and Dad had gone to live on the farm with my dad's parents as some kind of back to nature kick, and for a while I was too busy learning about the crops and the machinery to even surf the web. And what ten-year-old reads? But then I started to read a lot at night, when the internet bored me. There wasn't a whole lot else to do, and I found that I liked it. All the secrets of the soul are in these books, Nate. Revealed." When I just looked at him blankly, he sighed and continued.

"Then, when I was almost seventeen, I fell off the combine. Broke my leg in three places. Snapped my femur in half like kindling, fractured both tibia and fibula." He looked up and grinned at me. "Did you know you've got three bones in your legs, Nate?"

"I've had Anatomy, Wiley, you smug son of a bitch."

"So maybe you're not so dumb, after all." He released the top from Casey's phone, just like he had done with mine. He took the battery out of it, made some adjustments to its insides, then threw it into the drawer. "My mother was stricken with guilt – it'd been her idea to move out to the country, and here, her only child had almost bled to death before they could rush me to the nearest hospital. She wanted to set me up downstairs, but I said I'd prefer to be upstairs in my room. It was really a pain in the ass for her to bring all my meals up there to me, but she didn't seem to mind."

"My dad was then, and continues to be, an electronics genius. He also felt bad about his busted-up kid, and brought me all kinds of

23

toys to play with. X-boxes and Wiis and laptops, cellphones and tablets, and a big TV, not unlike this one. And when I got tired of messing around with them, he taught me how to take them apart. And then I learned how to *really* mess with them." He grinned at me, then went back to working on my phone.

"It took a while for my leg to heal up." He clicked the flex cables from the Casey's screen into place: snap, snap, snap; put the bracket back and began replacing the three screws. "That's why I'm behind in school. Not only am I smarter than you, Nate, I'm also older. What're you, seventeen?"

"Eighteen. Just last month."

"I'll be nineteen, right after I graduate. If I graduate."

"I thought you were smarter than everyone else, Wiley?" I said in surprise. "Why're you worried about graduating?"

"It's the math," he said – just like my grandmother, who always put a *the* in front of stuff she didn't quite understand: *the* Netflix, or *the* Facebook, or *the* gays. "Believe it or not, my brilliance is confined to electronics and literature and women –" he gently slid my phone back together, then looked up and grinned at me. "My brilliance is confined to just about anything else, except for math." He started putting the last two screws back in. "Are you any good at math, Nate, my savior? Can you help me?"

"No," I said. "I'm gonna get a C in math."

"A C passes," he said. "I'd give my front seat in hell for a C."

"I don't have the patience to tutor your condescending ass, Wiley." I thought a minute. "But I do know this girl named Brendee. She's great at math. She used to help me when we were kids."

Ah, Brendee! I had quite the little thing for little Brendee. She was tiny and blonde, like an elf, with bright blue eyes and a body that had no mercy whatsoever. She lived right around the corner from me, too, just like Wiley, although in a different direction. I always made it a point to pass by her house when I jogged.

I'd first noticed her in grade school – I think Brendee might've been the first girl that I'd *ever* noticed. We'd remained friends, or at least acquaintances, ever since, because sometimes she would notice me jogging by, and would come outside and talk to me. She'd also send me a *Hi, how ya doin?* text every now and then, and we'd gone out and had a pizza together once, but that was about it. She attended private school – she was an Honors Student, and didn't have any time to waste on the likes of me, someone who was just barely gonna make it out of public school, bound only as far as community college.

Wiley threw the screwdriver back in the drawer and handed my phone back to me. "I know Brendee," Wiley said. "She's Gary Comstock's younger sister, right? I haven't seen her in a long time, though. I don't talk to Gary too much either."

"Not, I imagine, since you told him to be smarter than the Xerox machine in front of about fifteen people. What was somebody like you doing in a public library, anyway?"

"I need to make some copies," he said and grinned. "For Bradley."

"You're a forger, too?"

Wiley shook his head. "I've told you too much already, my son." He paused. "Did Brendee tell you about that? At the library?"

"I don't talk to her too much, Wiley. She's busy with private school, getting ready for college and all. I was there at the library when you humiliated her brother."

Wiley shrugged. "It's our electronic world, my son. Paper confuses some people." He paused, then grinned again. "Brendee's all grown up since last time I saw her. She's what we'd call a spinner. Big girl, big pussy. Little girl, *all pussy.*"

"You're such an ass, Wiley."

"Better men than you have said so." He nodded at the phone. "Go ahead, turn it on. I know you can't live without it." I hit the power button and my phone came on, good as new. "You're welcome," Wiley said.

"What do you know about big girls and little girls, anyway?" I asked irritably. Now he had me thinking about *spinning* Brendee, and I didn't want to think about it when I was sitting there with him. "Like I say, I've never heard of you ever even having a date."

He grinned. "So there I was, stove-in, busted-up, on crutches, sixteen years old, confined to my room. I read a lot more during my convalescence, broadening my horizons, as did the consumptive poets of old." He gestured at his books. "All the world, right here, at my fingertips, gravy to my sponge-like soul. That's one reason I'm smarter than you, Nate, and anybody that even looks like you. I've read every one of these books. When I wasn't reading, I took electronics apart and put them back together, made *better* electronics. I gamed, I surfed the 'net –"

"That's where you think you know about girls from, then," I said. "That's where you get your filthy mouth. We've all seen porn, Wiley. That doesn't make you smarter than me."

I'd suspected that Wiley hadn't a clue what he was talking about – *Bev's talented mouth,* and all. I thought that, for all his bravado and disrespect, for all his almost criminal enterprises, he was really nothing more than a grown *boy,* like I was. He was just a more impolite, dirty-talking one.

Bradley had seen that he was just another kid, I was sure; and it was obvious to me now that Wiley's confidence and his disdain came from his luck in dodging that bullet, and from an oversaturation in porn. He thought he knew what he was talking about from seeing all that stuff, but in reality, he didn't know any more than me. Probably less.

I was no virgin; there'd been two or three friendly girls before Judy, and of course, there had been Judy. But still, I didn't count myself as a ladies' man, and either did any of them. And here was smut-talking Wiley – he'd gotten all his filthy lines from porn, from the internet, maybe from seeing the kind of shit that went on at Bradley's house – maybe he'd never even been with a girl.

"How do you watch your porn, Nate?" he asked me. "All by your lonesome, I'd imagine? With Pam and her five ugly sisters?" He splayed his hand in front of my face and I slapped it away. "I'm not much for porn, actually. At least not the scripted kind." He pulled his knees up, put his feet on the seat of the chair and spun it around, like a little kid. "Right after I turned seventeen, there was a girl. Her name was Kitana."

"Like the sword?"

"Like the video game character." Wiley grinned. *"Flawless victory."*

I smiled. My dad had showed me Mortal Kombat when I was a kid, when there were still a few guys left that played it online.

"She lived down the road from Grandpa's farm. Her dad was the local vet, and I'd met her at his office once, when we brought the dog in for his shots or something. I'd just turned seventeen, and Kitana was twenty – she was home for the summer from her first or second year of college. She was studying Eastern philosophy as a minor and her major was – cue the Gods smiling on the most fortunate Wiley Royce – Physical Therapy. So when she heard that I was all wounded and hobbling around on crutches, she decided that she could help me. That I'd be the perfect guinea pig.

26

"And help me she did. It turned out that she was rather an electronic genius in her own right, though from the Dark Side. While my dad might occasionally cage new software from one of his buddies on the down low – he'd tell be me was beta-testing it – Kitana could pirate whatever she wanted in a heartbeat. No encryption was too tough, no entertainment too obscure. She was a big fan of old movies – black and white – ancient, classic stuff, like you say, and she absolutely loved old music. I've heard as much shit from the 1980s as your grandparents. I watched Olivier's *Hamlet* for the first time in that little bed right there. In my grandpa's attic, with Kitana curled up, naked, next to me.

"My parents suspected nothing. Surely this gorgeous *woman* and their skinny, half-crippled boy weren't doing anything they shouldn't be doing, up there in the attic? Kitana talked electronics with my dad, so he knew we shared that interest. She talked about mending bones and stretching muscles and yoga and Tai Chi with my mom – my mom just considered her to be a kind and compassionate health care professional, who felt it was her calling to keep a lonely boy company, and to help him mend, straight and true.

"But Kitana put the *passion* in *compassionate,* Nate, my son. She used me as her completely willing sex toy, all in the name of physical therapy." He leapt up and assumed a crouching tiger stance. "I could have this if I'd just *reach* for it. I could have that if I'd just stretch out my wounded leg and *bend* for it. To this day, I'm as limber as a tight-rope walker." Wiley did a handstand, slowly extending his legs until they were nearly parallel with the floor, bare toes pointed like a ballerina. I had to admit that it was impressive. Then he leapt gracefully to his feet again and said, "Ta-da! You wanna see the trapeze?"

I blinked. "You've got to be kidding."

Wyle shook his head and pointed at the ceiling. I looked up and saw a black bar. It was attached to two thick off-white colored ropes, bolted through the ceiling on each side of the peak. The whole thing was gathered up with a smaller rope, also bolted through the ceiling, holding it up there with some kind of slipknot. "I just have to pull on the string to let it down," Wiley said. "I tied it up there, 'cause it blocks the view of the TV from my bed.

"Anyway, all through that summer, Kitana was there. Sometimes she'd leave after supper, then sneak back in and spend the night with me, after my parents had gone to sleep. 'You're mending like a tough old plow horse,' she'd tell me. Then she'd

27

climb on top of me and ride me like one." Wiley grinned. "She showed me all the finer points of Tai Chi and yoga. We built that trapeze –"

"What do you do with it?" I asked. "There's not enough room in here to –"

"It's called a static trapeze, Nate," he said, looking up at it again. "It comes down to about chest level. You do exercises on it. It swings, but not very much – I don't soar through the air and do somersaults off of it like Cirque du Soliel, or anything like that. Everything is slow, stationary. Muscle tension. And if I have a partner . . . Do you want me to draw you a picture, or do you have an imagination inside that little, tiny mind?" He slapped me on the side of the head and I slapped him back.

He again sat back down in the wheeled chair, what my grandma always called a *rolly chair,* and told me more about this girl. "We'd watch old movies, listen to golden oldies, read aloud to each other –" he again gestured at his books, "– and go to porn sites." Wiley positively leered. "She knew how to bypass where you're supposed to pay, and she showed me how to expertly erase the history when we were done. So well that even Dad couldn't see where we'd been, if he'd ever had a hankering to look. She'd have me pick some site, and we'd look at the pictures and the clips for a while, then she'd ask me if I wanted to try what I'd seen."

"You're full of shit, Wiley," I said.

Wiley shrugged. "Where do you think I learned to do a handstand like that? A little martial arts training –"

"You know Kung Fu, too?"

Wiley shook his head. "No. Just yoga and Tai Chi. It's really a martial art, too, but I never cared to learn the fighting aspects. Just the gentle movements. I'm a lover, not a fighter, Nate. Unless the situation calls for it." He made the crouching tiger hand gesture again. "A little Eastern movement, combined with some good old American porn . . . Kitana taught me to *do things to her,* Nate, my son, and *praise Jesus!* the things she did to me . . .

"But she also talked to me, for hours on end. She told me what girls like, what they want, how they think. Girls have been my favorite subject ever since. I like to study them, to *watch them.*"

I gestured at his room. "But not have any of them around, apparently."

Wiley shrugged. "Let's just say that, for the moment, mine is a hypothetical and not an applied study." He tapped the side of his head. "Planning and research as opposed to field work. Spiritual contemplation at this time, instead of physical consummation." He grinned. "Eastern philosophy teaches us that they are the Yin, the negative, the yielding, whereas we are the Yang, the positive; action. We are two halves to the whole. Equal. One incomplete without the other. Eternal."

"Thank you, Zen Master, for the insight."

"I'm no philosopher, Nate." Wiley grinned wickedly. "In the real world, there's not a lot of spirituality to it, now is there? What they want is for us to give it to them, just as rough and hard as they can take it. They're really very simple creatures. Just like us. They've just been taught not to let it show, and that amuses the hell out of me, because I know what they're really thinking. I know what they want."

"You're not supposed to let it show either, Wiley. You talk to them like you're a pervert."

"I know what they want, Nate," he insisted.

"Then how come you don't use this vast knowledge on any of them? Why do they cross to the other side of the hall to avoid you?"

Again Wiley shrugged. "Kitana went back to school in the fall. We talked online nearly every day – she made sure I was still doing my exercises; she encouraged me to keep reading Grandpa's books; she helped me pirate software, music, movies – I saw *Harvard's Henchmen* at least a good year before you did, right off the studio's in-house site. We read poetry to each other, and talked dirty to each other.

"She returned in June, just before I turned eighteen. I was completely, one hundred percent healed by then, and we were now equals. Teacher and student no longer. I showed her that I remembered all the things that she'd taught me, and she said she was my slave, and that she loved me. I was certainly her slave, and I just as certainly thought I loved her. We were simpatico, halves to the whole, like it's supposed to be.

"Then, on the Fourth of July, she told me that she was going to Europe at the end of the week. She was gonna go to school over there in the fall, on some kind of grant or scholarship or something. She asked me if I'd come with her.

"But when I asked Mom and Dad for a loan, they told me the joyful news: we were moving back home to Riverside at the end of July! Mom was tired of the farming life, she'd found a job here in town, and Dad had been offered a fairly good position at some tech firm. I'd get to graduate from Mom's high school alma mater. I'd get to see my other set of grandparents again. My parents would get to see all their old friends again. The upshot was, there wasn't any money to be sending Wiley on a European holiday that summer.

"Kitana's still over there – she's somewhere in England. I'm not sure where. That's something else I'm not brilliant at, besides the math – geography."

"So, I'm here with you and our ignorant, sheep-like peers. I may or may not ever see Kitana again – we don't talk as often as we used to, and she's made vague comments about staying over there. I might not even graduate, and even if I do . . . I don't wanna go to Europe, Nate."

Wiley sighed. "Maybe we've had our time, and maybe it's passed now. I've reflected on this thing called love, and . . . I just don't know. If we were together all the time, maybe things would get boring. Even the finest caviar might get stale, if you eat it every day. I think I could stand just about anything but that – I'd never want to wake up one day and find out that I was bored with Kitana. That she was bored with me. So, it's not even about the money any more. I've got plenty of money." He reached into the drawer and flung a huge roll of twenties at me, held together with a rubber band.

"Did you decide to sell Meow for Bradley after all, Wiley?" I asked and tossed the money back.

"You're not the only one with a busted cellphone, my son." He gestured at the electronic parts on the desks. "Or a broken tablet or laptop. Or a virus or an X-box that your buddy spilled a beer on, or a Wii that he tripped over, or a rolling TV or a computer that's stuck in an endless, *preparing automatic repair* loop." Wiley sighed again. "But like I say, I have no yen to visit the *auld sod.*

"I've faced the idea that Kitana and I may be nothing but a charming memory, and I'm willing to accept it. Life goes on. But to answer your original question – I'm certainly not going to waste my time and talent on any of the ignorant, transparent, uppity sluts we know. I'm not about to go chasing after any of them, make a fool of myself waiting around for them to decide to give me what they think I don't know that they want just as much, if not more, than I do."

"You're a snob, Wiley," I told him. "They don't usually make you wait too long, and it's all the same in the dark."

"That's where you're wrong, my son. It can be like touching the face of God, or, like Kitana used to tell me, it can be like scraping gum off your shoe. I have no yen to step in any of the girls we know." He grinned at me. "They all walk around like we'd give our eye-teeth just to hold their hands at the movies, nonetheless do anything more worthwhile. Like they're the deities, and we're the worshippers. But it's all bullshit, Nate. They don't want to be worshipped. They want to be dominated."

"Is that why you talk so much filthy shit to them? To dominate them? How's that been working out for ya?"

Wiley shrugged. "That's just me showing my disrespect. That doesn't have anything to do with –"

"I suppose that next you're gonna tell me that they secretly like it. That tramps like Bev like to have it pointed out to them that they're tramps, in front of everyone. I've heard this one before, Wiley. Girls liked to be treated badly – that's what Neal and Ed and their crew always say. *Treat 'em like shit, and they come running.*

"Now you're telling me the same thing. You're gonna tell me that Bev and all the rest of them really want to throw themselves at your bare feet, because of the way you talk to them. They just can't wait for you to *dominate* them. But I don't see Neal with too many dates, or you either. You're so full of shit, Wiley."

"You're not picking up what I'm putting down, Nate." He shook his head. "Anything I say to Bev – I'm not interested in Bev, Nate, not in this lifetime. Seriously. You've got to be kidding." He looked curiously at me. "Are you?"

"Am I what?"

"Interested in Bev?"

I considered for a moment. "The opportunity has never presented itself." I shrugged. "I'm sure that I wouldn't have any trouble –"

"Nobody has any trouble."

"Except for you."

Wiley grinned. "I seem to have painted myself into a corner, here. Touché, Nate. Maybe you're not as dumb as you look. If I say that I don't want Bev, you're gonna say that I'm just being sour grapes because she doesn't like me. If I say that I talk shit to her because I can, and because I don't want her to like me, then you'll say that's because I really want her and I'm just lashing out in resentment that she won't see what a perfect couple we'd make. Is that about it?"

"I don't think that you want Bev, Wiley. I don't even want Bev."

"But you wouldn't tell her no, would you?" Wiley grinned wickedly. "If you were at some party, and maybe you had a little too much to drink, and she took you by the hand and led you into somebody's parents' bedroom . . . you wouldn't turn her down, would you?"

I pictured it for a minute, then shook my head. "No. I probably wouldn't turn her down." I looked at him. "You're saying that you would?"

"Bev's not gonna be taking me by the hand anywhere. Unless it's to push me off a cliff."

"But let's just suppose for a second that she did. You're telling me that you'd tell her no?"

Wiley widened his eyes, nodded vigorously. "Yes, that's exactly what I'm telling you, Nate. How does the old saying go? I wouldn't fuck Bev with your dick."

"Why not?"

"It wouldn't mean anything to her. I'd like to think –"

"OMG, you're so full of shit, Wiley! Mean something? Who do you think you're kidding?"

"You don't understand what I'm saying, Nate. I'm not saying that it has to mean something to me." He laughed. *"As if.* But it wouldn't mean anything to her, either, seeing how she's been with every guy we know."

"Ah, Wiley, are you afraid you wouldn't impress her? Because she has so many to compare you to?"

"For the sake of this revolting scenario, if I was to attempt to impress Bev, trust me when I tell you that she'd be impressed." Wiley grinned. "I told you, they want to be dominated. I bet Bev doesn't even enjoy herself. She probably liked it the first time, but it probably isn't any good to her anymore, and that's why she keeps trying with any guy that'll have her."

"Now you're trying to tell me that Bev doesn't like sex?'

"Oh, I'm sure she does, but not as much as she wants to. She wants to be *conquered,* but she doesn't even try to resist. Where's the fun in that?"

I blinked in surprise. "You like them to fight you, Wiley?"

Wiley mirrored by surprise. "Why do you wanna make me out to be a pervert, Nate?"

"Maybe it's your disrespect."

"Here's a little story that I'm man enough to share with you. Kitana was very strong; there's no such thing as a weak physical therapist. They help people move all day long, they lift, they push, they pull. Besides that, she worked at it. She was in phenomenal shape.

"But I was stronger than her, through no other reason than that I'm male, and testosterone leads to bigger muscles. We were lying in bed, discussing this biological disparity one time. She started to touch me, in that way that always immediately captured my attention, but when I went to make my move, she said, 'You think you could force me, Wiley? Just 'cause you're stronger than me?'

"And for a minute, it was fun, wrestling around with her, trying to hold her arms and get her legs apart at the same time. She really didn't fight back that much; it was just a little harmless fun. But because I was stronger than her, after a little trying, I *did* pin her down.

I expected everything to just go as it usually did after that, but before I could let her up and do what comes naturally, as equals, Kitana cried, 'Please, don't, Wiley!' I was holding her wrists above her head – she struggled against my hands; she feebly tried to heave me off of her. "Please, don't hurt me!" she said, some rape fantasy bubbling up from God-only-knew-where inside of her. Or maybe she thought it was what I wanted.

"But the idea of forcing her, of *making her do it* – I certainly could've, like I say. I was stronger than her, I had her pinned down. There would've been nothing she could've done to prevent me . . . But the idea of forcing her, even if it was just role-playing, just pretending . . ." Wiley grinned ruefully down at the floor, shook his head. "I couldn't do it. I lost my hard-on so fast that it was like I'd never had one before. Poof! It just went away. Only time that's ever happened to me."

"Right."

He looked up at me and grinned. "I let Kitana loose, and after a minute of regular attention, when she wasn't screaming, 'Please, don't, Wiley!' everything worked out as it should've. My point in telling you this embarrassing story is this – I'm no rapist, Nate. That's not what I meant about dominating them.

"No girl wants to be hurt or coerced or forced or raped. But neither do they want to give in too easily – if they just give in, people think they're sluts like Bev, and then they get treated like sluts like Bev. Everybody knows they're gonna get a turn with her, without having to make any effort at all. She's gonna just give right in; she's given in for so long, she's forgotten how to say no, or even maybe.

And yet she keeps doing it, because it's not the dick she wants so much as she wants someone to make that effort, to believe that she might not just roll over this time. It's sad, really."

"Your pity overwhelms me."

Wiley smiled. "Nice girls have the self-control to put up that resistance, but they still want us to overcome it. It's not necessarily physical - *Please, don't, Wiley!"* He shook his head. "It's societal: *What kind of a girl do you think I am?* The first time, especially. They want us to talk 'em into it, Nate. They want to think that they're in control."

I frowned. "You don't think that they're in control?"

Wiley laughed. "Not only are they not in control – they don't even *want to be in control.* They want to give in. They say no for a while, they tease themselves . . . That just makes the surrender all the sweeter for them."

"And that makes you think you're better than them?"

Wiley shook his head. "Not at all. Their surrender, their yielding to our action is the name of the game. Everything's in balance, once they give in. Everything's as it should be.

"But they only resist the first time, or the first few times. That's why it's so good for them at first – they can't get enough of the ecstasy of that surrender. They've allowed themselves to be conquered, just like they secretly wanted all the time.

"But once you're all coupled up, going together, boyfriend and girlfriend – then no one expects her to say no out of some nod to chastity and good-girl-ness. She's your good girl now, and as long as she's not giving it to someone else, it's perfectly acceptable that she's giving it to you. Are you following me so far?"

I nodded.

"Okay, then you're going together for a while, and you're all equal – she wants you, you want her, blah, blah, blah. Then one day, you're late picking her up, or you don't return her text quick enough, or heaven forbid, you forget her birthday or some tragedy like that. And what does she do to punish you? 'I'm not in the mood, Nate. Go talk to Pam and her sisters.' It's really the only bargaining chip they have, isn't it? That, and crying. What's she gonna do, whip your ass? Arm wrestle you? No. She's mad at you, so she's gonna cut you off.

"Now the whole dynamic has suddenly shifted. Everything's out of balance again. Where before, you were equals, now she's the giver – or more importantly for my example, *the not-giver* – and you are reduced to the beggar. 'Oh, *puh-leese,* baby, just give me a little. I'll be a good boy from now on.'

"Now you've made your first mistake."

"How do you know all this, Wiley? You said that you and Kitana were always equals. Did she ever turn you down?"

Wiley shook his head. "No. Kitana always did the asking. And that is the point to my story, my son. Kitana told me that there was nothing more frustrating, nothing more of a turn-off, than when we beg, or wheedle. 'Here's my stallion,' she told me, 'once so potent, once so irresistible – suddenly reduced to a Shetland pony, his forelock hanging in his sheepish, beseeching eyes, begging me for a little ride.'"

"She was a poet."

Wiley nodded. "'But you, Wiley,' she said. 'You never beg.' The truth be told, she never gave me the chance. Like I said, it was more or less always her idea."

"What are you trying to tell me, Wiley? That they always want it to be their idea? That they just want us to stand around like so many *ponies,* and wait until they're in the mood?"

"No. Like I said, they want to be dominated. Sure, sometimes they are the initiators, and there is not one thing wrong with that." Wiley grinned. "But you can also tell by the way she looks at you when she wants *you* to make the first move. And I say, make her wait. I don't mean, make her wait until she has to ask you, if it's obvious that she wants you to ask her. But make her wait, anyway. Just a little while. If she wants you, make her want you a little more. Then give her what she wants, allow her to succumb to your more dominant will – because that's what she wanted to do all along. Balance is once again attained."

I thought about it for a moment.

"They want us to read their fucking minds, Nate. That's what Kitana told me. They don't want us to pester them when they're not in the mood, but they want us to be attuned to when they are. They don't want us to talk down to them or push them around – they want to be equals in the world. And well they should be – equals in jobs and pay and all that happy shit.

"I'm not saying that we're better than them, Nate. But in *matters of the heart,* shall we say, it pays to be a little *smarter* than them. It pays to be in control of ourselves. They've been taught that they've got what we want, and that there's something special about it – that we'll do anything to get it, that they can treat us any way they want. They've been taught that they're in control, at least behind closed doors. They can give or withhold at their whim. It's their prerogative to change their minds, no means no, blah, blah, blah.

"They want to be equals with us in society, and like I say, that's all well and good. But when we get behind closed doors, I'm telling you, they want us to be men. No matter what they say, they want us to be in charge. They don't want us to beg 'em for it. They want to *want us* – so, I say, always give 'em what they want. Make 'em wait."

"What if I don't want to make her wait?"

Wiley shrugged. "Then sooner or later, the dynamic is gonna shift, just like I said. Imbalance. She'll think that she can make *you* wait, just like her mama told her she could. And if she makes you wait long enough, if she sees that little pony look in your eyes, then maybe she'll make you wait a little bit more. Then maybe you might make some humble suggestion. Then she might still say no. How tiresome it is that you want her so much, when she's just not in the mood!

"Then you might get a little resentful, stand up for yourself a little bit. Then there might be an argument. Then she's *really* gonna say no. And so on and so on, until one day you wake up, and she's not so attractive to you anymore, or you're not so attractive to her. And you think about the little chippie that smiled at you in the grocery store. You figure that *she* won't make you jump through all these hoops, and then, well . . . people change. Life goes on."

"You sound like an old man, Wiley. Bitter."

Wiley shrugged. "I read a lot, Nate. And I had a very precocious teacher. She collaborated with the other side in the battle of the sexes. She told me all their secrets. She told me what they want." He tapped the side of his head. "And I've observed them. It's all true, I'm telling you."

"Why does it have to be such a game? Why can't we just be equals, like you said? I want her, she wants me – why can't we just leave it at that?"

"It's not the kill, it's the thrill of the chase, my son. It *is* all just a game. It's the best game in life." He paused, then said, "I went to a wedding one time, when I was just an innocent school boy." He batted his eyes at me. "I was only sixteen, before I broke my leg. I was sitting in the row in front of my mom. She commented to the woman sitting next to her that the bride and groom looked so happy and in love. The woman said, 'They just got married because they

can't keep their hands off each other. But you know how it is. If you put a penny in a jar every time you have sex for the first couple of years, then take one out every time after that, the jar will never be empty. It gets old after a while.'

"If you make it so she always wants you – that the idea that you might give her some today is just the most thrilling thought in her mind, 'cause there's also the possibility that you won't – if you make her wait sometimes, maybe it doesn't get old." Wiley grinned. "Trust me. I've given this a lot of thought. The idea of what women want – it's puzzled mankind for centuries, and you might say that the study of it is kinda my hobby." He gestured around the room. "What else have I got to do?"

"I dunno, Wiley. I don't see women lined up around the block, clamoring for you to make 'em wait."

"I just need one at a time, Nate. And I'm patient. Whoever the next one is, she won't be one of these high-and-mighty tramps we're forced to attend school with. I'm not sure of much in this life, but I'm sure of that. It'll be someone who appreciates me and everything I can do for her." He grinned wickedly. "It'll be someone who –" A door slammed downstairs, and a woman called his name. "Ah, my master's voice!" he said, not unkindly.

We went downstairs and he introduced me to his mother. She smiled, shook my hand, and then said to Wiley, "I finally got to have lunch with your Aunt Darlene today."

"Brendee's mom?" Wiley asked guilessly. His mom nodded, and I was again presented with that toothy Wiley grin. My mouth dropped open. "I'll be back in a minute," he said, and steered me by the elbow out the front door.

I was too dumbstruck to even tell Mrs. Royce that it'd been nice meeting her. *"Brendee's your cousin?* Why didn't you tell me that?"

"You didn't ask. We're not really cousins – not like blood relations. My mom and her mom went to school together. I used to call her mom *aunt* and she used to call my mom *aunt* when we were little. Like I told you, we moved away when I was ten. I haven't talked to her since then. I've talked to Gary." Wiley grinned, merciless as a shark. "Gary's my age, and Brendee's a year or so younger, right? I guess they have a brother and a sister that I don't remember at all."

"So you haven't seen Brendee since you were ten?"

"I haven't talked to her, or seen her in person, but I've seen her . . . *online,* shall we say?"

37

"Yeah, me, too," I said.

"Facebook stalker, are ya, Nate? Ah, the secrets we can learn from Facebook." He slapped me on the back. "But I'm not talking about that. I'm talking about something a little more secretive than a public forum. Come back tomorrow, and I'll show you. I didn't get to amaze you, this time, did I, my son? Except for our little side trip to the seedy side of town. But I've got other, more enjoyable amazements for you."

"Quit calling me *my son,* Wiley," I told him. I said thanks again for fixing my phone and left him standing on his front porch in his bare feet.

****

The following afternoon, I was once again in Wiley's attic room. He sat me in the same chair and again told me not to touch anything. He picked up a remote from the desk – it didn't have a back on it and had part of a circuit board, wrapped in electrical tape, sticking out of one side. He aimed it first at the tablet that was attached to the TV, then at the TV itself. The TV came on – it was filled with probably twenty squares, all the frozen frames of videos.

"This is my collection of . . . How shall I put it? Shall I call it amateur porn?"

"I don't wanna watch porn, Wiley. You said something about Brendee."

"I guess porn isn't the right word," he replied. "Porn is something recorded intentionally, something that the actors hope others will pay to watch. This, while indeed pornographic, is something else entirely.' He wiggled his eyebrows at me. "I've worked out a program to watch people through the webcams on their TVs, their tablets, their laptops, Nate. It's really quite simple, actually. You just have to –"

"You watched Brendee through her webcam?"

He nodded, and blinked innocently at me. "The one on her laptop. Many times. And I recorded it." He pushed a button on the remote and all the other squares disappeared, leaving just one, which enlarged and moved into the middle of the screen. "For your amusement, my – for your amusement, Nate." He pushed the button again. The video started and Brendee appeared in the square.

And I could see almost *all of her.*

The quality was great: I could make out some blonde singer looking back at me from a poster on the wall behind Brendee's bed. The singer was wearing fishnets and a studded black bra. She was sitting in front of a microphone, one leg crossed across the other, her arm raised, her hand like a claw. I recognized her – my dad had once showed me a picture of her on the internet. Her name was Baby Gaga, and she'd been popular when he was my age, he'd told me.

"I don't know why she's got that old poster," Wiley said. "My mom's got the same one, hanging in the bathroom. Very retro." He looked curiously at me. "Gaga says, *'What ya lookin' at, Nate?'*"

I was looking at Brendee, and trying not to feel too guilty about it. Like I say, I could see almost all of her, from the middle of her bare thighs on up. She was wearing an old, sheer white t-shirt, with a couple of holes in it. It wasn't a lace teddy, but it still left nothing to the imagination. She was lying in bed on her side, facing the computer, her head propped up on her elbow. She leaned closer to the screen, and her beautiful pixie face was framed there for a minute: her sparkly blue eyes, her tiny pink mouth; the blonde hair, damp, framing it all in curly ringlets. She was so cute, I felt a little poetic myself.

She hit a few keys, then leaned back again and closed her eyes. After a moment, she opened them again and watched the screen, and I noted that her pupils were now large, dilated with pleasure. She nodded her head – she was apparently listening to music, watching some favorite band.

"No sound?" I asked Wiley doubtfully.

"I haven't quite worked that part out yet," he said. "But who needs sound? Sound is overrated. Just watch."

Brendee raised her hand, then brought it down, then waited, eyes again closed, anticipating some moment in the song. The moment came, and I was amazed to see Brendee shudder, as if from some unseen lover's touch. She opened her eyes and drew her knees up to her chest, and I could just make out the curve of her fine, naked ass. She sang along soundlessly with the band, again raised her arm above her head. When she brought it down this time, she simultaneously threw her head back and straightened out her legs, the very picture of ecstasy. Then she curled up and opened her eyes, and sang along with the band again.

I glanced over at Wiley, who watched Brendee's silent performance with a somewhat clinical eye. I thought that all he needed was a lab coat and a clipboard to complete his aura of detachment. He really did study them. "How long does this go on?" I asked.

He looked at me. "It's not much, eh? Although sometimes she slides her hand between her legs, usually after that first pause there." He gestured at the screen.

"How long?" I asked again.

Wiley looked at the bottom of the screen. "Three thirty-five. That's how long the song lasts. Although sometimes she puts it on repeat. Then she might writhe around on the bed for ten or fifteen minutes. That's about it, though. Like I say, she sometimes snakes those little fingers between her legs, but she never takes off her shirt, so it's not like you can see what she's doing." The clip ended, and Wiley smirked at me. "But I can guess."

I asked the next obvious question. "What's she watching?"

Wiley blinked blankly, looked at the now dark square in the middle of the TV, then looked back at me again. "I haven't the slightest, Nate."

"You're kidding."

Wiley shook his head. "No. I have no idea what she's watching. Some music video, I'd guess, because she's not only listening and singing along, she's also watching it, when she's not –"

"You have no idea what it is, though?"

Wiley shrugged. "Some band that obviously gets her motor running."

"And it's always the same thing?"

"I'd say so, Nate. I watched her a couple of other times, when she's not doing anything but sitting there, using her machine. She only gets herself wound up over this – I can tell when she's watching it, because she lies in bed instead of sitting up, and she always makes the same gesture – that raised arm deally, and she always seems to pause at the same place. And it always runs about three thirty-five, unless, like I say, she puts it on repeat."

"How many times have you . . . When does she . . ."

"Calm thyself, my son," Wiley said and squinted at me. "Our Brendee is like clockwork. Every Friday night, between ten and midnight. I've caught this act maybe three or four times, but I only taped it once. There's not that much to it, compared to some of the stuff I've seen.

"Sometimes she makes herself a drink first. I can't tell if it's soda – but there's no ice in it, and it's always in the same goblet-looking glass. I think it might be white wine, to tell you the truth.

She sips, surfs around on the 'net for a while, then leans back and enjoys her three minutes. *Immensely.*"

Wiley pushed a few buttons on the ratty remote, and a list of video clips appeared on the screen. "I've got much better ones, Nate. The things these girls do in front of that little eye on the top of their telescreens. *My eye.*" He grinned at me. "They've all forgotten it's there, if they ever even knew about it. 1984 has long ago arrived, my friend. I'm just here to take advantage of it. I am the Thought Police."

"It's 2033, Wiley. 1984 arrived fifty years ago. What the hell is the Thought Police? What are you talking about?"

"It's a novel, Nate. Big Brother watched everybody through their telescreens . . ." He shook his head. "Never mind. It's not worth explaining it to you. Suffice it to say that, with a little electronic prestidigitation . . ." his fingers danced lightly over the remote. "By themselves, with their boyfriends, with their *girlfriends* . . . the TV's just there on the wall, or sitting on the desk; just another piece of furniture. They forget about that eye. Or they just leave some other all-seeing device open nearby, and forget about it, while they commence to do the most *entertaining* things. Brendee has whatever it is she likes to watch so much on a laptop, and she pulls it right up next to her bed. I think she's got it sitting on a chair or something, or maybe she moves the night stand.

"She's the only one I've ever seen that I actually know, but I think I've seen this one chick at the grocery store. She likes to sit and surf naked, you see, sometimes for hours, and I –"

"But you don't know what they're watching?" I asked again.

"Who cares what they're watching, for Christ's sake? *We're watching them!*"

"You're an evil man, Wiley." I said.

He shrugged. "I'm a product of my times, Nate, and it's not like I do it every day. Just when I'm bored on a Friday night sometimes. I'm what they used to call a hacker, and a bored hacker *is* a dangerous man. People should be aware of their devices." He nodded at the tablet hooked up to the television, and at the laptop sitting on the desk beside it, and to the TV itself. I noticed that there was a strip of masking tape across the webcams on all of them. "I'm not crashing their devices, scrambling their TVs, melting their phones, although I could. But what's the fun in that?"

"You're also an idiot," I told him, and slapped him on the back of the head.

"Better men than you have said so."

"Why haven't you found out what she's watching?"

"Who?"

"Brendee, for Christ's sake! *Your cousin!*" I looked at the list of files. "Don't you want to know what she's watching, what turns her on like that? Wouldn't you like to turn her on like that?" I said, and then immediately regretted it.

"I haven't thought about it, Nate, but I can see that you have." Wiley grinned. "I've no doubt that I could turn her on like that, my son. She's only human after all."

I must've frowned, because he continued quickly. "Brendee's a little tame for my tastes, though. Her clip is just one of many. Since you mentioned her, I thought you'd enjoy it." Wiley squinted at me. "Apparently I was right. But I much prefer the bare-breasted girl from the supermarket.

"My only interest in Brendee is her mind, Nate. The rest of her . . . That's all yours. Do you think you can get her over here to tutor me? If I flunk out of the math and don't graduate, my mama might take all these toys away from me." He hit a button on the remote and the screen went black. "And then you'd never get to watch Brendee . . . *dance* again."

"I think I can talk her into it," I told him. "Although I doubt that she'll like you any more than the other girls do."

Wiley endeavored to look hurt. "I'm sure she's a nice girl." He glanced at the TV. "Well, nice enough. Since you seem to like her so much, I'm sure she's certainly nicer than that uppity slut Bev and her uppity slut buddies. Did you want to see those pics from Eddie's phone?"

I shook my head. "Here's what I want, Wiley. I'll talk Brendee into tutoring you, so you get to graduate. I'll lie to her, convince her that you're a nice guy –"

"You don't think I'm a nice guy?" he said with a little fake pout.

"I think you're a heartless, filthy, voyeuristic son of a bitch, Wiley," I said and grinned at him.

He shrugged. "A fair assessment. It's the electronics, my son, the telescreens. They've rotted my brains. But like I say, I don't do it all the time. I'd rather watch them in person. But I wrote the program, so to test it out, I started to –"

"I'll convince Brendee that you're a nice guy, and you'll be a nice guy to her –"

"Scout's honor," he said. He folded the second to last finger of his hand across his palm, put his thumb on it, and held up the other three. I shook my head. "Seriously, Nate. Why would I want to piss her off? If she tutors me in math, she'll be saving my ass, just like you did." He made the proper Boy Scout gesture. "Scout's honor. I'll be a perfect gentlemen to her."

"If I get her to come over here and teach you, I want you to do something for me."

"Your wish is my command."

I nodded at the dark television. "Find out what she's watching."

BRENDEE

It was my mother's fault that I'd completely lost my mind.

I'd always considered myself to be a mature, sober-thinking young woman. I studied hard in school, but not too hard, because it all came easily to me. I was going to get a scholarship, and was going to have my choice to attend whatever college I wanted. I was considering some combination of law and computer science as majors.

I wasn't a druggie or a drunk or a tramp. I was very much in love with my boyfriend, Dave. Or at least parts of me were very much in love with parts of him, though I must say that he was *completely* in love with me. He talked about marriage and children and happily ever after, after we graduated from college and began our successful, well-paying journey through life. I let him talk, and made sure I took my pill every morning, so that there wouldn't be any unwelcome surprises after we had our weekly trysts on Thursday afternoons. Thank you, Planned Parenthood. We'd both arranged to have two study halls on that day, back to back in the afternoon. So we invariably snuck home to my house and did our thing, while my parents and brothers and sister were still out in the world.

I was content, the future was bright. Everything was going along per my carefully envisioned plans. I had no secret, drunken rituals. I had no secrets at all, except for my Thursday afternoons, and that wasn't anybody else's business, anyway. My mind was intact.

Then my mother showed me something, and quite unbeknownst to her, it put me completely around the bend.

One Friday evening, just before I finished my junior year last June, I came home to find her staring pensively at a dusty, black plastic box. "Can you make this work?" she asked me.

It was an ancient DVD player. I wiped the dust off of it, and considered the holes in the back for a minute. I had some old stuff in my room – cables and adaptors. I wasn't much for retro electronics, but every now and then, someone would ask if I could get music or info off one of those old-fashioned plastic things for them – *compact discs*, they were called. They weren't very compact, really, and didn't hold much data. They were once the best way to carry info between machines. But then streaming and thumb drives and TiVo and the Cloud had come along, and cellphones, and every other glorious technology, and it wasn't necessary to keep your data on a hard piece of plastic so much anymore.

A DVD was just another round piece of plastic like a CD – it just held a little more data, usually pictures or movies. I thought I might have an old laptop in the closet that might actually play it – but my mom had scared up its own dusty device, so all I had to do was find a cable to hook the technology of the past to our modern television.

Mom was drinking a glass of wine – it was date night for her and Dad, and she was getting in the mood a little early. She poured me a glass, as she did every now and then. She'd say, "Here, Brendee, have a drink. You work too hard. You have to learn to relax a little bit."

The wine was acrid and bitter to me, as it always was, but after a moment, it warmed my belly and began to gently befuddle my mind. I liked the sensation very much, and Mom knew it. She stood in the doorway to my room and watched while I searched for the proper connectors. "I want you to see something that's on this DVD, Brendee. It's from before you kids were even dreamt of, before I'd even met your dad."

Oh, how I dreaded Mom's trips into the past! For my entire life, she'd subjected me to old music and old movies, and every one of them had been awful. My older brother Gary had learned early to make himself scarce the moment he heard the strains of some godforsaken tune from the aughts and teens of our young century. My younger brother and sister were mortified that their mom would dance around in the living room, singing along to all that old shit. They'd made her promise to never do it in front of their little friends, lest they die of embarrassment.

My dad would just gently make fun of her. He was a musician, though not by trade; by trade he sold real estate. He'd tell us that our mom had always had what they called *mainstream taste* in music. Then he'd thank God that the mainstream stuff that she liked had gone over the falls long ago.

So it was with good-natured annoyance that I said, "It's not a movie is it? I don't have time for a movie, Mom. I have to study."

"It's Friday, and you don't have to study. School's out next week." She poured more wine into my glass. "It's just a little video. It's only three minutes long. I want to show you what passed for sexy when I was your age."

I rolled my eyes at that. I'd seen a few examples of what my mom thought was sexy when she was my age. She still had pictures in a little folder on her computer, along with her old music and old movies. Obscure foreign actors, long-forgotten – so many pictures! Throughout my life, whenever some celebrity of yesteryear would come up in conversation, Mom would say, "Let me show you a picture of So-and-so, Brendee! He was *so* fine!"

I'd never, not once, been impressed.

"I guess it's the least I can do, to watch it with you," I told her. "Since you're getting me drunk." I finished hooking up the old device to the TV, and held out my hand for the disc.

"Let me give you a little backstory on this first," Mom said. "I used to go see this band almost every weekend. They were *awesome.*"

"You must've thought so, to have kept this little piece of plastic all these years, to drag out – where did you find a DVD player, anyway?"

Mom waved her hand. "Your dad had it in the attic. I was looking for my high school year book – did I tell you your Aunt Amy's moving back to town?"

"Who?"

"You don't remember your Aunt Amy? She had a little boy, about the same age as Gary. His name was . . . Willie, I think. You guys all used to play together when you were little."

I tried to remember, but failed. I shook my head.

Mom waved her hand again. All that didn't matter. She wanted to tell me about this *awesome* video we were going to watch. Her enthusiasm was infectious, but I was immune. Mom was always enthusiastic about her old music and movies and videos, and since they'd never failed to bore me, I just rolled my eyes, and hoped the whole story wouldn't take too long.

"We used to go see this band, every weekend, at this little bar called *The Beachcomber.*"

"You went all the way to the beach to see a band? Every weekend?"

Now my mom rolled *her* eyes. "That's just what your grandma said. No. *The Beachcomber* was right here in town. They tore it down years ago. There's a *Baker's* there now. Anyway, a bunch of my friends and I really liked the singer from this band. I mean, *really.*"

She finally handed me the DVD case. On the front was a picture of a high-rise office building, and *Rolling Blackout's Hometown Debut* ran across the middle. The back showed a picture of some bar called *Mickey's* and a brief description of the band's start there. The last sentence caught my eye – *featuring the video to My Disgrace.* I figured that this was the hopefully mercifully short piece of *awesomeness* that my mother was going to subject me to. I opened the DVD case. *My Disgrace* was apparently the band's hit – the lyrics were printed on the inside of the front cover.

"Even your Great-aunt Rae liked him," my mom was saying.

My Great-aunt Rae was really a relative, unlike this Aunt Amy that I couldn't remember. Great-aunt Rae was my grandmother's sister, and was a jolly, happy old lady, in contrast with my grandmother, who'd always seemed to be rather a stick-in-the-mud to me. She wasn't married, and her niece's children seemed to be one of the greatest joys in her life. For as long as I could remember, Great-aunt Rae had never forgotten any of our birthdays; she'd never missed a Christmas; she'd always been there with presents for us. And she always had a smile on her face. No one in my life had every seemed more happy to me than my Great-aunt Rae.

"All of us liked this singer, in fact, except your Aunt Amy," my mom continued. Again, with this *Aunt Amy* person that I didn't remember. "She used to make fun of us, call us *groupies.* But then it turned out that your Aunt Amy married a man that looked just like him. We were all very jealous. Then –"

"Let's light this candle," I said, using one of my dad's favorite expressions. Mom's story was already beginning to bore me. Aunt Amy and ancient bands. I had other stuff to do than waltz down the Memory Lane of terrible old music with my mom. I pushed a button on the DVD player, and after what seemed like an eternity, the thing opened, and I gingerly dropped the disk into it. I pushed the button, and after another interminable pause – *my God, things used to be so slow!* – the machine swallowed the round piece of plastic.

It took me a few minutes of pushing buttons to get the video to start, because Mom hadn't been able to find a remote with which to control this antique, and she didn't want to see the other stuff on the disc. Just this *awesome* video. But at last, I got it going, and taking a big gulp of wine to deaden the pain I was sure was about to come, I sat down next to my mom on the couch.

The tune started, and I discovered that the unfortunately named Rolling Blackout was a four-man combo. I'd expected some kind of shaggy-haired musicians, and a discordant type sound – *metal,* I think they'd once called it – from the name of the band. But they were all fairly clean cut, a little older than I'd expected, and their sound was upbeat, poppy. There was a little drummer, a big bass player, and a guitar player with a big nose.

And then there was the other guitar player, who was also the singer.

He had curly black hair, not quite shoulder length, and the bluest eyes I'd ever seen. He was dressed to match his hair: tight black denim and a black leather jacket; he played a shiny black guitar that seemed to be a natural extension of all the rest of that dark sexiness. He wore snakeskin boots – the sale of such things had been outlawed about 2025, and such adornments had gone the way of ivory brooches – and a dark blue, V-necked t-shirt. The color enhanced his incredible eyes – I wondered if it was some kind of primitive special effect – nobody's eyes could really be that blue, could they?

The video cut away from the singer to show tall buildings and bridges and boats on the ocean; I didn't really get what the song was about that first time, because I was so shocked and amazed at the singer's entirely unexpected attractiveness. The video was lit well, for its time period, I thought; but the director had also used a lot of fuzzy, just slightly out of focus, completely annoying camera tricks.

The video ended, and my mom looked at me. "That," she said, "was Wes Thomerville, circa 2011 or 2012. He was the best looking man I'd ever seen."

I returned her thrilled look neutrally, completely emotionless. It simply wouldn't do for me to voice my opinion, to actually say out loud that I for once agreed with my mother. Especially not about something like the attractiveness of the opposite sex. If I did, then she'd want to open up that file folder on her computer and show me all those pictures again, and tell me about the movies that this one had been in, and how that one was really gay, and how this one had died of a drug overdose. It was really too dreary for words.

"Let's watch it again!" she cried in glee. She jumped up and pushed the right button on the DVD player on the very first try and sat back down. She was more familiar with this ancient technology than I was.

Wild horses couldn't have dragged me from the spot on the couch beside her. It couldn't have been as good as it had seemed, but

I aimed to find out. I slammed the rest of the wine in my glass, and displaying nothing but annoyed patience, I sat through it again.

Wes Thomerville, who had to be well into the middle of his fifties by now, had once been the most captivating man to have stalked the earth, or so it seemed from this video. How had I never heard of him before? Why didn't my mother have file folders full of pictures of *him*? The band was passable, the tune forgettable. Except that Wes sang it, and I'd eventually come to know every syllable of it, because he had this little hitch in his voice that seemed to caress my very soul. He yelped, he whispered, he paused and looked me right in the eye across the decades, and I was sure that the couch must've shook when I shuddered. How had I never before heard of someone that sang like this, that looked this good?

It was the sexiest thing I'd ever seen.

But then my mom played it a third time, and she started deconstructing, describing in intimate detail the things that *she* found sexy about it. I actually put my hands over my ears. It was disturbing enough to discover that this awful, ancient video of some tepid, unknown band had turned me on almost past my ability to sit still. I *could not* sit by and listen while my mother told me what exact parts of it had also touched her. That was just too weird. Seriously. Who wants to hear about what turns *their mother* on? I didn't want to discover if we agreed on any specific points.

Halfway through this third time, my dad walked into the room. Mom was watching with a little leer on her face. I was trying not to watch, but was unable to help myself. I kept my hands pressed to the sides of my head, so I couldn't hear Mom's commentary. Dad looked at us for a second, then he said, "Darlene." When Mom didn't turn away from the TV, he snapped his fingers in front of her face. "Darlene!" When she finally looked at him, he nodded at me. "You're tormenting your daughter."

Mom looked at me, with my hands over my ears, in disbelief. "You don't like it, Brendee?" She looked back at the screen, just as the video ended for the third time. "What are ya, nuts?"

Mercifully, Dad was also familiar with the workings of the antique plastic disc player. He pushed a button; the screen went dark, and after what seemed like absolutely *days* to me, the tray slid out. Dad plucked the plastic out of the machine and looked at the picture of sunny blue skies that was printed on it.

"Where *in the hell* did you find this?" he asked my mom. Then he grinned at me. "Where's the dog?" he asked. I pointed to the dog,

49

asleep by the front door. "It's a good thing she's deaf," Dad told me. "Wes Thomerville's voice has been known to cause house pets to throw themselves in front of moving cars."

"You're just jealous," Mom said. She stood up and took the disc from my dad, and stuck it back in its case. I observed where she put it, as carefully as might a junkie observe where the dealer hides his stash: she placed it carelessly on top of the dusty old DVD player.

"Me?" Dad said. "Jealous of – where did you find that?" he asked again.

"Amy and Alex are moving back to Riverside!" Mom said. "I was looking for my yearbook in a box of old stuff in the attic, and it was in there." She hugged Dad. "And you don't have to be jealous, Bo. It was a million years ago."

I was amazed, appalled. Were they saying that Mom actually *knew* Wes Thomerville? *Dated* him maybe? Had my mother actually *slept* with this incredible vision? Gazed into those depthless blue eyes, felt the touch of those long fingers? I had to know. "Why would Dad be jealous?" I asked, just a spark of curiosity amid my studied disinterest. "Was this guy an old boyfriend or something?"

Mom sighed. "If there truly was a God." She squeezed Dad's arm. "No. Like I say, he was just a singer that we all liked." She kissed Dad on the cheek. "And then your dad came along and saved me from my futile groupie-hood. I'd forgotten all about Wes Thomerville, until your Aunt Amy called. Your Uncle Alex looked just like him."

"Is this what I'm supposed to do on date night?" Dad nodded at the DVD player. "Listen to bad music from the dawn of time?"

Mom kissed him on the cheek again. "Not at all. We're going out to dinner."

"Let me get rid of this old thing for you, Mom," I said. I got up from the couch and began to unhook the old disc player. "Where do you want me to put it?" I carefully slid the disc in its case under the television. That way, my mom wouldn't notice it was gone, and take it back and hide it once more in whatever wondrous treasure box she'd found it in.

"Just stick it in the attic," Mom said. "Look for the non-dusty square on the shelf. That's where it was."

****

I put the DVD player back into the electronics graveyard in the attic, then sat on the couch and pretended to mess around with my phone. Just an average, almost eighteen-year-old girl, with nothing to do on a Friday night. The dog jumped up in my lap and I petted her. Gary came in and asked if I wanted to go to some party; normally, it would've sounded good, but I wasn't going anywhere right that minute. I told him that I'd love to, but that I had to study. He shrugged and ran off to take a shower and get ready to go. My younger brother Hal and my little sister Jen also came in, said hi to me, and then also wandered away when I proceeded to ignore them.

I was alone in the living room with the DVD then, and my eyes flicked up from my phone. I could just see the corner of the case underneath the television, but I knew no one else could see it hidden there.

At last, Mom and Dad announced that they were leaving, and I waved goodbye over my shoulder, carefree, preoccupied with my phone, with all the goings-on in cyberspace: everything that was so much more interesting to me than them. I didn't look up. I listened for the car to start, counted to ten. Then I took a deep breath, pushed the dog off my lap, and slowly stood up. Just as slowly, I crossed the room and retrieved *Rolling Blackout's Hometown Debut* from its brief hiding place under the TV. Then I couldn't stand to move slowly for another second, and dashed to my room and locked the door.

I found the old laptop in the closet – the one that would actually read and play these ancient plastic discs. I copied everything I needed, converted it to a modern format, then cavalierly sauntered back out to the living room and casually tossed the disc in its case onto the shelf beside the TV. My mom could do with it what she wished, now. I'd freed Wes Thomerville and his *awesome* video from its prison of unreadable plastic ancientness, and then moved it from the old laptop to a new one. The one I use every day.

Now I could watch him whenever I wanted. Alone, without my mother's disturbing commentary.

And watch him I do, every Friday night. There's a boring documentary, too. Just a bunch of interviews with him and his band. I don't want to hear him talk; *I want to her him sing,* want to watch him roughly, tenderly, manhandle that black guitar. I want to pause when he pauses, want to allow myself to feel it in the very core of me when he whispers.

Where I once thought of the bright, unknown future to come, now my whole week is more or less built around the anticipation of the ritual of watching this video. I am its most willing slave. There's school, life, living, all week; then a sweet and brief couple of tumbles with Dave on Thursday afternoon. I don't know if that takes the edge off; or if it puts a keener one on to my anticipation of what's to come the next day.

Dave, eighteen, my maybe-someday husband, is quite attractive in his own right, with reddish-brown hair and freckles, and the prettiest brown eyes. He's what my mother refers to as a *healthy, strapping boy,* and I'm pretty sure that Mom knows what we've been doing, for almost a year now, even though I bet she couldn't guess when, where, or how often – that's it's a weekly, scheduled event, just like her date night with Dad.

But since school let out last June, whenever I close my eyes and kiss my beloved Dave – whenever I close my eyes and do *anything* with my beloved Dave – I gleefully imagine that he's blue-eyed, black-haired Wes Thomerville, a man in his thirties. A man in his thirties before I was born.

I tell Dave goodbye and *I love you* on Thursday afternoons, and then I close the door and forget about him, in anticipation of watching Wes's video again on Friday night. Since it's Mom and Dad's date night, there's usually a half-full bottle of wine left sitting in the kitchen when they go out, and I never fail to fill up a big goblet and take it with me, if I can.

I drink my wine, take a shower, think about him. I drink a little more wine, and when I've got a good buzz going on, I set the laptop on a bar stool – no one has missed it from the den yet – and climb into bed. The quality of the video isn't the best – what with the artsy, un-focused camera-work and all – so I've discovered that the playback is better small, not even three by five, on the computer, instead of on the television. Up close, right there next to the bed.

There's one part where Wes raises his arm above his head, singing, *One slip and you'd be gone for good;* then he brings it down on *Not one single chance.* For a few weeks, I thought that this was the sexiest part. Never mind that the lyrics are stupid, that the song's too poppy: it's about pushing some woman off of a bridge or a cliff or a building, shoving her down a flight of stairs, or from the deck of a boat, for God's sake – couldn't they have shown a little more gravity in the tune? But no, it's just as bouncy and danceable as it can be, if you're into unknown, poppy and danceable from before you were born. Which I'm not; not in the least. Unless Wes Thomerville is singing it.

After a while, I came to the conclusion that the part where he looks directly at the camera and whispers is the sexiest part. Then, the part where he growls, *It will be from my shove* became the most anticipated moment for me. This appreciation shifted around as time went by: the beginning was the best, then the ending, then the middle.

Nowadays, it's the whole damn thing. Depending upon my level of anticipation, sometimes I just have to watch it once, and it's better than all afternoon with Dave. Sometimes I like to stretch it out and watch it over and over again – paying special attention to the way Wes holds his guitar this time, and his blue-blue eyes the next, and his flawless mouth the next. Never does it fail to get me off; it's the sexiest thing I've ever seen.

Sometimes, I think that I should attempt to wean myself from the insane influence of this video from before I was born – what had Dad called it – *bad music from the dawn of time?* It's nuts: I'm addicted to a person that doesn't actually exist anymore, at least not how he looks in this clip, and it isn't like I can go on doing this forever. But I'm not hurting anyone, and I like it. Very much. So no weaning has occurred.

I'd also toyed with the idea of putting it on when Dave and I were together on Thursdays, wondering if that would heighten everything, the reality combined with the fantasy. But I was sure that Dave would object if I suddenly insisted on playing this old-timey video in the background. Besides, I didn't want him to know about it. I didn't want *anyone* to know about it. It was my very own little secret. Even if it was insane.

And I was pretty sure that watching Wes over Dave's shoulder wouldn't make Dave's performance any better for me, anyway. I was already pretending he wasn't him, as it was. Dave and I did our thing in real life, and I closed my eyes and imagined that he had black hair and blue eyes, and that he played the guitar. And I did my thing alone with Wes's video, and I didn't have to imagine anything. I just watched it.

I'd completely lost my mind.

****

Now it was April, and I'd be eighteen in May and graduating in June, then going away to college in the fall. I wondered what my dorm-mates would think of my strange obsession. I was just thinking that whatever they thought, they'd just have to get over it, when my phone rang. It was Nate Osbourne. He was a nice guy. We'd gone to grade school together.

"I've got a huge favor to ask of you, Brendee," he said. "I want you to tutor your cousin Wiley, so he doesn't flunk out of *the math.*"

I laughed. "I don't have any cousins, Nate. My parents are both only children. I don't know anyone named Wiley."

Nate also laughed. "He says you're not really blood cousins. Something about your mom and his mom went to school together –"

"What's his mom's name?"

"I don't know, Brendee. But he says he knows you. That you and Gary and he used to play together when you were kids. Then he moved away. Now he's back, and he's flunking math. He'll pay you."

My mother had mentioned that aunt I didn't remember again, just the other day. I tried to remember what she'd said about this woman and her husband and her kid. It had to be the same people. "His name's Willie?"

"Wiley," Nate said. "I know it's a lot to ask, Brendee, but I'd hate to see him flunk out. He'll pay you," he said again.

What else did I have to do? It might be interesting to meet this pseudo-cousin. See if I could remember that lost moment of childhood. "When?" I asked Nate.

"How about tomorrow after school? Say, five-ish? You remember where I live, Brendee?"

That I did remember. Nate lived in the middle of the block, just around the corner from where we'd gone to grade school. "I'll be there," I told him. Nate said he appreciated it, and said goodbye.

My brother walked into the living room, and I asked him, "Do you remember our cousin Willie, Gary?"

He frowned. "Not Willie. *Wiley.* Yeah, I remember him. He's an asshole."

"Nate Osbourne wants me to tutor him in math. Says he'll pay me."

Gary shrugged. "Whatever, Brend. He's a big-mouthed asshole, and Osbourne's probably turned into an asshole, too, if they're hanging out together."

"I guess I'll find out," I said.

54

NATE

I walked over to Wiley's house to tell him the good news. He was again sitting in the recliner in front of the dark television. He looked hopefully at me and I gave him the thumbs up. "She said she'd do it. I told her you'd pay her."

"Gladly."

"I'll bring her over tomorrow after school."

"Great." Now Wiley grinned at me. "It's a small world, after all, did you ever stop to consider that, Nate, my son?"

"Stop calling me your son, Wiley," I said.

"After you left yesterday, I hacked lovely Brendee's laptop, as you requested, and obtained a copy of the file that so lights her fire. It wasn't difficult; it's the only video on her computer." He continued to grin at me. "You wanna see it?"

I looked at him warily. "What is it?"

"It's ancient. From like 2011. Some unknown local band."

"Really? Is that what you mean when you say it's a small world? Because they're local?"

"Something like that. Mom?" Wiley called. His mother poked her head out of the kitchen. "Tell Nate what you told me yesterday. About Rolling Blackout."

Mrs. Royce walked out into the living room and looked curiously at me. "Why are you boys suddenly so interested in a terrible band from before you were born?"

Wiley blinked innocently at her. "It's just like I told you yesterday, Mom. Some kid at school said his dad said, 'There used to be good bands in this town, son.' Then he mentioned this Rolling Blackout." Now Wiley blinked innocently at me. "We'd of course never heard of them, so I thought you might know. Tell Nate what you told me."

Mrs. Royce looked suspiciously at her precocious son. I'd only known Wiley for a few days – his mother had known him his whole life, and no doubt also knew that Wiley rarely asked meaningless, *oh, by the way* kinds of questions. She wondered why he could possibly want to know about some ancient local band, but she knew it wasn't just out of idle curiosity. She turned her suspicion upon me, and I blinked at her just as guilelessly as Wiley did.

"When I was in my early twenties, my friend Darlene –"

"My *Aunt Darlene?*" Wiley squinted at me.

"Yes. Your Aunt Darlene, and me, and four or five of our buddies used to go see this band called Rolling Blackout. Darlene had this huge crush on the lead singer, and so did everybody else. Everybody but me. I'd never seen them so nuts for anybody. He was about ten years older than us, and he was married. He wasn't interested in Darlene, or any of them, but she didn't care. She said he was the best-looking man she'd ever seen, and she dragged me out there every Friday to watch him sing. I thought he was okay, but like I say, he was married, and he wasn't interested in us, so I just couldn't understand why they were so interested in *him.*

"Then I met your dad, Wiley, and one night I invited him over to meet all my friends. We were all over at Darlene's aunt's house, and they were watching Rolling Blackout's awful video."

Wiley turned and grinned at me.

"Your dad rang the doorbell, and I brought him in to meet them. All conversation stopped, and they sat there, dumbfounded, gaping at him." Mrs. Royce grinned, looked sheepishly down at the floor. "Your dad, you see, bore a striking resemblance to the singer from Rolling Blackout. He could've been the guy's younger brother."

Wiley handed me his phone, but still paid attention to his mom. He'd called up a picture of his dad. Mr. Royce smiled – he was mostly bald, and what little hair he had left was now an iron gray. He was a little jowly; a pleasant-enough-looking, middle-aged man. Certainly nothing to thrill a teenaged girl.

"Darlene was so jealous," Mrs. Royce continued, with a little grin. "But she was my best friend, and she got over it. We both got married, and Darlene had a little boy, and I had you. Then she had a little girl, and then two more. You guys all played together when you were kids. Then we moved to the farm when you were about –"

"But what about the band, Mom?" Wiley asked, getting Mrs. Royce back on topic.

"Oh, Wiley," she whispered, "they were awful!"

"Were they – what did they call it? *Metal?* "

Mrs. Royce shook her head. "No. They had a poppy, completely forgettable sound. Stupid, inane lyrics."

"You said something about a video?" Again Wiley squinted at me.

"Yeah. *My Disgrace.* It was about revenge. It was terrible. Puerile." She grinned. "Your Aunt Darlene *loved* it."

"So I guess Andy was wrong, eh, Nate?" Wiley said. I blinked at him. I didn't know anyone named Andy. "About this Rolling Blackout being a great band?"

"Most definitely, he's wrong," Mrs. Royce agreed. "They were awful."

"Thanks, Mom," Wiley said, effectively dismissing her. She got the hint immediately, and with another suspicious glance at us, she went back out to the kitchen. Wiley grinned at me. "So . . . Ya wanna see it?"

"Do I? Your mom says it's awful."

Wiley shrugged. "I been told that I don't have a very discerning musical taste, so I can't say."

"You watched it?"

Wiley grinned slyly. "Of course." He stood up and stretched. "Come on, see for yourself. It doesn't really matter what I think or what my mom thinks or even what you think, does it? It only matters what Brendee thinks. And we already know how she *feels* about it, don't we?"

I considered Wiley and his crafty, shark's grin. "Why do I get the impression that I'm not going to like this?"

"You'll never know unless you watch it." He bowed and swept his arm toward the staircase to the attic.

****

Suffice it to say that I wasn't impressed with Rolling Blackout's video; I agreed with Wiley's mom, that their sound was poppy and forgettable, their lyrics inane. But the most annoying thing about the video wasn't their sound or their look. The most annoying thing about the video was the singer.

"What's this guy's name?" I asked Wiley.

He held up his finger, then typed something on his phone. A moment later he got a text. "Mom says his name is Wes Thomerville." He typed something on his phone again, then exclaimed in surprise. "Well, what d'ya know? They'll let anybody on *Wikipedia,* these days, I guess." When I didn't look amused, he cleared his throat and continued. "Wes Thomerville, born 1980. Damn, Nate, that makes him . . ." Wiley counted on his fingers. "Fifty-three? Damn!" He looked at his phone again. "Riverside's native son, lead singer of Rolling Blackout, one documentary video,

Rolling Blackout's Hometown Debut, featuring the video to *My Disgrace.* Married to Madeline Rearden since –"

"Is there a picture of him?" I asked.

"I'm sure there is," Wiley said, and looked down at his phone again.

I slapped him on the back of the head. "Is it like looking in a fucking mirror, Wiley?"

Because the main problem with Rolling Blackout, and the video that turned my pretty little Brendee into a writhing wildcat, wasn't their sound and it wasn't their lyrics. It wasn't even their singer, really, this Thomerville guy, who was now fifty-three and probably just as bald and jowly as Wiley's dad.

The problem was that Wiley, like his old man before him, *looked just like this guy.*

"What can I say, Nate?" he batted his blue eyes at me. "Don't hate me because I'm beautiful." I lunged for him and he dodged out of the way, and threw himself onto his bed. "How do you want to work this?"

"Maybe I should just kill you and bury you in the back yard." I collapsed into my assigned seat. If Wiley knew half of the stuff he said he did about girls . . . Hell, Wiley didn't have to know anything. He looked *just like* this guy. All he'd have to do was smile at Brendee, and she'd be his. Just what he needed, something else to stroke his insufferable ego.

"Then you wouldn't graduate, either." He threw a pillow at me. "I don't want this girl, Nate. I just want her to help me pass math." He smiled at me, genuinely. "You have my promise. Brendee's all yours. I won't touch her."

"What if she . . ."

Wiley considered his fingernails. "I'll just have to tell her thanks, but no thanks. I already have a girlfriend."

"You're a prince, Wiley, you smug, blue-eyed son of a bitch. You'll pardon me if I don't believe you."

"Look, Nate, you saved my ass. You're the only friend I've got. She's all yours. What do I want with some high school girl? And I do have a girlfriend, sorta."

"Yeah, on another continent." I threw the pillow back at him.

"I think it's an island." He smiled brightly. "Maybe I'm brilliant at geography, too, after all." He looked at me sincerely. "I promise you, Nate. I won't touch her. I'll turn her down if she asks to touch me." He grinned as another thought struck him. "Perhaps I should just be my normal charming self. You know how all the girls love my normal charming self."

What choice did I have but to believe him? He was a snob, after all. Maybe he wasn't interested in Brendee. Maybe he was my friend. "Just don't wear a leather jacket. Or a blue t-shirt."

"I think my mom's got a pair of snakeskin cowboy boots. Shush. They're contraband." Wiley swung his long legs over the side of the bed, and ran his hands through his curly black hair. "I'll be your Cyrano, Nate." When I looked blankly at him, he shook his head. "I'll talk you up to her. Tell her what a great guy you are, and all that bullshit. Trust me."

"I trust you, Wiley. Though I still might start digging that hole in the back yard."

****

The next day, as I walked the short distance to Wiley's house with Brendee, I felt like I was about to be strapped to the gurney and taken to the death chamber. But she was so cute, and she smiled at me, and touched me on the arm, so after a minute, I felt a little surge of confidence. My good friend Wiley, was, after all, somewhat of an asshole, no matter who he looked like. "Would you like to go get a pizza again, when you're done with your cousin?"

"He's not my cousin, Nate. I don't even know him. And I'd love to go have pizza with you, only . . . I have to tell you. I have a boyfriend. His name's Dave." She showed me a picture of him on her phone; he was a big, brown-eyed, dumb-looking redhead.

You had *a boyfriend,* I thought, all my glumness returning. *I'd bet my front seat in hell* – Jesus, I was even starting to *talk* like Wiley, even to myself – *you're gonna forget all about dapper Dave, the minute you see Wiley Royce.*

And I was right. The man himself was waiting for us on the porch. We walked up the concrete toward it, and when Wiley sauntered down the three steps, barefoot as always, Brendee stopped. Her mouth dropped open and I watched her sparkly blue eyes dilate, just like they had in the clip Wiley showed me. She wasn't seeing some friend of mine that she was coming to tutor in math, the cousin she didn't remember – she was seeing Wes Thomerville, in the flesh, the same age as she was.

Wiley was smiling at her, then his smile faltered a bit at the expression of naked desire on her face. He also stopped, and looked at me. Resigned, I nodded at him, indicating for him to come the rest of the way down the walk.

"Wiley, this is my friend, Brendee. Brendee, this is –"

"My . . . cousin . . . Willie," she said slowly, as if drugged.

"Wiley," he corrected, and extended his hand. Brendee clasped it, then looked down at it for a moment. It was the equivalent of pinching herself to see if she was dreaming, I thought.

"Well!" I said and clapped my hands together, making Brendee jump and drop Wiley's hand. "I'll see you kids later. Wouldn't want to be a third wheel to the studying. Call me when you're done, Brendee. We'll *all* go out for pizza. You, me, Dave . . . and ol' Wiley here."

Let's see how Dave likes the way you look at him, I thought. All was lost. I gave up in that moment. Sure, Wiley was my friend and all, and I believed that he'd been telling me the truth when he said he wouldn't touch Brendee. I believed that *he* believed it, at the time. But that was before she was standing right there in front of him, staring at him like he was on the menu. Who could fail to respond to that? He was only human.

Brendee seemed to get a hold on herself at the mention of her boyfriend's name. She looked down at the sidewalk for a moment, then said, "I'll call you, Nate. Later."

But Wiley said, "Don't go, Nate. I'm sure Brendee's just going to look at my book, and tell me what I need to study for next time." He looked significantly at me. "I'm sure there's not going to be any tutoring today."

Ah, Wiley, maybe you're my friend after all, I thought, and clapped him on the back. A little of my hope returned. Maybe all wasn't lost after all, maybe Brendee might still consider me . . . "If you insist," I said. We turned and walked the rest of the way up the concrete, up the three steps. As Wiley opened the front door, Brendee hurried to join us.

Mercifully, Mrs. Royce wasn't home from work yet, so I didn't have to endure all the *Look, how you've grown, Brendee! I haven't seen you since you were a little girl!* happy reunion joy. We followed Wiley up to his room at the top of the stairs. Brendee paused in the doorway, and glanced over at the desk by Wiley's bed. "What is that?" she exclaimed, pointing at the old desktop computer.

"That's a boat anchor," Wiley said.

"Does it work?" Brendee asked.

"Of course it works," Wiley said. "Only –"

"Very slowly," Brendee supplied.

She asked him some technical question about the pile of wires and cellphone guts on the desk, and Wiley smiled in surprise and answered her. It suddenly seemed as if they were speaking in Greek, long syllables followed by incomprehensible acronyms. I sat in my chair and put my head in my hands. He might be able to resist her if she was just pretty, but if she knew this electronic shit like he did? I got the impression that Wiley was a sucker for a woman with a brain.

They walked over to the other desk, still speaking like Spartans. I watched Wiley unplug the tablet that'd been attached to the TV – where he kept all his *telescreen* files, including the one of the girl standing next to him. Still talking tech to her, he plugged his laptop into the TV. He showed her the remote, and she laughed at it, then examined it closely.

"How much do you want me to pay you for your tutoring skills?"

"Oh, Wiley, you don't have to pay me!" she replied, flustered, looking down at her shoes.

"Are you sure?"

Brendee nodded and smiled up at him. "You don't have to pay me," she said again.

You just have do me, Wiley, you don't have to pay me, too, I thought. *Oh, fuck this.* I was just about ready to make my retreat again – they wouldn't even notice that I'd left – when I heard Wiley say, "I've written this little program that lets you spy on your friends through the webcams on their laptops." I looked up at him and he squinted at me. I noticed he didn't mention anything about televisions.

"What's your number, Brendee? I'll send you a copy of it." Brendee told him her phone number, and Wiley typed it into his phone, then hit *Send.* When I heard Brendee's phone beep, I thought, *You have no idea what a mistake you've just made. He's already in your computer. Now you've just let him into your phone.* What difference did it make, though? He was already in her imagination.

"How does it work?" she asked.

"Well, you plug in their IP address at the prompt. You know how to find their IP address, right?" Brendee shook her head. "Well, to find your own, you just go to *whatismyip.com* . . ." Wiley typed something on the laptop, then took the remote from Brendee. He pushed a button and a webpage sprang to forty inch life on the television screen. "There's my IP address," he said. "I'll show you how to find other people's later." He looked at the top of one desk, then the other one. "Shit. I left my book downstairs. I'll be right back." Wiley walked by without looking at me.

Brendee either didn't know or didn't care that I was watching her. She glanced at the TV, and surreptitiously typed Wiley's IP address into her phone. Then she looked over at me. "He knows his shit," she said, just for something to say, to cover up her sneakiness.

"Are you really going to spy on people?" I asked. *Or just him? I* thought. *Are you really too dumb to see that he's just led you to it?*

Brendee shook her head. "I don't know how to find people's IP's. And who would I spy on, anyway?" She laughed nervously.

Wiley returned and flopped down on his bed with his math book. Then he looked at me, and thought better of it. He jumped up, handed me his book, and held up his finger. We listened to his bare feet slap down the stairs. He returned a moment later with a folding chair. He sat in it, and indicated for Brendee to sit in his rolling chair. "Shall we begin?" he said.

BRENDEE

It was nice to see Nate again. He was cute and polite, and gutsy enough to try to ask me out the minute he saw me, even though I probably haven't said thirty words to him this year. He sends me a text every now and then, just to say hi, just to keep in touch. I might've gone out with him once, had he been more on the scene before I'd met Dave. They were a lot alike, actually: quiet and respectful, and neither of them were capable of hiding how much they liked me. Custom dictated that I could choose only one, and Dave had been in the right place at the right time.

Nate held absolutely no mystery for me: my curiosity was more than satisfied. One big quiet guy that clearly liked me was enough. But Nate was nice, and I was happy to help his friend for him.

We strolled up the walk to a large old Craftsman; a two-story. I glanced up at the porch, curious to see what my cousin Willie, who I couldn't remember at all, looked like.

Then the world stopped.

We've got that autonomic nervous system to control all those pesky things that we need to keep us alive, like respiration and heartbeat and all that. When he walked down the steps, barefoot, long and lean like some kind of cross between a blue-eyed white boy and a black jungle cat, my autonomic nervous system grew a voice. "Breathe, Brendee," it advised me sternly. "Take a breath, or you're gonna pass out."

I complied. He approached, and it seemed like it was in slow motion. The intellectual part of my mind faded into the background; it became like some kind of annoying tapping sound, like someone insistently sending out Morse code in another room. What remained of my mind became totally attuned to the visual, the visceral. *Oh my God, he's breathtaking!* The telegraph operator spelled out W-E-S at the periphery of my consciousness, over and over, like one of those old fashioned tickertape things. W-E-S, W-E-S, W-E-S . . .

Of course, he wasn't Wes at all. Wes wasn't real, not in any tangible sense of the word. He might still be walking around somewhere, but he didn't look like he did in his video anymore. Father Time had seen to that.

His video was a slice of witchcraft from across the decades that had enslaved my very soul, but if I thought about it, Wes from 2011 was just a tad old for me, anyway, no matter how absolute he looked.

But this guy was perfection distilled: he looked just like Wes, but he was real and breathing and barefoot and standing there in front of me, and he was my age.

Then Nate was introducing us, and the auto-steering in my mind suddenly sprang to life again, and replayed for me the conversation that I'd had with my mom, on that fateful day when she'd showed me the video to *My Disgrace*.

"You don't remember your Aunt Amy?" my mother had said. Maybe it was true that we never really forget anything we ever hear; that it's just stored away somewhere in the ninety percent of our brains that they say we never use. Because I was amazed that her words, which I hadn't really been paying that much attention to at the time, could still be recalled. "She had a little boy, about the same age as Gary. His name was . . . Willie, I think. You guys all used to play together when you were little."

"Wiley, this is my friend, Brendee," Nate was saying. "Brendee, this is –"

"My . . . cousin . . . Willie." I tried to remember what else my mother'd said, if she'd given some clue as to the alchemy that had made the child of her old school chum look so much like the singer that she'd lusted after.

"Cloning!" the insane part of my mind whispered, and then the more rational part reminded me again of Mom's words: "All of us liked this singer, in fact, except your Aunt Amy. She used to make fun of us, call us *groupies*. But then it turned out that your Aunt Amy married a man that looked just like him. We were all very jealous . . . I'd forgotten all about Wes Thomerville, until your Aunt Amy called. Your Uncle Alex looked just like him."

And through some miracle of genetics, his boy looked just like him, too. I considered that perhaps I'd actually enter a church and give praise to that God that I was now so positively sure existed, and who so obviously loved me, just like the Jehovah's Witnesses said He did. Because who else but a loving Higher Power could've made a walking, talking Wes Thomerville just for little ol' me, plopped him right down here in Riverside, made us practically family? My cousin, Willie . . .

"Wiley," he corrected, and extended his hand. I took it; and while it's true that most normal, sane people probably don't ever think about what it might be like to shake someone's hand, someone who wasn't even real . . . But Wiley's hand was hot and just the tiniest bit damp, just as I'd always imagined Wes's would be. I

looked down at his hand to see if he might also have those same long fingers . . .

Nate clapped like some kind of a lunatic cheerleader and made me jump. I dropped Wiley's exquisite hand and Nate was saying something about being on his way, and I thought he couldn't be gone quickly enough for me, unless the ground opened and swallowed him up on the spot.

But Wiley asked him to stay, and I stood there in disbelief, dumbfounded. I wasn't going to get to be alone with my cousin. How did he think he was going to learn anything, how did he think I was going to be able *to teach him anything*, with Nate hanging around? Insanely, I saw Nate holding up cards with score numbers on them, like in the old-time Olympics. I shook my head, wondering if I'd ever be in full control of my own mind again, and followed them into the house.

****

Wiley, incomparably attractive though he might be, was indeed an idiot when it came to math. I couldn't believe that someone who knew so much about electronics, someone with so many books in his room, someone who'd been favored by God with the appearance of a Grecian statue come to life, could be so damn dumb. I read a few problems from his Intermediate Algebra book to him, and he just blinked blankly at me and shook his head.

"How did you ever pass Beginning Algebra?" I asked in amazement.

He grinned at Nate, who was sitting in a chair with his arms folded across his chest, frowning. "You remember, last year, how they busted that big kiddie porn ring up North?" When Nate shook his head, still frowning, Wiley looked at me. His eyes were so blue that I might've flinched. "The perverts use file-sharing sites to disseminate all that sick shit to each other,' he said. "They have encryption sometimes, and codenames. But it's all still traceable. All you need is one IP address. The Feds found one, and started zeroing in on these guys."

"What does that have to do with –" Nate began.

Wiley held up his hand. "Let's just say that my Beginning Algebra teacher was suddenly nervous, and he'd heard that I knew a tiny little bit about computers. Maybe he'd also heard that I'm a discreet kind of guy. Without telling me what he wanted to make

65

disappear – I guessed on my own – he asked me if it was really possible to erase files and histories, so that they could never be recovered. Not even by the Effa Bee Eye." Wiley grinned at me. "I told him that it was, a mere bagatelle in fact, and wiped his hard drive for him so it was as clean and as innocent of sin as the day it was manufactured. I did Mr. Holstrap a little favor, and he did me one. Not much of one, however. He only gave me a C."

Nate continued to frown for the rest of the afternoon, while I asked Wiley more questions about his understanding of Algebra, and he continued to shake his head. Nate frowned, I say, except when I would catch him looking at me. When I'd catch that puppy-dog, hopeful look in his eyes, he'd quickly look away. These guys. These *boys.* They should really learn to hide it when they like a girl. All that obviousness . . . I guess I should've found it flattering. Nate wasn't a bad-looking guy – another *healthy, strapping boy*, like my mother said. Nate was all right. He was the same type as Dave, and he looked at me the same way Dave did. And Dave was all right, too.

But neither of them could hold the oft-mentioned candle to Wiley Royce. *My cousin.* I thought that maybe I remembered him from when we were little – I vaguely recalled going to visit a family with a yappy, black-haired kid a few times. It had to have been them.

But, my, oh my, sweet *Jesus,* how he'd grown. I wondered what my mother would think of *her nephew,* now that he was all grown up.

And why did Nate want to hang around anyway, mooning over me when he thought I wasn't looking? Didn't he have anything better to do? Wiley . . . Wiley didn't look at me like Nate did. He just smiled blankly at me – it was a friendly enough smile, I hoped – but if I didn't know better, I might've thought that *awesome looking* Wiley was a trifle dim, at least when it came to girls.

I realized that there was going to have to be some intense study, some intense tutoring on my part, if he was going to pass Intermediate Algebra and make it to graduation. He'd somehow managed to squeak by with D's this year, but he was utterly lost now. He was in the gutter, and it was a long way to that last D on the curb.

I thought it might be necessary to take him all the way back to the very beginning: *One plus one equals two, Wiley, insert Tab A into Slot B, oh, my, God, just tell me what I can do for you, you delicious, blue-eyed tomcat!* I thought it might be necessary to tutor him for several hours a day to get him to pass. *Every day.*

NATE

On Friday, Wiley gave me a ride home from school, because my shit-box Chevy was on the fritz again. When it wouldn't start the night before, my dad and I had opened the hood and peered in at the mysterious stuff beneath. Then after a moment, he said, "You're gonna have to get a job again, Nate."

"Why's that, Dad?" After my hand healed up, since I wasn't going to be playing football, I'd found a job hanging drywall on the weekends, busting my ass, just to scrape together the money to buy the damnable car. All in the name of integrity, Dad had said he'd subsidize my driving expenses while I was still in school, but I was going to have to buy the thing on my own. I quit my job the day after I bought it. It had turned out that I'd chosen poorly.

"What do I know about fuel cells?" Dad closed the hood. "I'm not entirely sure how they work, nonetheless how to fix 'em. You're going to have to pay somebody."

So the Chevy sat forlornly, inscrutably, in the driveway, and I rode to school and back with Wiley. Wiley, trapeze ballerina, well-read electronics master, black-haired, blue-eyed sex god that he claimed to be, knew absolutely nothing about cars. *Absolutely nothing.* He hadn't even read about them.

"You turn the key and push the pedal," he said. "This one, you plug it in at night. That's all I know."

We parked in front of my house and went inside. I made us both a bologna sandwich. Wiley squinted at me when I handed his to him, then shrugged and took a bite anyway. "What?" I said.

"You really shouldn't eat this shit, Nate." He held up the sandwich and took another bite. "White bread – no fiber. Bologna – Jesus, lips and assholes and too many chemicals," he said, his mouth full. "It's tasty, because they make it that way. But it's not good for you."

"What are you, a vegetarian?"

Wiley's black eyebrows shot up in amusement. "As a matter of fact, I am." He gestured with his sandwich. "Mostly."

"I can't see you as a crusader for the pigs and cows and chickens," I said.

"And you'd be right," Wiley said. "The bacon and the veal and the *moo goo gai pan*. I didn't claw my way to the top of the food chain to be worried about them." He finished his sandwich. "I'm not a vegetarian for them, I'm a vegetarian for me. And like I say, I'm not totally a vegetarian." He pointed to one of his canine teeth. "This little sharp one designates me as a carnivore. You have to have a little protein.

"But you? You eat like you're gonna go out and plow the back forty, Nate. And what're you gonna do? You're gonna sit on your ass and drive to school, then you're gonna sit on your ass *in* school. Maybe you'll jog around the track after school, or go to the gym." Wiley shuddered. "With all the other idiots.

"You don't need all that food, all that red meat. All that bread, pasta, Ranch dressing. People wonder why they're fat." When I didn't say anything, he continued. "Don't get me wrong, I like a good steak as much as the next guy. But you don't need it every day. It sticks in your guts. It makes you tired." He prodded me in the stomach, and I tried to slap him. He dodged my hand. "Makes you slow," he said with a grin. "Maybe a little fish or chicken, lots of veggies, a few whole grains. That's really all you need."

I finished my bologna sandwich, considering him. "You think you're a fucking Renaissance man, don't you, Wiley, you smug bastard? You really do think you're smarter than everybody else."

"And quicker, too." He batted his blue eyes at me, those eyes so like Brendee's geriatric singer. "I'm just not a sheep, Nate. *Baaa,"* he bleated, then grinned at me. "You want to find out what your girlfriend thinks of us? After just one afternoon?"

"What're you talking about, Wiley?" I asked, even though I was pretty sure I already knew. She'd given him her phone number, hadn't she? I was sure that was probably way more than he needed.

"I waited for ya, Nate. All damned day. Even though, I have to admit, I'm curious as hell. Come on, let's read it together." He walked out to the living room, flopped carelessly down on the couch, and began scrolling through his phone. "Let's see, Brendee . . . Who does Brendee know, that knows us? Besides Gary?" His long finger flicked across the screen. "Ah, my blushing Deneen." He looked up at me. "Do you know she's anorexic, Nate?"

"I know she's skinny. I didn't know she had a problem with it."

Wiley's grin bloomed. "Oh, she doesn't have a problem with it. She digs it! *Quod me nutrit me destruit.* It means, *What nourishes me also destroys me.* I've seen the history on her computer, Nate. She's pro-anorexic. There's a million sites for them. *They're our bodies, we'll do what we want to them* and all that. They don't do it because they have a poor self-image, and all that shit. Or at least that's not why they *think* they do it. They do it because they like it.

"I could tell her a few things about what nourishes her, if she'd give me the time of day. She's so fucking stupid."

"Are you in everybody's business, Wiley?"

"What kind of computer you got, Nate?"

"I use my phone," I told him.

"That's the easiest of all," he said, without looking up. "You want me to send a copy of Brendee's video to your phone? So you can watch it with Pam and her sisters?"

"Fuck you, Wiley. I don't want a copy of it." I didn't wanna watch her get off to some guy older than her father.

"If you change your mind, just let me know." He paused. "Ah, here we go. This was from last night. 7:20. Right after you dropped her off, I assume. Brendee says, *'Hi, Deneen, how r u?'*

"'Deneen texts back, *'Fine, Brendee, how r u? Haven't talked to u 4 a minute. Since Hilda's party.'* That was quite a party, Nate. I never did show you the pictures –"

"What else does Brendee say?"

Wiley squinted at me, then looked at his phone again. *"'Do u remember Nate Osbourne? From grade school?'* she asks.

"Deneen says, *'Yeah. I have English w/him. He's cute. Nice ass.'"* Wiley looked up at me. "Turn around, Nate. Let me see." I flipped him off. "Maybe you should forget about Brendee. It looks like maybe Deneen's the girl for you. You could make her a bologna sandwich." He grinned.

"Brendee says, *'He's nice. Do you kno his friend, Wiley Roice?'* She spelled my last name wrong, Nate. What kind of a cousin is that?"

"At least she's not calling you *Willie* anymore," I replied.

Wiley nodded. *"'Yeah,'* Deneen says. *'I kno him. He's an asshole.'* Why Deneen, you wound me. *'I don't kno y Nate hangs around w him.'"*

I wondered that myself sometimes. "Better men than she have said you're an asshole," I said.

"You, for example. *'U don't think he's cute?'* Brendee asks.

"'Maybe if he'd keep his fat mouth shut,' Deneen says. So she likes the strong, silent type? I think we've found the girl for you, Nate. Aren't you the strong, silent type?"

"I don't want Deneen, Wiley."

"I know what you want, Nate. It's as plain as the nose on your face." Wiley scrolled forward and then back again. "I dunno. *If you can't be with the one you love . . .*" He looked up at me and waited. When I didn't say anything, he sighed and looked back at his phone again. *"Love the one you're with."*

"What is that?" I asked in annoyance. "Poetry? Byron?"

Wiley shook his head. "Some ancient song."

"Do you have any vinyl, Wiley?"

He looked up at me. "What?"

"Do you have any vinyl? Records? You know all these old songs, these old singers. Baby Gaga –"

"*Lady* Gaga. She wasn't on vinyl, though. That goes way back."

"Yeah. I asked my dad if he'd ever heard of her, and he said, 'Yeah. She looked just like that Mikkelea, that one you all listen to these days.'"

Wiley looked up at me again. "Who?"

"You really don't know anything about music, do you?"

He shrugged and looked down at his phone again. "Nothing you've ever heard of."

"Anyway, Dad says, 'I wanna show you something,' and takes me out to the garage. He pulls out this milk crate from under a bunch of Christmas lights, and pulls this cardboard sleeve out of it. 'This was Debra Harry,' he says, and hands it to me. She looked a lot like Mikkelea, and a lot like that Lady Gaga. 'There's a blonde singer for every generation,' he said. 'This one was from your grandma's time.' And then he went on to tell me about how, once upon a time, everything was on these big, black plastic discs, and they came in different speeds, and you had to have a needle to play 'em –"

"Did you ask your dad if he'd ever heard of Rolling Blackout?" Wiley asked innocently, not looking up from his phone.

"I did not," I said.

"Brendee says, *'Well, I think Wiley's cute.'* Why, thank you, Brendee. So does my mama.

"Deneen says, *'What about Dave? I like him. He looks like he's a handful, just like Nate.'*" Wiley grinned at me. "Are you a handful, Nate?"

"Fuck you, Wiley."

"Who's Dave? Brendee didn't text *Dave* yesterday."

"Dave's her boyfriend."

"Is he now?" Again Wiley grinned. "Are we so sure about that? Brendee says, *'I'm beginning to think I might b ready 4 a change.'*

70

" 'Ur not thinking of that asshole Wiley?'

" 'I dunno. He's cute.'

" 'U can have him. I'll take Dave off ur hands. Or maybe we can double – u and Wiley and me and Nate. If u can get Wiley 2 keep his filthy mouth shut, LOL.' " Wiley looked up at me. "Does anybody really text *LOL* any more, Nate?"

"Apparently."

"I think Deneen's the girl for you," he repeated. "What do you find so special about Brendee, anyway?"

I thought about it, shrugged. "I dunno," I said. "She's not all that special, I guess. I've known her since we were in grade school." But she was beautiful, and for long as I could remember, I'd thought about her. Even when Judy occupied most of my time, Brendee had always been there, at the back of my mind . . . Whatever it was I liked about her, I didn't feel like discussing it with Wiley Royce, of all people. He was not the romantic type.

"You just want to *get at her,* is that it?" He squinted at me. "Who's the snob now? Weren't you the one that said it's all the same in the dark?" He looked at me seriously for a minute – it was the first time I'd ever seen Wiley serious. He even said, "Seriously, Nate. I don't think Brendee's gonna all of a sudden think you're the one. You're not her type." He batted his blue eyes at me.

"Go fuck yourself, Wiley," I said, starting to get pissed off.

"Don't think I haven't tried, my son," he said, and sighed again. "I'm just saying – here's another old song lyric for you – *You can't always get what you wa-ant.* So why waste your time?"

"I knew it!" I stood up. "Get outta my fucking house, Wiley, before I kill you."

He looked up at me, smiled mildly. "Why would you want me to do that?"

"You want me to forget about Brendee because *you* want her! I knew it!"

Wiley shook his head. "You're the only friend I've got, Nate, the only one that's not an ex-convict. I value that friendship. It's great to have someone to talk to."

"All you do is talk down to me, Wiley! Get the fuck outta my house."

"Calm thyself, my son."

"I swear to *Christ,* Wiley, if you call me *my son* one more time, I'm gonna cut you."

"I'm trying to pay you a compliment, and you threaten me?" I noticed a slight edge of anger to his voice, something else I'd never heard before. "I'm trying to tell you that I value your friendship, that I'm not interested in this silly bitch that you've got a hard-on for –"

"Shut up, Wiley," I said, and sat back down.

"I'm just saying, you're barking up the wrong tree. Why waste your time, when there's so many *other* trees? Skinny trees, like Deneen?"

And this was after only one afternoon with her, I thought, *with me sitting right there with them. What's going to happen when they're alone?* Maybe he was right. Maybe Brendee wasn't the girl for me.

"Will you at least think about someone else?"

"Yeah, Wiley, I'll fucking think about it. But you said you wouldn't –"

"I won't touch her. I promised you. I don't want her. She's all yours. But I don't think she's having any." He looked at me, and I saw that ol' Wiley wickedness. "I won't touch her. But if you wise up and find someone else . . . *We must not promise what we ought not, lest we be called on to perform what we cannot.*"

72

BRENDEE

As I walked over to Nate's house to meet him and Wiley, I thought about Deneen. She was between boyfriends at the moment, and it appeared that perhaps she was zeroing in on Nate as the next candidate, although she'd also obviously be amenable to giving Dave a whirl if I dropped him. Deneen always was partial to those *strapping, healthy boys*. But if she picked up my leftovers, then we wouldn't be able to hang out together – it would be awkward – so I thought that she'd prefer Nate right at the moment.

I'd known Deneen since grade school, too, as had Nate; but Nate had forgotten the chubby green-eyed girl from fifth and six grade. There were two middle schools in our area, whose district boundaries overlapped; Deneen and I had gone to one and Nate had gone to the other. Deneen transmogrified during middle school, shedding the baby fat, and every other ounce of fat that she'd ever carried. So quickly did she lose it, it was as if she'd caught some wasting disease. By the time she started freshman year, the chubby little girl was someone else – Deneen was the skinny girl now, and that's how everybody knew her. I'm sure that Nate never made the connection between the two; Nate didn't remember Deneen from grade school. But she remembered him.

All the girls where I went to school were serious and scholarly – their parents, like mine, were paying through the nose for them to attend there, so it would've been unusual for them to be otherwise. And I'd always been serious and scholarly, too, even though I'd been fortunate enough to find Dave, and to realize that there was a little bit more to life than virginal study, and looking down on all the public school girls that were having more fun than us.

And that's why I liked Deneen. She was pretty and frivolous – she liked to take me to the mall. She was awed and delighted by clothes and make-up and bright, shiny things. She brought a little flash and color into my life, and if she didn't care about Occam's razor or the plight of the third world, that was all right with me. We talked about boys – she'd already chosen her share, and I enjoyed her down-to-earth descriptions of them. Passion was a huge part of her life – unkind people might have deemed her to be a little bit of a tramp – but she showed me that there was incomparable enjoyment to be gotten from it, once you dispensed with all the good girl/bad girl societal unfairnesses.

"Why should they get to have more fun than us?" she asked archly. "I don't care what you think, or what the other girls think, and I certainly don't care what *they* think. If I like some guy, why shouldn't I let him know it? In a hundred years, nobody will know the difference."

Deneen was always enthusiastic about her newest boyfriend, whereas I thought of Dave as just a nice, weekly diversion. He was fun and all, don't get me wrong – I never failed to enjoy myself – but he wasn't the incredibly sexy Greek god to me that Deneen's newest conquest always was to her. Dave was just Dave, the person that had the opposite equipment to mine, with whom I put the whole mechanism to enjoyable function. But each new boyfriend thrilled Deneen to the bone, until he didn't anymore, and the next one arrived. "Haven't you ever seen a guy that is just so damned cute that you just gotta have him?" she'd asked me. "You just can't live another moment 'til he touches you and kisses you?"

No, such a thing had never occurred for me. "Not this week," I'd tell her.

"You don't love Dave?"

I shrugged and told her that I certainly loved parts of Dave, but overall he was just okay. He served his purpose.

"Maybe I'm just in love with love," Deneen said. It was the distillation and extent of all the philosophy she possessed. I thought that she was just in love with boys, interchangeably. "And maybe you just haven't seen the right one yet," she said.

"This is what it's like when you see the right one, Brendee. Imagine yourself sitting on the edge of a boxcar, that's open at the top." Deneen held her hands out in front of her, fingers splayed. "The whole boxcar is filled with . . . Oh, I dunno, let's say . . . the whole boxcar is filled with marbles. Thousands of them; *millions of them.* White ones and blue ones, red ones, green ones, purple ones." Deneen ran her hands through the make-believe marbles, sifting them with her fingers. "But all of them are pretty much the same. These are boys. So you start eliminating them."

Deneen mimicked throwing marbles over her shoulder. "Oh, you're okay, and you're okay, but nothing to write home about. You're boring. You're dumb. You're mean. You're obnoxious. You're ugly." Deneen threw imaginary marbles over her shoulder – rejected boys. "Then one day . . ." she clasped her hands together for a moment, then reached out delicately with her thumb and forefinger. "There he is. A marble like no other." She turned the invisible marble over in her fingers; glanced back into the depths of the imaginary boxcar for a moment, over her shoulder again. "The most beautiful, perfect marble you've ever seen." Deneen closed the non-existent marble up in her fist.

"This week."

She grinned at me, then held it up between her thumb and forefinger for me to examine. "This is the marble for you, the one you're gonna wanna keep." She carefully put it into a pocket on her shirt that wasn't there.

"And what if I find out after a while that he's not the one I wanna keep? Like you do?"

Deneen rapidly took the non-existent marble out of her non-existent pocket and threw it over her shoulder with the others. She looked in the boxcar again. "There's plenty more where he came from." And she pretended to sift through the marbles again, tossing the culls over her shoulder.

"You just haven't seen the right marble yet, Brendee. When you do . . . you won't be so calm and collected. It's so much fun to think about him, all the things that you want him to do . . . The one for you – he's out there. I'm pretty sure it's not Dave. Dave doesn't thrill you – he can't be the right one. Just wait 'til you see him."

How prophetic those words had turned out to be. And when I saw the right marble, the one that made me shudder at the very sight of him, the one whose banal yelping song touched the very core of me – it was a man who didn't exist anymore, a man that I could never possess as anything more than a secret, ridiculous fantasy. I'd finally felt that all-encompassing lust, just like Deneen enjoyed with each new guy that struck her fancy, except that the man that did it for me wasn't real.

I'd understood Deneen's analogy with crystal clarity, the moment I'd seen Wes Thomerville. *A marble like no other. The most beautiful, perfect marble you've ever seen.*

I was satisfied with my vision of Wes, too, until I saw Wiley Royce: now here was a flawless marble, and I longed to roll him around between my palms, to carry him in my pocket. Now I sighed in delighted anticipation, just because I was going to get to see him again. I pushed the button beside Nate's door.

NATE

The doorbell rang, and we both looked toward it. Wiley sprang to his feet, no less graceful for the fact that he was wearing shoes for a change. He smiled genuinely at me again. "I promise – I won't touch Brendee. You're my friend, and I give you my word. I can't give you anything more than that."

"I need to start digging that hole, while the ground's still soft," I said, but I smiled back at him. What choice did I have but to trust him?

I opened the door and let Brendee in. She smiled at me, then looked at Wiley, and immediately, her pupils dilated, huge and black. Maybe he was right. It wasn't like he was doing anything to take her away from me. He was just standing there, doofy fucking Wiley, looking like Wes Thomerville, some guy from before she was born. That was all it took. I thought about suggesting he get a haircut, but that seemed a little desperate. Besides, his hair would grow back. Maybe he was right. Maybe I was reaching for something I couldn't get. But she was so *damned* cute.

"Are we gonna do this here?" she asked.

"My book's at home," Wiley said.

"You're supposed to take it with you to class," she said, and pushed him playfully.

"It's still all Greek to me," he said. If he said something in Greek, I thought I'd drop him right there in my living room.

"Well, let's go see if we can translate it for you," Brendee said and smiled sweetly at him.

We went out the door and Wiley paused on the sidewalk next to his car. It had once been white, or beige, maybe, but now it had a black door and a black hood, both dented. Whatever his other qualities, he'd never impress anybody with his car.

"Ah, the backseat's full of shit," he said, bending over and peering in at it. "Unless you guys want to squeeze together in the front seat . . . I'll take it home and walk back and meet you." Not waiting for us to answer, Wiley jumped into his Prius and drove off.

Brendee and I started walking toward his house. After a moment, she asked me if I knew Deneen. I said that I did, and she smiled and said, "She likes you, you know." I feigned surprise, tried to appear flattered. They were friends, after all. "You should ask her out sometime."

I told her I'd think about it. We rounded the corner to Wiley's block, and when she saw him walking toward us, Brendee stopped, just to watch him. I said, "Maybe you and me and Dave and Deneen could go out and get that pizza tonight."

"Dave's out of town for the weekend," she said, not taking her eyes off Wiley. "He's checking out Cal State San Diego with his parents. But that sounds like a good idea, Nate. Maybe Wiley –"

"Wiley's a vegetarian, Brendee. I don't think he's too big on pizza."

The man himself had arrived, and said, "Maybe when Nate gets his car fixed, he can drive you over here."

Or she can drive herself, I thought, *and just cut me out altogether.*

"What's wrong with your car?" Brendee asked.

"It no go," I said, and shrugged. "I don't know much about cars, and nothing about fuel cells."

She looked at Wiley and he also shrugged. "Gary knows about fuel cells," she said. "I'll see if I can get him to come over and look at it tomorrow."

"I'd definitely appreciate that," I said.

"Tell him, if he can fix it, we'll pay him," Wiley said. "It's spring, *when a young man's fancy lightly turns to thoughts of love.* It's also the time when people seem to start dropping cellphones and spilling shit on their tablets." He looked blankly at me. "I'll pay for it, Nate. I'm flush right about now."

I remembered that wad of twenties in his desk drawer. "I'll let you," I said.

****

Wiley took off his shoes on the front porch.

Brendee looked at me. "Should we take our shoes off, too?" she asked.

In surprise, Wiley asked, "You mean, like the charming Chinese tradition?" Brendee nodded. "You can if you want. But it's not a house custom or anything like that. I just like to be barefoot."

"I'll pass then," I said.

We filed upstairs and I sat in my accustomed chair in Wiley's room. He handed me a gigantic softcover book: *The Collected Works of William Shakespeare.* I blinked at him.

"Too much?" He put it back and handed me *Oscar Wilde and the Yellow Nineties,* then sat down next to Brendee in the folding chair, at the desk under the television. He opened a three-ring binder. Brendee sat in the rolly chair next to him.

I looked into the book he'd handed me. There was a picture of a dark-haired guy, wearing a cape, holding a hat: Oscar Wilde. The next page informed me that the book had been published in 1940, for God's sake, nearly a hundred years ago. I looked at the table of contents. Chapter XII was entitled *The Love That Dare Not Speak Its Name.* Right. Like I was interested in any of *that.*

I watched them, feeling entirely more the guilty voyeur than I had when I'd watched Brendee by herself. They had their heads bent over the desk; Wiley was writing something, and Brendee leaned in a little closer to him. I watched her slowly, deliberately press her knee against his. Wiley just as slowly, just as deliberately shifted away from her. Maybe he was a good man after all, but this was just entirely too much. I sat up straighter in the chair, and scraped my foot across the wooden floor.

Wiley looked over his shoulder at me. "What's a'matter, Nate? Oscar Wilde's travails not to your liking either?" He got up and took the book from me, stuck it back on the shelf. "How about this one?" He handed me *Brave New World,* by Aldous Huxley. "It's not *The Doors of Perception,* but I don't know if you're ready for that yet." He sat back down beside Brendee again, taking the opportunity to scootch a little farther away from her.

I opened the book he gave me. *Chronic remorse, as all the moralists are agreed, is a most undesirable sentiment,* the foreword began. *Right, Wiley,* I thought. *This is much better.*

But I endeavored to get into the story of decanted sub-castes and *soma.* It was intriguing, and I found that when Wiley stood up on his toes and stretched, three hours had passed.

I watched Brendee look all the way up at him, her face solemn, her pupils once again black and round. I imagined her reaching up, slowly, tentatively, and running her hand across his belly . . .

Fuck, I thought. *Now I'm just tormenting myself.*

It appeared that Brendee felt a little froggy, and even though she didn't touch him, she jumped: "You want to go to a party with me tonight, Wiley?" Forgotten was Dave, forgotten was pizza with me and Deneen. Brendee wanted *to get at* Wiley, as he'd so un-poetically put it, and it looked like she was getting tired of waiting. Al-fucking-ready.

"What are you doing tonight, Nate?" Wiley asked as he finished his stretch.

"Lemme check my calendar." I took my phone out of my pocket, then put it immediately back. "Not a fucking thing," I said, and nastily enjoyed Brendee's little flinch at my profanity. *Fuck her,* I thought. *She didn't ask* me *to go to the party.* "You wanna play poker?"

"I cheat at poker," he said.

"Of course you do," I replied, and considering Brendee's hopeful face, still looking up at him, I said, "Teach me."

"It'll be my pleasure." He looked down at Brendee. "Maybe some other time, Brendee. Nate and I are gonna play cards." He didn't invite her, because he knew, and I knew, and she knew, that she'd say yes. "Come on, let's use the dining room table."

We went downstairs, and Wiley paused in front of the door. "Thanks so much for helping me, Brendee," he said. "Do you want Nate to give you a ride home?" He looked over at me. "You can take my car."

"That's okay, Wiley. I just live a few blocks away from Nate's house," she said, talking about me like I wasn't standing right there. "What time do you want me to come over tomorrow? We should get an early start."

"Not too early," he said. "I work out for a while in the morning, especially on the weekends. Besides, my brain hurts. Maybe noon-ish?"

Brendee tried mightily to hide her disappointment, but failed. "Noon-ish sounds good," she said.

"Just call me," Wiley said, and opened the front door. "Thanks again, Brendee!" He was dismissing her, just as curtly and completely as he'd dismissed his mother the other day. Brendee got the hint as surely as Mrs. Royce had. She seemed to notice me standing there for the first time, and said goodbye. Then she smiled at Wiley one last time, and left.

Wiley pushed the door closed, then went into the dining room. He fished around in a cabinet for a minute, found a deck of cards, then sat at the dining room table. He took his phone out of his pocket and put it on the table. "I give it ten minutes," he said.

I sat down across from him and asked what he was talking about.

"Poor Brendee, all alone. She told me her boyfriend's out of town, did you know that?"

"When did she tell you that?"

"While we were studying. While you were absorbed with Huxley."

"What else did she say?"

Wiley shrugged. "Not much. She said I was picking up the math pretty well." He looked at his phone. "Maybe five minutes."

"Five minutes 'til what?"

Wiley shuffled the cards and started to lay out a hand of solitaire. I only knew what he was doing because I'd seen my grandmother do it. It was probably something he'd picked up during all that time he was alone in his attic room with a busted leg, although I didn't know why he'd bothered to learn how to do it with actual cards, when the computer would deal them for him.

"Her boy is out of town. She's all alone. She's gonna wanna talk to someone. People can't go much more than five minutes without talking to someone, nowadays." Wiley tapped the side of his head. "It's that short attention span. Lack of self-awareness. Gotta see what everyone else is doing."

The front door opened and Wiley's parents came in. He introduced me to his dad, and he was even a little balder and a little grayer than he'd been in the picture on Wiley's phone. It was absolutely no consolation whatsoever for me to realize that someday, Wiley's black-haired good looks would fade, and he'd just be an average-looking old guy like his father. Because that was all still a lifetime away, and right now, Wiley was just as hot as July. At least to Brendee.

"You wanna play poker, Dad?"

"You cheat, Wiley," Mr. Royce replied and winked at me. "Don't let him take all your money, Nate."

"I already have all his money, Dad. I fixed his phone." Father and son had a little laugh over that one, then Mr. Royce left and joined his wife in some other part of the house.

Wiley resumed his solitaire game. He hummed. I opened my mouth to say something, and his phone made a *Ta-da!* sound.

"Ah!" he said. "The lovely Brendee speaks!" But he didn't make a move to pick up his phone. After another moment, I reached for it, but Wiley grabbed my wrist. He grinned evilly at me. "Don't ever touch my phone, Nate. It might blow up in your hand." I couldn't tell if he was kidding or not, but I could imagine him installing little worms of plastic explosive, nestling them among the components inside, and I withdrew my hand. He dealt another row of cards.

"Well?" I finally said. "Are we gonna find out what she's saying?"

"Give it a minute, then we'll start from the beginning. We don't want to have to sit here and wait for 'em to answer each other." Wiley looked at his solitaire lay for a minute, then sighed and scooped up the cards. He shuffled them, then began to lay them out again. "I'm just kidding, Nate," he said, and set the deck down. "We don't have to wait any more."

He picked up his phone. "She's texting Deneen again," he said. Then Wiley giggled, like a little girl – he put his hand up to cover his mouth and everything. "Oh, you're gonna love this, Nate! Brendee asked Deneen, *'Have u ever heard anything about Wiley being gay? Or Nate?'*" Wiley giggled again, then he endeavored to look seriously at me. "I have heard you've got a nice ass."

I frowned and he looked back at his phone. "Deneen says, *'I don't kno about Wiley, but Nate's not gay. He used to go with Judy. She said he knos what he's doing and he's hung like a horse.'*"

"Do people still say *hung like a horse*, Wiley?" I said, feeling a little smug myself.

"Giddy-up," Wiley said and squinted at me. "Deneen asks, *'Y do u ask if they're gay? Did u c something?'*

"Oh, boy, Nate, here goes our reputations. A few choice words from your little Brendee and we're branded as lovers forever." Wiley scrolled his phone up. "Brendee says, *'No. I didn't c anything.'* Then there's a question mark from Deneen. Brendee didn't say anything for . . ." Wiley peered at the screen, counted on his fingers. "For a minute and twelve seconds. Then she says, *'Can you keep a secret?'*"

He grinned brilliantly at me. "I know I can. What about you, Nate? Can you keep a secret?"

"That depends on the fucking secret, Wiley." I had a pretty good idea what the secret was going to be. Just like he'd said, Brendee had to talk to someone. This thing she had for Wiley was starting to get to her, and we all know how much girls like to talk.

"'Of course I can keep a secret,' Deneen says.

"'I love Wiley Royce!'" Wiley Royce said. Then he looked innocently at me and grinned. "I'm just kidding, Nate. That's not what she said." He looked down at his phone. "She said, *'I think I'm going 2 break up w/Dave.'*

"*'Y?'* Deneen asks.

"*'I dunno. I think I'm bored.'*"

Apparently Brendee wasn't ready to discuss *The Love That Dare Not Speak Its Name* just yet. At least not by his name. But I was pretty sure it was coming. "What else does she say?"

Wiley read the texts. "Deneen says, *'I'm bored 2. Come on over 2 my house. We'll find something 2 do.'* Then Brendee says, *'K.'*

"That's it." He giggled again. "You wanna go upstairs and make out, Nate? Since Brendee thinks we're gay?"

"Brendee thinks *you're* gay."

"Better men than she have suggested it, but it's not true. I'm just very, very picky. And I've made a solemn oath." He gathered the cards together, shuffled them, and set them on the table in front of him. "You don't really want to play poker, do you?"

"Not on your life."

"Maybe you are smarter than you look. So what d'ya wanna do? You wanna scare up this party Brendee's talking about?"

"I'm not going to any parties with you, Wiley. People might think we're gay." I winked at him.

"Oh, I wasn't going *with* you, Nate. Are you kidding? The liquor flows, tempers flare, I feel compelled to open my big mouth . . . I just avoided an ass-kicking. They'll all be there together, the little teammates. Rah-rah. I can't take 'em all. Even you and I both together can't take 'em all. Your knuckles aren't all the way healed up from the last time. Do I want to go to a high school party? *As if.* But speaking of partying – do you want a beer?"

"Sure, Wiley. If your parents won't object."

Wiley shook his head. "Dad won't miss it." He went out to the kitchen and returned with a Grolsch beer. He expertly opened the flippie with one hand and handed it to me.

"You're not having one?"

Again Wiley shook his head. "Defiles the temple of the spirit."

"Are you kidding?"

"Yes, Nate. I'm kidding. I only drink if I've got something to celebrate. What have I, or you, for that matter, got to celebrate?"

"Any day above ground is a good day, my grandma says," I told him and sipped my beer.

"So you don't want to go to the party?"

"And listen to Brendee talk about you?"

"She hasn't said too much about me. Only that I'm cute. Which I am." He batted his eyes at me.

82

"That's all she's said so far." Now I sighed. "What kind of movies have you got?"

Wiley grinned. "Anything you want." He put one hand over his eye. "I'm a pirate, and I have the fastest connection in town."

He brought a few more beers along and we went up to his room. There was a picture of a large red ball in the middle of his laptop, which was still hooked up to the TV. I watched him glance up at the masking tape covering the webcam on the TV, and satisfied that it was still there, he turned around and said, "Suggest something, Nate. The internet is our oyster."

BRENDEE

I was beginning to think that Wiley had to be shy. Every time I tried to get close to him, he moved away from me. How could he look like he did and be shy? Maybe it was just me. Maybe he just looked like anyone else to everyone else. Maybe he was only irresistible to me.

But, I thought, with a little self-congratulatory pat on the back, *he hasn't a clue what he does to me.* After that little stutter upon meeting him, I'd maintained my cool.

My mother hadn't caught on that seeing Wes Thomerville sing from the mists of 2012 had put me halfway around the bend. And Wiley and Nate couldn't guess that meeting Wiley had put me the rest of the way around it. I was just that much in control.

True, I had tried to ease a little bit closer to him. He hadn't responded to that, which surprised me. The first time I'd eased a little bit closer to Dave, he'd grabbed my hand and kissed me. Dave might be quiet, but he wasn't shy.

Wiley just *had* to be shy. Or maybe he didn't want to leave Nate out in the cold. Guys are weird with their friends. I'd always admired how they seemed to stick together through anything. A girl, on the other hand, wouldn't hesitate to stab her friend in the back over some guy. Witness Deneen, ready to catch Dave when I drop him, if she couldn't get Nate to bite. And drop him I shall, if Wiley . . . Maybe I should've invited Nate to the party first – I know *he* would've jumped at the offer. Then I could've just invited Wiley along, too. Maybe he just didn't want to leave his friend by himself.

Or maybe they're gay.

But, unlike my mother, I'd like to believe in God. And if Wiley Royce is gay, there is no God.

I'd told Deneen that I'd go over to her house; she'd have something to drink, and I needed something to drink, after spending all afternoon mere inches away from Wiley. My fingers positively *itched* to touch him. But he was obviously shy; I was afraid I might scare him, and it's not like I could've touched him with Nate there, anyway. But I've got Nate's number; I know how to take care of *him.*

Before I went over to see Deneen, I transferred Wiley's spy-program to my computer. While we were studying, he'd asked if I'd tried it yet. I said I hadn't and he mentioned again that he'd show me how to find people's IP addresses sometime, and that's what reminded me of the program, still on my phone, when I got home. The idea of it had always been in the back of my mind, anyway, to tell the truth. I didn't need anyone else's IP address. I had his.

As soon as the download was complete, the computer went blank for several seconds, and it freaked me out a little bit. I've never been very good at using a command prompt, and Wiley's program had thrown me completely out of Windows. There was just a blinking cursor on a black field. I hit *Enter*.

The command line said, *Enter IP address:*

I looked at the numbers on my phone, and nervously entered them, then hit *Enter* again. The command line responded immediately, returning *Connecting . . .*

A rectangle appeared in the middle of the dark screen, a little under three by five, the same size as Wes's video. But no picture appeared. There was just a whitish glare that faded in and out. It looked like the reflections you see through a window at night, when someone inside is watching television.

I'd hoped to see the view from Wiley's TV, since he had the laptop whose IP I'd entered hooked up to it. I'd hoped that I'd see the glorious view from the TV: the TV that faced his bed. I'd hoped to see him there, in bed, hopefully not with Nate or anybody else. But all I got was a white glare. I was pretty sure that the program had connected me to something, but it wasn't what I wanted to see. I couldn't imagine that Wiley had written a program that didn't work and had given it to me without testing it. Maybe I was just getting the laptop webcam; maybe it was closed and the flashes of light were from something playing in the room. Maybe it hadn't connected at all.

I hit the *Enter* key again. The command prompt asked: *End view y/n?*

Again, I was sure it'd hooked up to something . . . but it wasn't Wiley, and it wasn't much of a view, so I hit *y*. Immediately, my Windows desktop reappeared. I closed the laptop.

There was just enough time to go over to Deneen's for a few drinks. Then I could come home and watch Wes . . . Somehow, I didn't think I'd be thinking about him.

NATE

When the credits rolled on the second movie, Wiley jumped up and turned on the lights. "Oh, fuck, Nate! What time is it?"

I looked at my phone. "It's 10:02."

He grinned. "You wanna watch Brendee? It's about time for the Wes Thomerville show."

I didn't even hesitate. "No. I do not wanna watch Brendee. Hell, no," I added firmly.

Wiley's smile didn't dim. "I didn't really think you would."

"Why would I want to watch her? Now that I know what she's watching? What she's thinking about?"

"What do you think she's thinking about?"

"That singer. Wes Thomerville."

Wiley shook his head. "Not anymore. She's thinking about me now, Nate, my son. You said it yourself – I look just like him."

"But you're not him, Wiley."

Wiley grinned. "He's not even him anymore, now is he? He's an old man. The closest thing to our yelping singer from yesteryear that Brendee's gonna find around here is me."

"Fuck you, Wiley," I said. I was amazed at how anger and resentment rose and fell in me like the tide. One minute, Wiley was my buddy and Brendee was beautiful, and the next minute, I hated them both.

"Imagine what it would be like, Nate." Wiley stood in the middle of the room and looked at the television. The silent credits ended and the screen went dark. "Kitana and I, we got to be equals after a while . . . But the best thing about it was, there was always a challenge to satisfying her. It was almost like a contest between us. She knew what I liked and I knew what she liked, but the challenge was always to try to keep it fresh, incredible, unbelievable . . . to make it better than the last time, every single time . . . It never failed to get me off, just to get her off, to feel that surrender . . ." He looked over his shoulder at me. "But it was *work* sometimes, let me tell ya.

"But imagine what it would be like . . ." Wiley turned back and looked at the blank television, imagining. "Brendee's already more than halfway there, on her own. All I'd have to do is touch her . . . How awesome would that be, to make her come just by touching her . . . kissing her . . . Imagine how good it would get from there." Wiley stood looking wistfully at the dark TV for another heartbeat, then turned around and grinned at me. "Goddamn, Nate!" He sat in his wheeled chair and pushed off, sliding all the way across the room. "The shit I don't do for my friends!"

"Like I said before. You're a fucking prince, Wiley."

"That I am. I gave you my word. But I've every confidence that you're gonna release me from this promise. Some other girl's gonna come along, and you're going to say to yourself, *How could I possibly want anybody that wants Wiley?* You're going to ride off into the sunset with Miss Right . . ." Again he looked at the blank TV. *"And leave the world for me to bustle in!"* He found the remote and pointed it at the laptop. A list of files appeared. "In the meantime . . . what d'ya wanna watch next?"

****

Brendee called me at 11:45 the next morning. "I'll be there in a few, Nate. I'm bringing Gary with me. He says he'll be glad to look at your car."

I barely had time to walk outside before they squealed up to the curb in Gary's shiny black and chrome Chevy Sequel. It was a sleek and immaculate SUV, and I would've been impressed, if such things impressed me. They got out and Gary took a dented red toolbox out of the back. "Show me to the patient," he said, and slapped me on the back. "The doctor is in."

Brendee actually walked halfway up the driveway with us before she stopped. "Well," she said, a little breathlessly. "I've gotta go. Can't keep Wiley waiting."

"Wiley's an asshole," Gary said, opening the hood of my car.

Brendee shrugged, smiling lightly. "Whatever. He needs my help, and I said I'd help him. Call me when you guys are done."

But not too soon, I thought, watching her skip up the sidewalk. My next thought wasn't very charitable: *The sneaky bitch!*

"Do you have a drop light, Nate?" Gary asked. He'd crawled under the car. "I can't see shit."

"A drop –? I've got a flashlight." I went into the garage and found it for him, again thinking that maybe Wiley was right. What kind of a nice girl used her own brother like a decoy, just so she could keep me occupied, just so she could be alone with him? *The sneaky bitch!* I thought again.

I handed Gary the flashlight, and he started talking about the finer points of hybrids and fuel cell technology. He said that it

87

probably wasn't anything to do with the cells themselves, why the shit-box wouldn't start. He said something about some kind of connections. He asked me for a screwdriver and I found one in his toolbox and handed it to him. I pulled the toolbox over by the front tire and sat on the ground next to it.

I tried to pay attention to what Gary was saying, but I couldn't possibly care less. I was again seeing Brendee, how she'd looked up at Wiley, like some kind of feral cat in heat. I was just again imagining her reaching up and touching him, when my phone beeped.

Fear not, my son, Wiley texted. *We're studying in the dining room. I told her I was having my room redecorated. LOL*

Ur a prince, I wrote back.

Mom's in the kitchen, making veggie tacos. We r chaperoned. It's all good. TTYL

Do people still text TTYL, Wiley, you smug bastard? I thought. But he was a good man.

****

I was effectively cut out of sitting in on the tutoring sessions after that. If I kept showing up, it would've just seemed weird, like I was trying to keep Brendee away from Wiley, which was exactly what I would've been doing. But Wiley assured me that they always studied in the dining room now.

At lunchtime the following Thursday, Wiley and I were sitting in the cafeteria. Bev and Deneen and Bobbi were sitting two tables over from us. Deneen smiled at me and waved, and I waved back. She whispered something to Bobbi, and Bev looked over her shoulder and scowled at Wiley.

He ignored them. He was eating baby carrots out of a plastic bag, and he was unusually pre-occupied, frowning at his phone. He'd always maintained that it was not only rude, but simple-minded, a sad commentary on our times, to be staring at your phone when there were living human beings sitting right there with you.

"What the fuck, Wiley?" I said. "Who are you talking to?" I was convinced that he was talking to Brendee, that he was making an exception to his rule of interpersonal versus phone etiquette for her. I was a little bit surprised at my own paranoia.

He pushed *Send* and put his phone in his pocket. "Ah, the inconvenience of modern conveniences. So delightful when they're functioning properly."

The span of perhaps five heartbeats passed, then, from across the room, I heard Deneen exclaim, "I don't know! It was working fine three minutes ago!"

"Such an expensive pain in the ass when they fail." Wiley grinned at me. "I told you I'd be your Cyrano, Nate. I'm just changing Roxanes on you." When I looked at him blankly, he said, "I need you to be my wing-man. Just stand there and look pretty. Follow my lead."

Wiley arose and approached Bobbi and Deneen and Bev, who all had their heads together now, looking down at Deneen's iPhone. I followed him.

"What seems to be the trouble, ladies?"

Bev looked up. "Fuck you, Wiley."

"Let me check my schedule, Beverly, my dearest. I'm sure I can pencil you in."

"There's something wrong with my phone!" Deneen wailed, as if some friend or relative was dying.

"Lemme see it," Wiley commanded. When they just looked up at him dumbly, he walked around the table until he was peering over Deneen's shoulder. Deneen handed the phone to him, and he examined it closely, pushed a few buttons. "I can fix it for you, Deneen. But I'm gonna have to take it back to my workshop at the North Pole."

"You're outta your fucking mind, Wiley," Bev growled, and I was put in mind of another feral cat, this one about to claw Wiley's eyes out. "Deneen's not giving you her phone."

"Suit yourself." He set it on the table and started to walk away.

"Wait, Wiley," Deneen said. "Can you really fix it?" I recognized the same hope in her voice that I'd felt when he'd said he could fix mine. We really couldn't live without them.

"Of course," Wiley replied. "Ask Nate. His was a lot worse off."

Deneen looked hopefully at me, her green eyes huge and sparkly in her thin, pretty face. I nodded.

"But you're gonna have to bring it over," Wiley said. "I'll text you my address. Oh, wait. Your phone's broken." He produced a Sharpie from I knew not where, and before any of them could move to stop him, he wrote his address and number right on the screen of

Deneen's phone. They all blinked at him in disbelief. "Just call before you come over, say, later this afternoon? Borrow my darling Beverly's phone. I'd love to have her number." He pursed a kiss at Beverly, and she flipped him off.

"Thanks, Wiley," Deneen called gratefully after him as he walked away. "Bye, Nate!" she said to me as I followed him. I waved goodbye to her.

"Fags," Beverly said.

****

I was outside washing my car after school – Gary had got it running like a champ again, and it had only cost Wiley seventy-five bucks – when the man himself texted me.

I need you to get over here right now. It's important.

I frowned, wondering what the hell he could want. I turned off the hose and jogged over there.

Mrs. Royce opened the door. "He's upstairs," she told me. "But you might want to knock. He's got a girl with him." Mrs. Royce grinned, and I wondered if it was out of relief. I was sure that I wasn't the only one that had noticed that her son never had a date. Maybe she'd been thinking he was gay, too.

The door at the top of the stairs was closed, and I suddenly wondered if Wiley wanted me to save him from Brendee, if he needed me to make sure that he kept his promise. Or maybe he just wanted me to *catch them*. I paused and listened at the door, hating myself, hating him, hating Brendee. I heard him laugh, and it felt like he was laughing at me. I swung the door open, and it crashed into the wall.

The two of them blinked at me, at the sudden noise. But it wasn't Brendee sitting at the desk with Wiley. It was Deneen, gleefully clutching her iPhone, which I assumed that Wiley had effortlessly repaired for her. It was effortless, I was sure, seeing as how all the evidence suggested that he'd just as effortlessly, wirelessly, broken it for her.

"Easy on that door, Nate." Wiley motioned for me to come in and I walked across the room. He pointed at my chair, and I sat. "We were just talking about you."

"Hi, Nate," Deneen said, and smiled winningly at me. I said hi and smiled back.

"I was just talking to our lovely Deneen about the Mikkelea concert tomorrow night."

"It's sold out," I said, wondering where he was going with this. Wiley didn't know Mikkelea from milquetoast.

He smiled and winked at Deneen. "A lot he knows, huh?" He picked up his tablet from the desk, and handed it to me. There was a text from Ticketmaster, detailing the purchase of two tickets to see the blonde singer.

"I have two problems, however. One: I don't have a printer to print out the confirmation. I understand that they still require that ancient tradition. Ah, the dead trees!" Wiley lamented theatrically.

"You don't have a printer?"

"What could I possibly need to print?" He squinted at me. "Secondly, even if I did have a printer, my mom says I can't go. I'm grounded, you see. My poor grades and all. I didn't realize that she'd be such a hard-ass about it, and our greedy friends at Ticketmaster don't give refunds.

"So I was wondering, Nate, if you might like to go see Mikkelea. With Deneen. If you're not busy." Before I could answer, Wiley's phone beeped. He looked at it and said, "Ah! My tutor's gonna be here in a minute. Let's go downstairs and meet her. No big lesson today. She's just gonna give me a test." Wiley squinted at me again. "Then we can all go get something to eat. Let me forward this to you, Nate. So you can print out the confirmation."

So before I had a split-second to object, I had a date with Deneen to see Mikkelea. All courtesy of Wiley Royce. The slick, conniving bastard.

BRENDEE

A small thundercloud of anger formed behind my right eye when I saw Deneen standing there beside Wiley. It made me blink, like a tic. But then it dissipated somewhat when I realized that she'd probably just wrangled some way to be there because she liked Nate. Wasn't that cute? Then the thundercloud disappeared entirely, evaporating as quickly as it had formed, when she said, "Oh, my God, Brendee! My phone just all of sudden stopped working at lunch today. It was still on, but it just went blank! Wiley fixed it for me!"

"Free of charge," Wiley said. "I hear you guys are friends, and any friend of yours . . ."

I was surprised to see Nate glower at him. I said to Deneen, "I wondered why I hadn't heard from you all afternoon." But enough of Deneen, and frowning Nate. I wanted to look at Wiley, so I said to him, "Sorry I'm late, Wiley." *You incredible, blue-eyed masterpiece.* "Are you ready for me to test you?"

He smiled blankly at me and said, "As ready as I'll ever be."

I went out and sat with him at the dining room table, where he'd insisted that we study, ever since I gotten rid of Nate. He was shy. But I wasn't. I was just waiting for some afternoon when his parents weren't around . . . and then I'd show him that it didn't pay to be shy in the big, mean world. I was amazed at how calculating I'd become lately, but the thought of touching him, running my fingers through all those black curls, kissing him . . . It was keeping me up at night.

"Are you hungry, Brendee?" Nate asked from the living room, and I reluctantly left Wiley to *the math,* and the fairly simple test I'd devised for him. I knew he could ace it, and I thought his success would give him confidence. It was obvious to me that Wiley lacked confidence. It was probably an outgrowth of being shy.

Deneen looked closely at me, her face a mask of concern. She said, "Are you okay, Brendee? You look like you've been crying!"

I waved my hand, indicating to her that it wasn't something I wanted to talk about in front of Nate. I said to him, "Yes, I'm hungry. What did you have in mind? Chinese sounds good." I thought Deneen could pick at some Chinese for a little while, and no one would notice when she didn't really eat any of it.

"I haven't had Chinese in days," Nate said, brightening a little bit. "*Peking Cavalcade's* pretty good." He frowned again. "But my car's at home."

"You can take mine," Wiley called from the other room, without looking up. He was chewing on the end of his pencil, the eraser's pink nub clenched lightly between his white teeth, and looking at him made me shiver. Just for an extra thrill, I glanced down at his bare toes, curled adorably into the rug beneath the table. Still not looking up, he reached across the table for his keys and arced them through the air.

Nate caught them and said, "What do *you* want from *Peking Cavalcade,* Wiley?"

He took the pencil out of his flawless mouth and wrote something. Still concentrating on the test, he said, "Pick something for me, will ya? Something small. I'm not that hungry."

"I'll split mine with you, Wiley," Deneen volunteered. "I'm not very hungry either."

Wiley smiled and wrote down another answer. "That's very kind of you," he said.

We told Nate what we wanted from *Peking Cavalcade* and he departed.

Deneen whispered to me, "Let's go out on the porch 'til he's finished, Brendee. Tell me why you've been crying."

I'd been crying because I'd broken up with Dave. I actually hadn't been crying *because* I'd broken up with Dave; I'd been crying because it'd been necessary for me to cry *in order to* break up with Dave. But he didn't know that, and I wasn't going to explain it all to Deneen, either.

He'd arrived for our weekly romp, but when he hugged me, I found that I could pretend that his big, strapping, brown-eyed, redheaded, freckled self was long, lean, blue-eyed, black-haired, exquisite Wiley no longer. When he gave me one of his sloppy kisses, it was just like when the dog would jump up, catch me unaware, and plant one on my face: just as disgusting, just as not-thrilling; and I'd pushed him away, just as quickly. He gave me the same wounded look that the dog did, and asked what was wrong.

The lies unspooled from some black well within me, a dark, still pool that I hadn't even known existed. "I've been sad, lately, Dave. I really don't know why . . . Maybe it's hereditary. My mother's struggled with depression for years." After my always-cheerful Great-aunt Rae, my mother was the next happiest person I knew. She completely loved me and my brothers and sister and my dad, and her job, and all her memories of the good old days. Mom wouldn't know depression if it bled to death on our front lawn.

Dave blanched at this sudden admission to mental instability in the family.

"I really can't explain it!" I wailed, and let the crocodile tears fall. "You've decided on Cal State San Diego, and I . . .." *I would go wherever Wiley was gonna go.* "And I haven't decided where I'm gonna go yet. I'm might just stay here in town –"

"And go to UCR?" he asked incredulously.

You're such a snob, Dave, I thought. *Just because I can get in anywhere I want doesn't mean there's anything wrong with UCR, with staying local.* "I've been thinking that I want to stay close to Mom. She needs me to cry with her sometimes . . .."

I peeped at him to see if he was buying this load of bullshit, and he was. It suddenly occurred to me that Dave didn't really know my mom, or any of the rest of my family. He'd always been eager to see me at school, and take me out, and have sex with me on Thursdays, but he'd never been the type to want to hang around and have dinner with the family. It surprised me that I'd never noticed his shallowness before.

"So, I've been thinking . . . maybe we should just end it now, and save ourselves the heartbreak come fall. I don't think I could stand all that stress hanging over my head 'til then." I had enough stress, but it was of a delightful kind, trying to decide what I would first do to shy Wiley, the minute I could manage to get him alone.

I burst into tears again, and when Dave moved to comfort me, I held up my hand and stopped him, as unyielding and frigid as an iceberg. "Just go, Dave!" I sobbed. "I can't do this anymore!"

He looked at me in bewilderment, but through the mist of my fake tears, I noticed that he didn't seem all that broke up about it. Maybe he'd only loved parts of me, after all, and I'd just granted him all those new vistas to explore, without any monogamous guilt, once he moved to San Diego. He left without saying a word, without a backward glance. It had been *entirely* easier than I'd expected it to be.

Once he was gone, I'd wiped away the rest of the phony tears, and thinking about how I'd word my Oscar acceptance speech, I hurried over to see sexy Wiley.

"You just *broke up* with Dave?" Deneen asked in amazement. "Just like that? Why?"

I shrugged, and gave her the stock, meaningless answer: "It wasn't working out, Deneen."

Perhaps I'd felt a tiny twinge of guilt that I didn't want him anymore. But mostly, Dave had been taking up space in my mind that Wiley could be using. I couldn't entertain the thought that I might never get Wiley – why couldn't I have him, once Dave was gone?

But regardless of how long it took to snag Wiley – I was convinced it was only a matter of getting him alone – I was done with Dave right now, and permanently. I couldn't be with him when my fantasies about someone else were better than my realities with him; when I got off more from *just thinking about Wiley* then I did from actually *being with Dave.*

"Well, I'm sorry to hear about that," Deneen said. Then she looked at me uncertainly and added, "If you're sorry."

"I'm not sorry."

She smiled brightly. "Then that's great! Wait 'til I tell you my news! Wiley had two tickets to go see Mikkelea tomorrow night, but then his mom wouldn't let him go because of his grades. So he talked Nate into taking me!"

Before I could stop it, a small curse slipped from my mind and sought out Mrs. Royce. Maybe Wiley had gotten those tickets for *us.* Maybe it was going to be a surprise, maybe he was going to show me how much he appreciated all my help by taking me to rock out to Mikkelea's awesomeness. And Mrs. Royce had ruined it for me!

"The more I look at him, the more I like him, Brendee," Deneen said, and I stared at her in shock for a moment. How dare she look at Wiley! How dare she tell me how much she liked him! But then I realized that she was talking about Nate, and I thought again how easy it was to lose one's mind.

"Would you be mad if I told you that I told Nate that you like him?" I said, feeling like I was in grade school.

"No, I'm not mad! That's great, Brendee! Thank you." Deneen rubbed her hands together and did a little dance on the porch. "I'm gonna get to see Mikkelea! With Nate!"

"So you don't think Wiley's such an asshole anymore?"

Deneen stopped dancing. "He's okay, I guess. He fixed my phone and he didn't charge me, so I guess he can't be all bad. I haven't heard him say anything dirty lately."

The thought suddenly occurred to me that maybe it was all a scam, and I guiltily rescinded my curse upon Mrs. Royce. Wiley didn't have bad grades in anything but *the math;* he'd bitched about the fact that it wasn't fair that he could be prevented from graduating for flunking just one class, when he was going to pass everything else, and swimmingly. But credits are credits, and they have to add up.

And Wiley was trying to succeed; his friend had obtained for him the most dedicated, secretly-worshipful tutor on the planet. And it was just one night. It seemed like a ridiculously unfair punishment.

And I reflected that Wiley had never mentioned a fondness for Mikkelea before. He never mentioned anything about modern music at all, and I remembered thinking that it was a shame that he didn't play guitar, but then I thought that would've been entirely too much. I was just being greedy. I didn't want him to play guitar for me, or even sing to me, anyway. I wanted him to . . .

I looked at Deneen again, and remembered how Wiley had turned me down to go to that party, because it would've left Nate with nothing to do. Maybe Wiley had set them up, got them tickets to this show, because he was hoping that his friend and my friend would get together, and then he wouldn't have to worry about Nate being left by his lonesome anymore. It seemed a stretch, but from what I'd heard, Nate was the only friend Wiley had – that was no doubt another product of being shy – and maybe Wiley wanted to do him a favor.

Maybe he'd fixed Nate and Deneen up, because he'd decided he didn't want to be quite so bothered with his buddy all the time anymore. Maybe he'd made up his little shy mind that he wanted to be *with me.*

I wished Deneen luck and dared to hope.

Wiley materialized in the doorway, holding up his test. "All done," he said, and smiled at me.

He'd gotten every answer right.

NATE

When Wiley and I walked out to the parking lot after school, we discovered that all four of his tires were flat. Not just flat: they had been shredded, filleted –

"Like Caspian sturgeons," Wiley said. *"What mightst thou do, that honor would thee do, were all thy children kind and natural!"*

I blinked blankly at him. "More Byron?"

"Shakespeare, my son." He kicked one of the ruined tires. "I ask you, Nate: what kind of a man is it that attacks a defenseless car?" I looked across the parking lot to see Neal and Ed, leaning against the building. Neal was nervy enough to be cleaning his fingernails with a good-sized knife. I nodded in their direction, and Wiley followed my gaze. "Ah. The boys that can't take a joke. I'd forgotten about them."

I was amazed at Wiley's calmness, while my own anger churned. He was right: what kind of an asshole attacked a defenseless car? And over what? Someone pointing out the truth about his slutty sister?

"Come on, Wiley," I said. "There's only two of them. Let's go wipe that smile off of Ed's fat face. Make Neal eat that knife."

"Revenge is for suckers." I could always tell when Wiley was quoting something, because he'd pause and wait to see if I got the reference. When I just blinked at him, he shook his head. "A million reasons spring to mind, Nate: that's what they want; it's not worth it. They're armed, we're not. But mostly: fuck 'em."

Wiley smiled and waved at Neal and Ed, then turned his back on them and hopped up and sat on the fender of his car. He took out his phone and called for a tow. Then he texted Brendee and told her that something had come up, and that he'd have to miss their lesson today. Then he rather abruptly put his phone back into his pocket

"But you could do something, Wiley," I said, not willing to let my fury dissipate, hanging on to it, savoring it. "You could wreck their phones –"

"You're telling me that *revenge is a dish best served cold,* is that it, Nate?"

"You could do something, Wiley," I repeated. "I know you could. Make them sorry they fucked with you."

Wiley shrugged. "I could cancel their parents' credit cards, drain their bank accounts. But that would be illegal –" he blinked innocently at me "– and I've sworn off illegal pursuits. For the most part. Besides, I have no beef with their parents. I'm sure that it's not entirely their fault that their girls are sluts and their boys are assholes."

"But –"

"I appreciate your loyalty, Nate, *my brother and only friend,* and I appreciate your confidence in my skills. It's true – I could cause Neal's phone to melt in his hammy hand, make it seem like it was his sweaty touch, instead of my control, that made every single device around him malfunction, if he as much as looks at it. I could volunteer Ed to be the star of any number of unspeakable gay websites, post his number on their walls, and tell the subscribers to come get him. But if I did any of those things, while they wouldn't know for sure, and while they couldn't prove it, they'd always suspect that it was me who'd masterminded it.

"And that would make it look like they'd affected me – which, past an annoying inconvenience, and missing my lesson with your girlfriend – they have not. It's just tires, Nate." Wiley grinned gleefully as another thought struck him. "Or I could always call your favorite Meow dealer. You know how much Bradley loves me. He'd be more than happy to help me out, and I'm sure he'd enjoy every minute of it. I imagine that he'd handle such a thing personally, in fact. But as worthless as Neal and Ed are, I'd feel almost bad to see them die, or wish they were dead, over a set of tires." He smiled again, maddeningly serene.

"Will you stop fucking with them behind this, though?" I asked. "Stop talking shit about their sisters and girlfriends?"

"Not on your life."

That was the Wiley I knew, serenity be damned.

"Will you follow me over to the tire place?"

"Sure, Wiley." I leaned against the car next to him.

It must've been a busy day for broken-down cars, because by the time the wrecker arrived, the parking lot was empty. More than a few of our peers were probably also headed to the Mikkelea concert, and wanted to get an early start. We stood around in the tire place for another half an hour. Wiley picked out a set of tires, then told the guy that he had to go home and get some money.

I took him to his house and followed him up the stairs and waited while he rooted around in the drawer for that rubber-banded roll of twenties. I looked at his laptop: a large white circle took up almost the entire screen, just like the red one had before.

"What is that?" I asked him and nodded at the computer.

Wiley looked over at it, and grinned his ol' toothy smile. "That's security, my son. It lets me know when someone's trying to get into my system. It's a waste of time, because my system is fucking impenetrable; but people still try. In this case, it's alerting me to my own program. The prompt is red when the connection is open. It goes white after it's disconnected. She's looking for me, Nate. Trying to find out what I'm doing."

"Who?" But I already knew.

"I didn't actually give her the whole app. What I gave her will only hook her device into this laptop, and to the TV, if I set it up that way. It'll say, *Connection not found*, if she puts in anybody else's IP. She can't spy on anyone but me." He nodded at the covered webcam on the TV. "Right now, she wants to know why I cancelled our lesson today. But this is the second time she's tried to watch me."

"What're you gonna do?"

"What would you do?"

I shook my head. "I dunno, Wiley. I don't think I'd like being watched."

"Really?" he exclaimed in disbelief. "I think it's absolutely awesome. It shows she's just as evil as I am. She's just wondering where I am today, but that first time . . . That was at night. Maybe she thinks I've got a little video like hers and I do the same things she does while I watch it." He wiggled his eyebrows at me. "Maybe she wants to watch me while I . . ." He clapped his hands in glee. "That's fucking diabolical. I love it!" He looked at the taped-over webcam. "Oh, Brendee, you nasty girl!"

"I'm sure she doesn't want to watch you –"

Wiley looked at me, black eyebrows raised. "What else then? What else could she want to watch me do, late at night, when she figures I'm all alone, that would be even remotely interesting?"

"Maybe she just wants to watch you, regardless of what you're doing, because you look like Wes Thomerville."

"Does she think I secretly pay the guitar? All by myself?" Wiley grinned brilliantly, then walked over and ran his finger over the masking tape, assuring himself that it was secure. "If you knew someone was watching you, you couldn't look directly at the webcam," he mused. "I imagine that'd be the hardest part. If you look right at it, then you're looking right at *her,* and then the gig's up. She'd know you knew she was watching you.

"I could run it so I was watching her at the same time as she was watching me . . . but I don't think I could pull it off. I'd look at the

webcam sooner or later. And why would I wanna watch her while
she was just staring at her laptop, watching me?"

"What're you gonna do?" I asked again.

He blinked innocently at me. "Maybe I should just let her watch
me. Let her see that there's nothing special about me." He grinned
wickedly.

"There isn't anything special about you." I added uncertainly,
"Is there?"

Wiley sang, *"I make a smart woman beg/And I make a good
woman steal/I make an old woman blush/And I make a young girl
squeal."* He grinned at me.

"I know that one. My grandpa used to sing it. Jesus, Wiley. You
and your ancient music. But you got it wrong. It's *I make a rich
woman beg."*

His eyebrows went up again. "I don't know any rich women,
my son. But I do know a smart one." He looked at the TV again, then
shrugged. "There's nothing special about me that you don't already
know about, Nate. I don't secretly play the guitar. Scout's Honor."

"Well, I don't have time to sit around and discuss your
specialness or lack of it. I've got a date."

"You're welcome."

"Thanks, Wiley," I said sincerely. "It's gonna be fun."

"Remember, your reputation precedes you, from – what was her
name?"

"Judy."

"That's right. Be nice to our sweet Deneen. *The gentler
gamester is the soonest winner.* Tease her a little bit. Make her wait.
Don't just drive right in there for the kill."

"Gee, thanks for all your swell advice, Wiley," I said, "but you
can just fuck right off."

"Have fun. Don't do anything I wouldn't do."

"You don't do anything."

I thought it seemed like an effort for him not to turn around and
look at the TV again. "Not yet," he said.

"I gotta go, Wiley. We're going out to dinner first."

"I guess I'll just call Brendee and ask her to take me back to get
the car. If she's not too busy trying to spy on me." He smiled slyly,
and I was amazed at how much he suddenly thought he could fuck
with me about this. But where before I might've felt compelled to try
to smack him, now there was just a tiny spark of jealousy, and that
also amazed me. I discovered that I was truly looking forward to

100

going out with Deneen. "I'm just kidding, Nate," he said. "Go. Have fun. My dad'll drive me over there."

****

The crowd to see amazing blonde Mikkelea was massive, but Deneen and I fought our way through it, until we were standing right in front, right on the rail. But a concert crowd is a jealous monster, and its many arms and legs continue to push and surge from the back, even when there's no hope of the individual units moving forward. Deneen weighed maybe a hundred and twenty pounds – she could use a bologna sandwich, just like Wiley said – so I stood her in front of me, to protect her from the unceasing shove of the crowd.

She braced her arms against the rail and leaned back into me when Mikkelea came out on stage, to the deafening roar of her fans. The crowd pushed; I was molded into Deneen's back. My nose was in her hair, and she smelled so good that I felt light-headed for a moment. But I got a hold of myself. That's all I needed – to pass out from delight and be trampled to death, leaving Denny and her glorious smell, unprotected, to also be crushed by Mikkelea's mindless, pushing fans.

But I couldn't maintain complete control, I discovered after a few minutes. My nose was enveloped in Deneen's scent, and I could feel every inch of her, pressing back against me, as I was pressed forward against her by the people behind me. Her thin shoulder blades were against my chest; her soft, pliant ass – Denny was skinny, but she had an ass that just would not quit – her ass wiggled and jumped and pressed back against me, just below my beltline.

Feeling it was great, and was bad enough – but thinking about it made it even better, and even worse. I felt the first twinge of a hard-on, and I knew that if I didn't do something, and quickly, she'd feel it, too. I didn't think it would bother her very much. Deneen was no blushing virgin, even though I knew she wasn't as big of a slut as Bev and Bobbi; and she liked me. She might even take it as a compliment.

But seriously, how rude would that be? How would it make me look, that I was too immature to control myself, just because a pretty girl had to be pressed against me, because she couldn't get away in the crowd? It wasn't like she was doing it on purpose, or at least not entirely. And if I let this happen, she'd tell, or worse, *she'd text* Brendee about it, and Wiley would read it, and he'd never let me live it down. *You need to practice yoga, my son,* he'd say, *try to be a little more Zen.* Or something like that. *Seek to achieve some self-control.*

Denny took one hand off the rail. She looked up at me and quickly caressed my cheek. Yeah, she liked me, and I wasn't going to let her know that I was suddenly liking her, too, and quite a lot. So before nature could advance its course any further, I reached down and grabbed Denny by the hips, and lifted her over my head, and set her on my shoulders. She exclaimed in delighted surprise, and again touched my cheek.

She weighed next to nothing. Her hot thighs lightly squeezing my neck and her tiny feet digging gently into my back did nothing to relieve my hard-on, but at least she couldn't feel it now. I put my hands on the rail and held on, and sang along with Mikkelea, while Denny bounced gently on my shoulders and sang along too. Mikkelea was absolutely awesome, and little bitty Denny wasn't so bad either.

I carried her all the way out to the parking lot on my shoulders, like she was some prize I'd somehow been fortunate enough to win. She had to duck when we went through the doors. When we got to the car, I again lifted her by the hips over my head. When I set her down she turned and hugged me. She wrapped her arms around my back and positively *squeezed* me, and now her nice firm front was molded to my front. The hard-on had long ago retreated – I do have some self-control, after all – but it was still nice. She smelled like heaven.

Then she looked up at me with her enormous green eyes and I didn't hesitate, didn't think about Brendee for a change. I kissed her, and it didn't matter that there were a million still-whooping Mikkelea fans eddying all around us. For the span of that kiss, we were the only two people in the world. We stopped kissing and looked at each other in surprise at the splendidness of it. We panted for a second, then Denny shivered, and I was sure it wasn't entirely from the brisk air. I unlocked the car door for her, and she got in.

I was glad that I had to concentrate on not running over or crashing into any of these idiots as we threaded our way out of the parking lot. Denny's smell, her hot, hard body (all hard, except for that cushy, round ass), her unbelievable kiss, had befuddled me quite more than a little bit, and making sure we didn't meet any of our fellow concert-goers gave me the opportunity to come down, to get the helm once again under intellectual control.

"What do you wanna do now, Nate?" she asked. I looked over at her: her beautiful green eyes sparkled, the pupils huge and black. But her expression was girlish and happy – she didn't smile seductively or with any kind of slyness. It was just an innocent question. She didn't want to go home yet, because she liked me, and she hoped I liked her.

We went to a large, brightly-lit diner downtown, a place that catered to the college crowd and was open twenty-four hours a day. To my surprise, Denny ate almost half of the burger she ordered, and nearly three-quarters of the French Fries.

We talked and laughed and even held hands across the table a few times. It was just like one of those scenes you see in the movies – it was perfectly fun and enjoyable, and we realized that we liked all the same things, and with each passing moment, we liked each other a little bit more. Every now and then, a little spark of desire would peep out from behind her eyes, and she would lower her lashes shyly. I don't know if the shyness was real or not, but it was still adorable.

At two in the morning, the tired, annoyed waitress told us that if we didn't order something else, we'd have to leave. Denny giggled and looked at her phone. She was amazed at the time, and said that this was our cue – if she didn't get home right away, her mother would kill her.

I walked her to her door and she kissed me again, and I kissed her again, then I said that I'd call her in the morning – it really was already morning – and I asked her, if she wasn't doing anything, if she might like to hang out tomorrow. She said she'd love that, and then we kissed a little more, and I finally left.

I went home and did what young men do to maintain their mental health, especially after a first date. For the first time in a very long time, I didn't think of Brendee. Brendee didn't even cross my mind.

BRENDEE

I almost dropped my phone in surprise and excitement when I saw that Wiley was calling me. Wiley never called me. He hadn't even called to cancel today. Just a short text. Maybe he was calling now to tell me that whatever had kept him had been concluded. Maybe he was calling to say I could come over now. I looked at the time on my phone. It was 8:52. A little late for studying, but not too late for . . .

"Hello?" I said, way too breathlessly.

"Hey, Brendee," he said neutrally, like he was talking to Nate or some other dude. He told me about what had happened with his car, told me that he was sorry that he'd missed our lesson. He told me that he'd just been studying for a few minutes on his own, and had already come to a stumper. He read the problem to me, and I guided him through it. After a minute, he understood.

"I'm really glad you're helping me, Brendee," he said softly, with what seemed like a little edge. Now it seemed like he was talking to me like I was a girl, like he might be trying to communicate that he was *really* glad. Like he just might want to show me *precisely* how glad he was.

I responded by lowering my voice a little, too. "I'm happy to do it, Wiley." *I'm happy to do anything you want,* I thought, *if you'd just quit being so damned shy and ask.*

There was a little pause; I hoped he was thinking about showing me that appreciation. But then he asked brightly, "Did you try my spy program yet?"

I looked over at my laptop, perched on its barstool, in its ready-to-watch-Wes position. It was Friday night, after all. I'd run Wiley's app earlier, trying to see if he was home, wondering why he'd canceled today. But all I got were the same white flashes, and had escaped back to Windows in disappointment.

"As a matter of fact I did," I told him. "It doesn't work."

"Really? Where did you get an IP?" he asked.

I'd already thought up what to tell him, just in case this question came up. "My brother went to the Mikkelea show tonight, so I went into his room, and looked up his IP on *whatismyip.com*, just like you showed me. I wrote it down, plugged it into your app. I wasn't really planning on spying on Gary – how boring would that be?" I laughed nervously. "But it didn't work."

"What did it do?"

"It said *Connecting*, but all I got was a blank screen."

"I don't know why it wouldn't work, especially right there in the same house. Did you look at the code? Try to debug it? Maybe you could find something I missed."

"I looked at it, Wiley," I lied. "But the code is a little –"

"Dense?"

"I'm not much for creating apps codes from scratch, like you do. Or debugging them."

"Well, I've streamlined it. Let me send you the newest version, and you can try it again." He paused, then said. "I'm gonna finish the rest of the problems on this page, then I'm gonna go to sleep. My brain hurts." His voice lowered, and I once more thought that I heard that sexy edge to it. He said, "See you tomorrow, Brendee," then he said goodbye and hung up, and my mind wanted him to whisper to me some more. But I thought that maybe Wiley was like a lot of guys I'd talked to, who were brave on the phone or online, but just became boys again in person. Or maybe I was only imagining a sexiness to his voice, just because I wanted so badly for it to be there.

My phone beeped. He'd sent me the revised app. *See me tomorrow, will ya, Wiley?* I thought. *Not if I see you first.*

I sat on the side of the bed and hopefully loaded the program onto my laptop, sitting on its barstool. If it worked this time, there'd be no Wes tonight. If this worked, and I got to see Wiley, depending on what he was doing, whether he slept naked or not, there might never be any Wes again.

Windows vanished, and when the cursor started to blink in the corner of the dark screen, I hit *Enter.*

The command line said, *Enter IP address:*

I looked up his numbers on my phone again, typed them, hit *Enter* again. *Connecting . . .*

Hallelujah and praise Jesus, *it worked!* And whatever tweak he'd given it to make it work also made it even better: instead of a little three by five square, the wonderful vista of Wiley Royce's bedroom filled the entire screen.

The room was dim; it seemed to be suffused with a pale green light, somehow reflected from the walls. There was a shaft of moonlight coming in through the skylight, but I thought that there had to be more illumination, coming from somewhere else – maybe the television was on. Wiley was lying on his bed, looking down at some book. He glanced across the room, in the direction of his laptop. Then he stood up, taking the book with him. It was his Algebra text, and I just had time to think about what a good little studious boy he was, until looking at him blotted out all thought.

He was wearing a black robe, belted loosely at the waist; it had a grinning yellow tiger, embroidered, climbing down from the shoulder. The material was thin, shiny, almost feminine. I could tell that he was shirtless underneath it, and wore some kind of white sweatpants. He crossed the room, and set his book down on the desk, looked over at the laptop (which was off camera). He didn't look at the television at all, so maybe it wasn't on. He turned and walked back toward the bed, and I saw that there was a garish green dragon sewn into the back of the robe.

Then – saints be praised! – he took off the robe and threw it casually onto his bed. A little shiver shot through me at seeing his naked back for the first time: his shoulders were broad, blades lightly sculpted; his black hair curled to just below the nape of his neck. I followed the line of his spine down to the curve of his superbly fine ass; I'd noted that Wiley had a nice ass before, but the gathers of the white sweats limned it perfectly.

He turned around and stood up on his toes, and reached up and tugged on something above his head that I couldn't see. I looked at the outline of his ribs; the curve of his impeccably formed lats; his shoulders and biceps, perfect, flawless, not overly muscled, but muscled enough. Quite beyond my conscious control, my hand reached out, as if I might touch his collarbone, faultlessly formed. Or run my fingers across his smooth, hairless chest, or down across his flat belly.

Wiley wasn't bulky like a bodybuilder. He was simply lean; his muscles were spare and lightly defined like a swimmer or a diver. Half-unclothed, he was breathtaking. Standing there, he looked like a younger, leaner, healthier Wes, not ready to sing and play guitar, but to engage in some more enjoyable *physical* activity. My fingers positively itched to touch him, to feel those muscles ripple and move. But of course, I couldn't touch him, not yet, not through the screen of this indispensable electronic contrivance. For the moment, I had to be content with just watching him.

He gave whatever he was pulling on a final sharp tug, and to my utter amazement, a trapeze dropped down, just like in the circus. The black bar was a little lower than his chest; thick beige ropes snaked up, out of sight, to the ceiling. How had I not noticed such a contraption, the few times that I'd been permitted into his room? A trapeze? *Seriously?*

Wiley reached up and grabbed the ropes, leapt and sat on the bar. Still holding onto the ropes, he leaned back and put one bare foot on it, then the other, and stood up, sliding his hands upwards along the ropes. The light and shadow of the room played off his arms and chest and incomparable belly, and my nervous system suggested mildly that I might want to breathe again.

He lifted his legs out to the sides and pointed his toes until they were almost parallel with the ground, then wrapped his legs around the ropes, and slid down until his knees rested lightly against the bar. The ropes formed a V against the juncture where his thighs joined his body, then on up his chest and shoulders and in front of his still upstretched arms. He put his elbows through the ropes and leaned forward, released them, then held his arms out from his shoulders, again parallel to the ground. The ropes were behind his shoulders, and now he bent his elbows and grasped them at his waist and leaned all the way forward, balancing on the bar with his knees. Then he straightened up and sat on the bar. He pointed his toes at the TV, then leaned back until his torso was parallel with the floor. It was amazing: how *strong* he must be!

Then he grabbed the ropes, pulled himself up again, unhooked his legs from behind the bar; he crossed his ankles in front of it and leaned back again. Then he grabbed the bar between his legs, pointed his toes out to the sides and behind him, then brought them together and slowly lowered them to the floor.

Wiley let go of the bar and walked over to the desk. He picked up his Algebra book, walked back across the room to his bed. He picked up the shiny black robe and threw it on, transferring the book from one hand to the other as he did so. Then he padded slowly out of the room like a jaguar going to study his equations.

I'd never seen such a breathtaking example of balance and muscle control in my life. I'd seen gymnasts' routines on rings, of course, but they hadn't been entirely shirtless; they hadn't looked like Wiley Royce, like a leaner, younger, stronger, incredibly perfect Wes Thomerville. I longed to run my fingers across his obliques – Deneen called them *boy muscles* – those just slightly contoured strips below a guy's waist that, like some kind of God-designed vanishing point, led the eye and consideration ever lower, made one's mind and soul wonder about the shape and dimensions of what lie just below the waistband of his sweats.

And when I'd seen gymnasts, I hadn't been watching them when they didn't know they were being watched. They hadn't been alone in a dim, green-litten room on a trapeze. I'd never had a barely-controlled desire for any of them.

And their routines had always seemed very quick, with lots of large flips and swings. This had been so gloriously slow, just one fluid motion after another, like some kind of teasing foreplay. I blinked at the empty room, surprised at the term. But that's just what it'd been like: some slow, acrobatic dance. For his next trick, I imagined Wiley performing another act, perhaps a little less slowly, but no less acrobatically. I shivered, and stared at the empty room, willing him to come back and show it all to me again.

After about five minutes, he returned. He glanced in the direction of his laptop, then picked up that funky remote from the desk beside his bed. He pointed it in the general direction of the TV, and the room went black, except for the shaft of moonlight shining through the skylight onto his trapeze.

I watched for several more minutes; but it was too dark to tell if he was still there (perhaps naked, crawled in bed) or if he'd left his room again. I heaved a mighty sigh and hit the *Enter* key. The command prompt asked: *End view y/n?* And I thought that here was a view I wanted never to end; but since there was nothing more to see tonight, I hit *y*.

NATE

When I woke up and looked at my phone the next morning, it was already ten o'clock. There was a text from Wiley. *Show up at my house like 1-ish, will ya? I need a chaperone.*

I frowned. The first-date thrills of the night before evaporated. Deneen wasn't here with me and Brendee wasn't here either, so Brendee once again filled my mind. Sure, Denny liked me, and she smelled good, but Brendee . . . I'd wanted Brendee, dreamt about having her, for so long. She had her own little address in my head, while Deneen was a newcomer to the neighborhood. I might eventually allow Brendee to pack up and move away – I imagined for a moment that I could still taste Denny's mouth on my tongue – but I wasn't ready to send my tiny blonde crush on her way just yet.

I texted Wiley and said that we'd be there.

We?

Deneen & me.

Did u ignore my advice? Have u stepped in our lovely Deneen already? Does she already hang like a new-married wife about ur neck, hardly 2 b shook off?

Fuck u, Wiley, and ur poetry. I'll c u at 1.

BRENDEE

The next day, *noon-ish,* I rang the doorbell, and I heard Wiley's voice tell me to come in. I opened the door and stopped dead. He had his back to me, and I saw that green dragon again, prancing on its field of black across Wiley's broad shoulders. The memory of him from the night before sprang to my mind, from after he'd ditched the robe: shirtless, wearing nothing else but those amazing white sweats, consummately balanced on that totally unexpected trapeze, muscles positively gleaming in the moonlight . . . I looked down: he was barefoot, as always, but denim curled under his heels a little bit. He was wearing jeans. He turned around – he'd been looking at his Algebra book – and smiled at me. He was – and the Gods did weep – fully clothed beneath his robe.

We sat at the dining room table and I handed him another test. This one was more difficult, and he seemed to be having a little bit of trouble with it. He kept biting on his pencil, and stretching his head to one side, as if he had a crick in his neck. At last he finished the test, and handed it back to me, smiling.

I checked his answers. One by one, they were coming out correct, and without looking up, I said, "You got 'em all right again, Wiley. Pretty soon, you won't need me anymore."

"Oh, I need you, Brendee." Like on the phone the night before, his voice was low, but not soft this time – it was like a growl. Or maybe I'd just imagined it, had just wanted it to sound that way, to mean that he needed me as much as I wanted him, because when I looked up, he just smiled blankly at me. His voice was back to its cheerful, neutral Wiley normality when he said, "It's still a long way 'til exam time."

I told him that he was doing so well that he could take the rest of the day off. "You wanna go to the mall or something?"

"Maybe. Nate and Deneen are coming over."

He did that neck-stretching thing again, and I realized that it wasn't some unconscious tic, brought on because he was nervous about the test. "What's wrong with your neck, Wiley?" I asked. *Do you want me to rub it for you? Bite it, maybe?*

He twisted his head again. "Ah, I'm just a little stiff. I missed my workout this morning."

In hopes that he'd correct me and then elaborate, I said, "What gym do you go to?" Maybe he'd tell me about his trapeze. Maybe I could ask to see it, and when he showed it to me, maybe I could talk him into showing me what he did with it. Maybe he'd strip down to only those white sweats again, then maybe I could talk him into taking them off, too . . .

"I don't go to a gym, Brendee," he indeed corrected me, as if I was a child and he was telling me that I was too old to still believe in the Tooth Fairy. Such a belief was ridiculous, as ridiculous as Wiley Royce going to a gym. "No need to prance around in public. I do Tai Chi and a little yoga, right here at home, in my room."

"Tai Chi?" I repeated. The term sounded familiar, but I couldn't seem to associate it with a trapeze.

"Have you ever gone to the park on a Sunday morning? Have you ever seen a group of people, standing in rows, doing exercises together? Usually they're older people, but not always."

I nodded. "I always thought it was some kind of interpretative dance."

Wiley smiled. "No. They're doing Tai Chi." He typed something on his phone, then read the *dictionary.com* definition to me: "It's *a Chinese system of calisthenics, characterized by coordinated and rhythmic movements.*"

But where did the trapeze come in?

"And you do this every day?" *I hope,* I thought, because I was certainly willing to *watch him* do it, every day. *And three times on Sunday,* like my dad always said. "By yourself? Not with a group of other people, like in the park?

"I'm not big on other people too much, Brendee. I'm sort of a lone wolf." To my utter surprise, Wiley threw his held back and howled, then grinned at me.

"And you do this every day?" I repeated.

"I try to," he said. "I broke my leg a few years ago, and the physical therapist taught me yoga and Tai Chi as part of strength and stretch training, so I wouldn't lose my range of motion."

Your range of motion is phenomenal, I thought, and pictured it again, for a second too long, because there was a pause in the conversation. I hurried to fill it. "Why did you miss doing it today?"

"I had to take my parents to the airport. They flew up to see Grandma and Grandpa. It's like a little vacation. They'll be back on Wednesday. They wanted me to go, but I said I probably shouldn't miss three days of school this close to the end. I told them I had to study."

Before the idea that Wiley's parents were gone had a chance to sink into my head – before I had time to consider that I'd been here in the house with him, alone, for a good forty-five minutes, and had failed to take advantage of it – the doorbell rang. Wiley said, "Come in," and Nate and Deneen walked into his parentless house. They were holding hands. Wasn't that cute?

Nate said, "What the fuck are you wearing?"

Wiley glanced down at himself, at the tiger on his shoulder. "It's a mandarin robe. It's silk."

He offered his elbow to me so I could feel the texture, an offer that was entirely too good to pass up. I slid my hand across the top of his arm, feeling the hard muscle underneath the slick fabric, and it took every ounce of self-control I had not to shudder, not to just continue running my hand up and around and across the dragon on the back. But I stopped, and when I looked at Nate, I noticed he had a little disgusted frown on his face. I removed my hand from Wiley's arm, thinking, *Haven't you ever seen a guy wearing a silk mandarin robe before?*

"It was a gift from my physical therapist." Wiley smiled and Nate rolled his eyes.

"You're not wearing it out in public, are you?"

"No." Wiley stood up and slid out of the robe, and tossed it onto the recliner. "I just felt a little chilly when I got back from the airport this morning."

"Maybe you should've left your shoes on," Deneen observed.

Wiley shrugged, then said, "Brendee says I'm doing so well that I can take the day off. She suggested that we go to the mall . . . but I was thinking of a little fresh air. We were just talking about the park. What d'ya say, Brendee? You wanna go down to the park? Walk around the lake? Feed the ducks?" He didn't wait for me to answer. "Nate?"

"That sounds like fun!" Deneen said. "I haven't been to the park in days!"

Oh, joy, I thought. But I'd get to be with Wiley, out in the world for a change. And maybe he would get the hint from Nate and Deneen, so obviously newly a couple, and want to hold *my* hand.

NATE

We walked around the lake, and I put my arm around Deneen's shoulders, and she put her arm around my waist. She was a nice girl, and I did like her, but I just couldn't seem to concentrate on the things that were starting to happen between us, because I kept watching Brendee and Wiley, walking a little bit ahead.

Brendee would push him playfully, and Wiley would dutifully stumble a little bit to one side. It was an obvious game: Brendee hoped that he would overcorrect and lean back into her, but Wiley, ever graceful, refused to play. She'd touch him lightly on the shoulder, look up at him and smile. Giggle. All the girlish tricks that I'd always hoped she'd display to me. But Wiley, good man that he was, wasn't having any. He looked over his shoulder and grinned at me, making sure that I was noticing his indifference.

We found a playground on the other side of the lake, complete with a sand bottom and those industrial-strength fiberglass swings, suspended from heavy chains across a massive steel frame. Wiley immediately took off his shoes and wiggled his toes in the sand, then leapt up and stood on one of the swings. I sat on the next one over, and Deneen and Brendee perched on the wall behind us.

"Did you guys ever bump the swing set when you were a kid?"

"I beg your pardon?" Brendee said and smiled her cute, sparkly-eyed Brendee smile at him.

"Maybe you were even there, Brendee," he said over his shoulder to her, reminding her that they'd known each other as children. "We had this flimsy, rusty old swing set, and if you got to swinging really high and fast, the legs would come off the ground a little, then clomp back down. My mom would yell out the window, 'Wiley, quit bumping the swing set! You're gonna turn it over on yourself!'"

Brendee shook her head. She didn't remember bumping the swing set as a kid with Wiley, but I knew she wanted to bump something with him now. Deneen didn't comment because she was looking at her phone.

Wiley looked at me.

"We had a tire swing," I said. "Couldn't bump the tree."

He looked over his shoulder at the girls again. Now Brendee and Deneen were both looking at their phones. Wiley wrapped his arm around the chain for balance and took his own phone out of his pocket. He scrolled up and down for a minute, then typed something and looked at me. Now my phone beeped, and I took it out of my pocket.

They're talking about us, Wiley's text said. I looked over at Brendee and Deneen, heads still bent over their phones. My phone beeped again.

They're 2 close 2 actually speak out loud, Wiley's text said. *But they're still talking about us. Read it.*

He handed me his phone, then pulled on the chains until the swing started to move.

I looked at Wiley's phone. Brendee and Deneen's conversation was all on it, with colons after their names, like a script.

Brendee: *Well?*

Deneen: *He kisses like a god.*

I looked up at Wiley, but he was swinging back and forth, to the limits of the chains and of gravity. I thought he might be trying to bump this set, even though its legs were set into the concrete under the sand, to prevent such lunacy.

Brendee: *Did u kno Wiley has a trapeze? He does exercises on it.*

Deneen: *How do u kno?*

Brendee: *I watched him.*

Deneen: *He let u watch him? I thot u said he was shy?*

I watched Wiley hurtle thru the swing's arc. He was a lot of things, some of them not at all likeable; but shy was definitely not one of them. I looked back down at his phone, scrolled it up a little bit.

Brendee: *He is shy. He didn't kno I was watching him. He gave me an app to look thru people's webcams. He prolly didn't think I'd use it 2 watch him.*

Deneen: *That's nasty.*

My sentiments exactly, Denny, I thought, and it made me like her a little bit more.

She texted again: *Y would u want 2 watch him?*

Brendee: *I think he's awesome, Deneen. I want to eat him.*

Deneen: *Really?*

Brendee: ☺

Deneen: *He's all right, I guess. He's a little 2 skinny 4 me. I like em with a little more meat on em.*

Brendee: *Like Nate?*

Deneen: ☺

114

I smiled to myself. She was all right.

Brendee: *I need u 2 do me a big favor.*

Deneen: *?*

Brendee: *I need u 2 keep Nate occupied 2night.*

Deneen: *?*

Brendee: *Wiley's parents r out of town. I want 2 go over and c him 2night, & I don't want u and Nate hanging around. I have 2 go to Jen's recital at 7, but it should b over by 9, & then I'm gonna call Wiley.*

Deneen: *And eat him?* ☺

Brendee: *If there is a God.*

Deneen: *I'll tell Nate I want 2 go 2 the movies or something. It's so nice 2 have a boyfriend again!*

Brendee: *I'm in the market. And I have just the model picked out.*

Deneen: *I'll make sure Nate's out of the way. I kno how 2 keep him occupied.*

Brendee: ☺

I resisted the urge to turn around and look at them, thinking that if I did, they'd surely be looking at me. At least Deneen would be. Deneen would be looking at me, her big green eyes all bright and sparkly, the pupils round and black, like they'd been after Mikkelea's show. I realized with a little start of surprise where I'd seen that expression before. Deneen looked at me the same way that Brendee looked at Wiley. I dared a peek at them. Deneen was still looking at her phone – but I'd seen that look in her eyes last night, and I smiled a little to myself.

Brendee was indeed watching Wiley, flying through the air like a tall, blue-eyed blackbird. I thought about how much she'd gotten into that awful old Wes Thomerville video, and then I imagined how much she must've dug secretly watching Wiley, so much closer to her own age, while he did God-only-knew-what on his trapeze. While all the time, courtesy of the red ball on his laptop, he knew that she was watching him.

I thought about Deneen and her big green eyes, and it struck me that she wanted me, just as much as Brendee wanted Wes Thomerville and this walking, talking, present-day embodiment of him. I admitted to myself that Brendee wanted Wiley in a way that she'd never want me. I thought that even if, in some different future, I did somehow manage to get her, I'd never, ever be able to shake the idea – it would always be in my mind, unremovable – that she

115

was thinking about Wiley. Maybe she wouldn't be thinking of him at one exact minute, but maybe she would be the next. I'd seen the autonomic, uncontrollable, subconscious action of her eyes dilating when she looked at him. They say the eyes are the windows to the soul, and I'd seen the same expression in my pretty Deneen's eyes when she looked at me. What more could I ask for than that?

It was time I stopped torturing myself about something I wasn't going to get, and started appreciating what was being offered to me. *Fuck it,* I thought. *Wiley can have her.*

I walked out into the sand, where he could see me. I nodded up at him, indicating for him to stop swinging. Then I took out my phone and sent him a text: *She's all yours.*

Wiley eventually got the swing stopped and while he was still standing on it, I handed his phone up to him, nodded at it.

He read my text, and sent one back: *R u sure?*

She wants to eat you.

Wiley's eyebrows shot up at that, but he didn't look at me. He texted: *Very discerning tastes. A connoisseur. But r u sure?*

I'm sure.

No take backs, my son. No kicking my ass cuz u changed ur mind.

She's all urs. I know I'll wanna hear about it someday. But not anytime soon.

He jumped down off the swing and grinned at me, that ol' toothy, wicked Wiley grin. He said, "Then *let's kick the tires and light the fires, big daddy!"* Then he waited, like he always did, for me to get the reference. When I just looked at him blankly, he shook his head and clapped me on the shoulder. "Someday, we're gonna have to get you to watch some old movies, Nate."

****

I expected Wiley to glom onto Brendee immediately, but as we walked back around the lake, he was just as aloof as he'd ever been, ignoring her little attempts to lean in closer to him, to get him to lean in closer to her. I hugged my new girlfriend a little tighter to me, and when she asked if I'd like to go to the movies tonight, I kissed her on the cheek and said, "Whatever you want, Denny. Your wish is my command."

Brendee couldn't sit as close to Wiley as she wanted to in the backseat of my Chevy, either, because the seat belts prevented it. She

116

still smiled and giggled at him, and endeavored to touch him on the arm as much as possible. Wiley continued to more or less ignore her, looking out the window, and only giving her the most perfunctory of answers. When I dropped her at her house – she had to get ready to go to her little sister's spring dance recital – she leaned in through Deneen's window, and said to Wiley, "When do you want me to come over tomorrow? For your lesson?"

Wiley didn't even look up from his phone. "Noon-ish is good. Call me."

Brendee and Deneen shared a glance, then Deneen shrugged, shook her head a little. We said goodbye to Brendee, except for Wiley, who just waved in her general direction, not looking up from his phone. When we pulled away from the curb, he put in in his pocket and said, "What're you guys doing tonight?"

"We're going to the movies," Denny told him. "What're you doing?"

"Oh, the same old thing," Wiley said. "I have to study. Might watch something on TV."

We'd reached his house. He got out of the car and said, "You kids have fun. Don't do anything I wouldn't do." He squinted at me, then skipped up the walk, bounded up the steps, and disappeared into his house.

BRENDEE

I went home and took a bubble bath, shaved my legs, as if I was preparing for a special date instead of just going to see my little sister's dance recital. I'd made up my mind that I'd have Wiley, shy or not, come hell or high water, and tonight. His bitterly brief performance in his white sweats, suspended in the air, toes pointed at the walls, had firmed up my resolve, had whetted my purpose.

Visions of him had filled my head since I'd first laid eyes on him, and like an untreated disease, they'd only gotten worse. I was becoming absent-minded. More than once, I'd looked over at someone, only to realize that they'd been talking to me, and that it was my turn to say something. I'd have to say, "What?" and tell them, "Say that again," because I hadn't been paying attention. Where once I might've been thinking about Wes and his video, now I'd been thinking about Wiley, just as blue-eyed and black-haired as Wes, just as incredible to look at. But unlike Wes, Wiley was *right here,* and I could do so much more than just look at him, if only I could talk him into seeing things my way.

The idea of lying beside him and running my hands over his taunt body frothed in me. I frequently caught myself rubbing my fingers together, because they itched: they hungered, like they were independent entities. They wanted to tangle themselves in all that black, curly hair. They wanted to touch him, everywhere, wanted to seek out and hold everything that my eyes had not yet seen.

I imagined, heartily and repeatedly, the things that someone so limber could undoubtedly do. I'd only been with Dave – big, strapping boy that he was – and I'd enjoyed him very much. When we'd first met, I'd been very much attracted to Dave – he was bright and funny, and he was cute. I used to like the way the sunlight would play off his dark red hair, burnishing it to a million different tawny shades of coppers and auburns. I used to like the way he appreciated my body, like I was some amazing God-given creature, and he was the luckiest man on earth to be allowed to possess me. I used to like the way he'd hold my small hand in his big, meaty one, how he would nibble my ear.

But all that was forgotten, like old love letters shut up in a box, the minute I saw Wiley. My attraction to Dave had been on the wane since I'd started watching Wes's video – I'd already begun gathering up those letters, tying them in bunches with ribbons, setting them aside. Only rationality had prevented me from dumping Dave then: Wes wasn't real. No matter how much he and his video owned my imagination, I'd never see him dressed in anything else but that scrumptious collection of black leather and denim; I'd never get to touch him or kiss him or hear him say my name.

I often congratulated myself: keeping Dave around after I'd become besotted with Wes proved that I wasn't completely insane – if I would've been completely insane, I would've gotten rid of Dave right then, and just concentrated all my efforts on the care, feeding, and maintenance of my fantasy of Wes's perfection. But that was just nuts; Wes wasn't real, would never be real, and while my attraction to Dave had faded, almost from the moment I'd hit the right button on my mother's dusty old DVD player, Dave was there and actual and we might've had a life together. Normal people thought about a future with their boyfriends; they didn't lock themselves up forever with just a goblet of wine and a three by five video of a man that no longer existed.

But my cousin Wiley was also alive and breathing, unattached and right around the block. He was intelligent (except for some brain lesion of stupidity when it came to math, but he was overcoming it, and how could I possibly care about that?); his understanding of electronics was unparalleled in my experience. His sense of humor, what little I'd seen of it, was wry. Deneen said that Wiley could say the filthiest, most disrespectful things; that nobody liked him, that he thought he was better than everybody else. But I'd seen none of that. Wiley had struck me simply as a watchful, shy *boy,* even if he did make the occasional, playfully derisive comment about the world around him.

And then there was the inescapable fact that he looked just like Wes, and that he had the body of a god; and there was the fact that my mind would not rest, I wouldn't be able to think clearly or concentrate on the banalities of life ever again, until I found out for myself if he could really do all the things that I imagined he could. I would have him, or he would tell me why not.

Jen's recital concluded at 9:09. She'd been adorable: she was thirteen, still a little girl. The instructor was not one of those that dressed little girls up in skintight outfits; she didn't have them paint themselves up like drag queens, or have them writhe around on the stage like animals in heat. She insisted instead on perfect synchronization; flawless discipline. They were more drill team than dance troupe.

I'd been a good big sister – Gary had bailed, gone to see Mikkelea again, her second show – but now it was time for me to think about myself. I gave Jen a bouquet of roses to celebrate her talent, kissed her on the cheek and told her she was great, then I'd left her in the care of my parents and little brother. I'd taken my own car, telling Mom and Dad some lie about having to attend Deneen's eighteenth birthday party. This convenient untruth had occurred to me because my own eighteenth was coming up – I knew what I wanted for my birthday, and nobody could give it to me but Wiley. I bid them farewell, and started calling him as soon as I walked out to the parking lot.

He didn't answer, so I sent him a text: *Hey, Wiley, what cha doin?* But he didn't text back. I put my phone in my purse and got into the car. Then I took it out and looked at it again, just to make sure – sometimes I missed the beep, right? But he hadn't texted back. With a force of will, I put it back in my purse and started the car. I would seem like a crazy stalker nutball if I called him too many times. I wondered if, since I realized this, did it make me any less of a crazy stalker nutball? *No,* I thought, *it did not.* It just made me a self-aware crazy stalker nutball, and somehow that seemed infinitely worse.

I returned to our empty house, and just like it was commonplace, just like it was the thing to do, as if it wasn't concrete proof of my crazy stalker nutball-ness, I loaded Wiley's spy program onto my computer. It connected immediately, and there he was in his green room, reclining invitingly on his bed, studying. I called him again, and it was surreal to see his phone light up, right there on the desk next to him. But he ignored it, or he didn't hear it. Maybe he had it on silent, or maybe he was listening to loud music. I doubted that, though; I'd never known Wiley to play music while he studied.

I dared to call again – that was three calls now, and one text, all unanswered. Too many more, and I'd really start to look desperate. He was again dressed in his black robe and white sweats, and I decided that it wasn't entirely unfulfilling to just watch him lying there for a few minutes. I didn't want to watch him, I wanted to touch him, to be there with him; but I couldn't just march over there to his house and attack him.

Wiley had never responded to my gentle flirting; not in the slightest. Except perhaps for those little changes in his voice – and there was a possibility that I'd only imagined that – he'd always been friendly, but oblivious to any little smiles or nudges that I attempted to send his way. Yet I was assured: Dave's appreciation and the longing looks of the likes of Nate and others had led me to have confidence in my own attractiveness. There was no reason whatsoever why I couldn't have Wiley. I knew that he didn't have a girlfriend, and barring some latent homosexuality that I couldn't guess at, I was sure, once I got him alone – I might have to be the initiator, because he was shy – he would respond. Once I started to touch him and kiss him, I was sure that he'd realize what he'd been missing; I was sure he'd be eager to make up for all the time he'd wasted in his ignorance.

But he obviously wanted to study right now – I'd just have to be patient. I was sure that he wouldn't study all night, and maybe when he was done, he'd pick up his phone to turn the ringer on, and he'd see that his tutor had called three times. He was always saying how grateful he was for my help – surely he'd call or text back to see what I wanted? Then I would finagle some reason to go over there.

But in the meantime, I'd have to just be content with watching him. Maybe he'd let the trapeze down again.

After a few minutes, Wiley closed his Algebra book, and leapt out of bed. He tossed his book on the desk beside it, and with his back to me, shook himself out of the black robe. I shivered in anticipation, thinking, *I'll give him another call after this is over.* He walked to the center of the room, again into that shaft of moonlight. But he didn't look or reach up; he didn't let the trapeze down.

He stood with his feet together for the span of a heartbeat – I had to again remind myself to breathe. Then he moved his left foot, like I'd seen the silent groups in the park do, when they were practicing Tai Chi. Then Wiley moved his hands, gracefully, oh, so slowly upwards. He swayed, moving his arms and his hands through the air, palms up, then palms down.

Next, he sinuously slid his left foot to the side. Bending at the knees and elbows, he put his palms out flat, then did the same movement as before, arms moving across his body, palms first up, then down. He pointed his heel, then stepped to the left and swung slowly around, crouching, moving. It was absolutely nothing like the little old men and women in the park, even though he was doing the same slow, deliberate movements. Watching Wiley do Tai Chi, shirtless, in his white and shadowed sweats was like watching a jungle cat move: supple, slow, whispery; all muscle, tension and release. It was breathtaking, mesmerizing. His movements hypnotized me: he was the snake charmer, the slow sweeps of his limbs like the swaying of the flute.

Limitless poise, fluidity, an extended leg, a bent knee, an arm lifted slowly skyward, as he swept and slowly turned, then backed up again, knees bent, hands describing gentle arcs before his face. Then advancing, heels and toes pointed, knees deeply bent, arms moving in circles, wide or short. It was a dance, it was a martial art; he was a *ballerino,* a *danseur;* he was a ninja. He pushed outward, he pulled backward, all with infinite slowness and flexibility. His arms caressed the air like a lover.

His broad back to me, he stood on one foot, then pointed his other foot up to almost shoulder height, then slid it slowly down and out to one side until he was almost on the floor. Then he raised that knee and stood again, and continued the same arcs and turns. This went on for maybe ten minutes; it seemed like I held my breath for the whole time, even though that wasn't possible. The exercise ended when he described another small circle in the air in front of his exquisite chest, and drew his legs together, until he was standing in the same position in which he'd begun.

I expected him to bow, but he did not. Instead, he turned sideways and bent over at the waist. Again, I had a moment to study the perfect curve of his lat, the shadow of his ribs in the moonlight. He put his hands on the floor and walked his feet toward his hands, until he paused on tiptoe. Then he slowly raised his legs until he was doing a handstand. It was absolutely phenomenal. He let his legs back down, *ever so slowly,* then turned until he was facing the TV again. This time he bent and moved his feet out to the sides a little bit, and did the handstand with his legs spread; he brought them up, bare toes pointed at the ceiling, and held them that way, for what seemed like an eternity; then he opened his legs wide again, and slowly lowered them back to the floor. He jumped up, and reached for something on the desk.

Then Wiley, who hadn't even broken a sweat, who wasn't even breathing hard, looked at the webcam at the top of the television. He looked me right in the eye. He held up a small piece of white cardboard, a little bit bigger than a sheet of notebook paper. Written across it in black Sharpie were the words: *Hi, Brendee!*

He held it up long enough for me to read it, then discarded it on the floor.

The next one said: *Do you like me? Circle yes or no.* It had a little yes or no at the bottom. Wiley look down as if reading it himself, then grinned and quickly, confidently discarded that one.

He looked at me again and smiled slowly, slyly, his blue eyes smoky in the dim greenish light. I finally got to see the one expression that I'd dreamt of, that I knew had to be there all along. Wiley wasn't shy at all; he wasn't as innocent and boyish as he seemed. The sign he held up said: *I know what you want.*

The next one said: *I'm here all by myself.*

The last one said: *Come get me.*

He let it slide to the floor. He turned his back to the webcam, crossed the room. He picked up the remote from the desk and, over his shoulder, he pointed it at the TV. The room went dark.

****

As I drove the short, interminable blocks to Wiley's house, my mind was aswirl with all the commonplace, annoying, everyday things that try to assert themselves and take control when one is on the brink of doing something on the down low, something that promised to be dark and wet and just a little bit dirty. What would his neighbors think when they saw my car parked there overnight? Would they tell his parents? What would his parents think? Would they be shocked to learn that a girl had spent the night with their shy son? Were the neighbors really that nosy, that they would notice a strange car? Were they that friendly with the Royces that they'd mention it? The neighbors didn't know who I was, wouldn't recognize my car. Whatever the neighbors thought, it sincerely didn't matter, really, because Wiley . . . *OMG, Wiley!*

The thought never crossed my mind to worry about what Wiley might think of me. He'd summoned me to him, and I was responding as if he was my vampire master, as if such a summons was quite undeniable; because it was. I was finally going to get to have him; if my eagerness cast my morality in some kind of unkind light to him, I couldn't possibly care less. I'd never even kissed him, never even held his hand. But now consummation was imminent; regret and recrimination could come later. The dream was about to be realized – if there were nightmares on the horizon, I would, as my dad often put it, burn those bridges when I got to them. For the moment, I was going to *use Wiley up.*

I paused on the unlit front porch, took a deep breath. I ran my hand through my hair, straightened my clothing a little bit. I didn't think; I didn't consider conversation, what I would say or what he would say to get the ball rolling. We were strangers, after all. But the time had come for action; it was time to employ the universal language.

The house, too, was dark. I knocked, received no answer. I hesitated only a split second before turning the knob; of course, he'd left the front door open for me.

I climbed the stairs quickly. The door was open, and he was standing in that shaft of moonlight in the middle of the room, waiting for me. I paused in the doorway to just look at him: he was not wearing anything under the silk robe now. I could see his smooth chest, the muscular curve of his calves. There was a small but wicked scar on his left shin, halfway between ankle and knee, like something out of a bad Frankenstein remake. A thick white line, flanked on either side by white dots: stitches. I'd learned something new about him already. It had been his left leg that he'd broken.

I'd never been so excited in my entire life. I panted, although I wasn't out of breath. The very air on my skin seemed to caress and tease me. No presents on Christmas morning, no hot fudge sundae, no first day of school or first car or first date or first kiss – there was no comparison – I'd never anticipated anything, ever, as much as I'd anticipated this.

I walked over and stood in front of him, looked up into his blue-blue eyes, so much like Wes's. Poor Wes, once again relegated to the dust heap of obscurity, once again forgotten. I would think no more of Wes. How could I, when I was standing right here in front of Wiley, mere inches, mere moments away from him?

Wiley put his long fingers lightly on my cheek, and ran his thumb over my mouth. I shivered, waiting. But he didn't move any closer to me, and soon dropped his hand from my face. He said, "Show me what you want, Brendee."

What I wanted, more than anything I'd ever wanted in my life, was just to touch him. I'd looked at him, *watched him* for so long, and now that culmination was almost at hand, the thing that would bring all that longing to its first level of fruition would be to *just touch him,* to feel his skin beneath my fingers. Somehow Wiley realized this, so he just stood there.

I splayed my fingers out, and they trembled. Like in so many fevered fantasies, I caressed his chest, just below the collarbone, and electricity seemed to jump from his skin, arcing through to the most secret parts of me. I shuddered uncontrollably, and Wiley asked me if I was cold.

"Yes," I said, and I expected him to offer to warm me up, to enfold me in his arms.

But he just continued to stand there, aloof, apart. "Touch me," he said. But it wasn't a command; it was a permission. It had been inappropriate, denied, forbidden to me for so long . . .

He must've felt that I hesitated too long, so, to facilitate such adventures, Wiley untied the cord at his waist and shrugged the robe off his shoulders, never taking his eyes from mine. It whispered to the floor. Perhaps he thought I'd look down, then. He sensed how much I wanted to touch him, and he undoubtedly thought he knew how much I wanted to *see* him, also. But I resisted the urge . . . I'd be seeing all of him soon enough, *praise Christ,* and for right now, I just went with my initial desire.

I ran both hands across his chest then, over his shoulders and down his hard-muscled upper arms. The hair on his forearms felt like velvet. I grasped his wrists lightly for a moment, then slid my palms firmly under his palms; they were moist and hot, just like when we'd first shook hands. He trembled, ever so slightly, but still he didn't move. I laced my fingers between his and he squeezed my hands – at last, some reaction. But it wasn't much, and after a moment, he released my hands, leaving them free to again explore.

I put my palms and thumbs on either side of his waist, on his obliques; but I didn't look down, didn't take my eyes from his. Again he trembled. I left my right hand where it was and put my left on the curve of his jaw, his cheek, seeking the hair just behind his ear. I wrapped a curl around my finger.

"Are you shy, Wiley?"

His eyebrows shot up and he grinned. "No," he said, barely restraining a laugh. "I'm standing here naked, Brendee, how can you still think that I'm –"

I raked the fingers of my right hand lightly across his belly and Wiley gasped. I'd found the end of his endurance. He pulled me to him and kissed me then, not tentatively, not gently. No. Wiley wasn't shy. I put my arms around his neck and kissed him back.

If I live to be a hundred, two moments will live above all others in the Chronicles of Brendee's Orgasms. The first was the incredible, implausible, completely unexpected shudder I'd experienced, sitting there on the couch, the first time I saw Wes Thomerville sing. He'd go on to engender many others, but that first one – that secret, public, unbelievable moment, will remain enshrined in my memory forever.

But Wiley put it in the shade. My knees failed when he kissed me; I clung to his neck, and he wrapped his arms around me and crushed me to his hard, feverishly hot body. The combination of his mouth and the floodwaters of my desire for him, pent up for so long and now so suddenly loosed, served to work an indescribable magic upon every cell in my body. Whatever happened next, whatever happened *ever,* nothing would be able to take away the glory and inconceivable release that came with kissing him for the first time.

Somehow, we made it over to the bed. Wiley jumped onto it, in all his naked perfection, and grinned up at me while I struggled to remove my clothes. When I was finally free of them, I fell upon him. For a moment, I again thought that he was shy, because he simply allowed me to explore his body with my mouth and fingers, his only response being trembles and appreciative moans. But he didn't touch me back. Then I realized that his restraint by no means indicated shyness – he knew what I wanted, and he was allowing me to have my fantasy first: the one that involved doing whatever I wanted to him for as long as he could stand it.

And at last he could stand it no longer, and I just had time to wonder how some guy who'd never had a date to anyone's knowledge could be so knowledgeable about just how I wanted it, just how I needed it . . . Then bliss blotted out everything but the blood thrumming in my ears and the smell and taste and touch of his body.

****

I awakened slowly, as if floating up from the bottom of a warm pond. My body and mind were languid, sated, satisfied, a most absolute sword had been put to all the agonizing, awesome, unfulfilled, hurts-do-good desire that I'd shouldered so stoically for so long. I remembered every moment from the night before, how Wiley had finally allowed me to exorcise all my demons upon his incomparable body; how he'd then proceeded to answer every question I'd ever imagined about just what he could do for me with it. Heaving the most contented sigh in the history of the world, at last I opened my eyes.

Where there had been moonlight the night before, now a shaft of sunlight streamed happily in through the skylight in the tilted ceiling. Wiley was wearing his white sweats again. He had his back to me, and was doing his Tai Chi. I laid my head back on his pillow and watched him.

He'd expertly rounded off the stiff, near-desperate edges to the desire that I'd harbored for him: it seemed like I'd wanted Wiley all my life. But watching him move was no less intoxicating, even though I now knew, and thoroughly, what every part of that perfect body felt like. His arms, his chest, his incredibly strong back. I knew that he had another scar on his left leg, longer and uglier than the first, that ran down the outside of his thigh.

"All three bones," he'd told me. "Snapped like kindling."

He finished with another spectacular handstand, then leapt up and smiled at me. "Tell me, Brendee," he said. "How d'ya like me so far?"

I told him, "I think that's the sexiest thing I've ever seen. *You're* the sexiest thing I've ever seen."

Wiley grinned. "You must not get out much." He held up one long finger, as if a thought had just occurred to him. "I know something you'll like even better." And he came immediately back to bed.

NATE

I went to the movies with Deneen on Saturday night, and we held hands in the dark. Afterwards, she brought me home and introduced me to her parents and baby sister. The little girl, named Delia, was about five, and took to me right away. While Denny and her mom made popcorn, and her dad and I sat down in the living room to chat, Delia climbed into my lap, with no awkwardness whatsoever. I was her new friend. She clutched the remote to the television in her tiny hand. "Let's watch cartoons, Nate," she said, and pushed the button.

The TV lit up with bright colors and catchy jingles, and her indulgent father just shook his head and smiled. He asked me how I liked playing football. When I told him I didn't play anymore, he seemed a little relieved, and said, "That's good. Getting hit like that scrambles your brains."

Your beautiful, green-eyed daughter is scrambling my brains, I thought.

I watched another movie with Denny and her family. She sat next to me on the couch, but Delia sat on my lap, the tiniest chaperone. There would be no secret hand-holding with her there. She was like a house cat: it was her house, and her couch, and just because I was sitting there didn't mean she wasn't going to sit there, too, and because she liked me, there was no reason for her not to sit on my lap. It was the most adorable thing I'd ever experienced. She gave me a big hug when it was time for me to go.

My car was parked around the corner, out of sight of her house, and when Denny walked me out to it to say goodbye, she pushed me hard up against the door and kissed me just as hard. It was obvious that little skinny Denny wanted me very much, so I spun her round and pushed her up against the car door, too. I whispered, "What are you doing tomorrow afternoon?"

She lightly pulled on my bottom lip with her teeth. "What did you have in mind?"

I picked her up and she wrapped her legs around me, right there in the street, and kissed me again. "It's entirely up to you," I said.

"I'm sure I can think of something." Then she kissed me quickly on the nose, all lust gone, replaced by playful affection. It was nice to know that Denny liked me, besides just wanting to do me, and it occurred to me that it wasn't a very macho thing to think, but it was true, nonetheless. And it wasn't like we could do anything about it right then, anyway. I set her down, and she told me that she'd promised to go to the mall with her mom and little sister in the morning, but she said I could pick her up around one o'clock. She once again promised that she'd think up something for us to do. I kissed her goodnight and reluctantly went home.

BRENDEE

Wiley asked me if I was hungry, and I discovered that I was ravenously so. He hopped up and put his sweats on, and handed me his robe. "It's awesome," he said simply, and he was right: the silk felt indescribably delicious against my skin, and I shivered in pleasure.

Wiley observed my enjoyment, and told me, "Nabokov said, *'It is strange that the tactile sense, which is so infinitely less precious to men than sight, becomes at critical moments our main, if not only, handle to reality.'* I like those moments the best, I think." He smoothed the agreeably slick material down over my shoulders, and I shivered again. Wiley grinned, delighted with the way his touch affected me. "I'll order you one. What color would you like?'

"You pick it out," I told him, and hugged him to me.

Wiley said, "All right." He picked his phone up off the desk and put it in his pocket, and we went down the stairs arm in arm.

He told me to prepare to be amazed by his culinary skills. I doubted that he could amaze me any more than he already had, but I sat at the dining room table as directed, and watched him through the doorway as he made us something to eat, dancing around in the kitchen, barefoot as always, humming some unfamiliar tune.

I heard his phone beep. "Nate says hi," he said.

"Tell him hi back," I said.

Nate's text to Wiley had reminded me that there was another world outside, and that I still had a role in it. It took me a minute to locate my purse; I remembered nothing from the night before that didn't involve Wiley: touching Wiley, kissing Wiley, *OMG, had it really finally happened?* I retraced my steps and found my purse on the floor next to the desk in his room, where I must've dropped it and forgotten it when I saw him standing there in the moonlight.

I texted my mother; I told her that I'd had a little too much to drink at Deneen's birthday party, and had stayed overnight at her house. I told her I'd be home for dinner.

Then I texted Deneen. *If anybody asks, I stayed at ur house last night.*

Did u eat Wiley?

☺

☹ *I don't kno what u see in him. Was it worth it?*

He's incredible. When I tell u the things he does, u won't believe me.

I already don't believe u ☺

Wiley set a plate in front of me; it was a Denver omelet. He returned a moment later with a glass of orange juice, then went back into the kitchen and came back with his own.

"I thought you were a vegetarian," I said in surprise.

"Who told you that?" he said, tucking into his breakfast.

"Nate."

"I am but a vegetarian north-north-west: when the wind is southerly I know a hawk from a handsaw, and I know when a little protein is healthy for you." He nodded at my phone and smiled. "Are you telling your mom about me?"

I blinked, then grinned at him. "Not yet. My mom just might lose her hillbilly mind when she sees you."

His eyebrows went up in surprise. "Why is that?"

"Aunt Amy's little boy, *Willie,* all grown up. Now you look a lot like someone she used to know."

"Is that a fact?" He sipped his orange juice and looked curiously at me. "Anybody I know?" When I shook my head, he said, "Well, your mom's just gonna have to wait her turn." He grinned. "I'm afraid it might be a long wait."

NATE

I woke up to the sun streaming in the window, and decided that it was a damn shame that one o'clock in the afternoon was still so many hours away. I didn't want to bother Denny while she was out with her mom, so I texted Wiley.

What r u doin?

Up til about 5 minutes ago, I was doin ur girlfriend. Now I'm making brunch. What r u doin?

I'd forgotten all about him and Brendee. I waited for the surge of jealousy to hit me like it'd always done before, to blindside me like a scalding hot towel, smothering me in helplessness and disgust; hatred of them and self-loathing for myself. But none of that came this time.

It appeared that I was cured. If I played my cards right, I might be *doin my girlfriend* myself this afternoon, so how could I possibly care what Brendee and Wiley were doing?

My girlfriend's at the mall, I texted. *How was it?*

It's not something that should b discussed via text. People might b reading this.

R u kidding?

Yes, I'm kidding. But I need 2 make gestures, maybe draw diagrams. Suffice it 2 say, I've fallen madly in bed with her. ☺ If u don't c me at school 2morrow, don't worry about it.

Y won't u b at school?

My parents r out of town til Weds. Do I have 2 draw u a picture?

I couldn't imagine that Brendee, Honors Student that she was, would be so irresponsible as to cut school just to be with Wiley. Studious girls with scholarships just didn't do stuff like that, did they? But then I remembered how she'd always looked at him, how she'd told Denny that she wanted *to eat him. They have appetites,* Wiley had told me. *Just like us.* I intended to feed Denny whatever she wanted at the first opportunity.

Have fun, I texted. *Don't do anything I wouldn't do.*

Not a chance. TTYS

BRENDEE

Wiley and I stayed in bed the rest of the day. It seemed like I'd wanted him for my entire life, and now I couldn't get enough of him. He made me feel as if the whole thing was just an exercise in my pleasure. While it was true that I was inexperienced beyond Dave, I'd found him capable enough. I'd enjoyed myself with Dave, most of the time.

But Wiley . . . *OMG, Wiley* was like a mind-reader; he anticipated my every whim. If it pleased me to touch him – which was still my chiefest delight: nothing flipped the switches quicker for me than just to run my hands over his bare skin – if I had a mind to touch him, Wiley held perfectly still and let me do it. When I wanted him to touch me, he knew it immediately, and always came across with precisely what was required at the time. He was tender and gentle if the moment called for it; but he was also commanding, he was demanding, he was aggressive; he murmured sweet nothings and whispered the most filthy suggestions – all at just the appropriate time. Wiley knew what I wanted, like he knew the moves to his Tai Chi; he made nary a misstep.

When I reluctantly left to go home to put in an appearance for dinner, he said, "Rest. Come see me in the morning."

"Wiley, I have to go to school –" But he kissed me, and the thought of school disappeared, as if by some magician's trick. Poof! School? What was that? Wiley wanted me. Anything else could wait.

"Come see me in the morning," he repeated. "I think the world won't miss us for one more day."

****

We cut our respective classes the next day, and again spent the entire time in bed together, pausing only to eat and bathe, again together. If I thought what he did upstairs was phenomenal, what he did under the running water in the shower was absolutely sublime. We didn't talk a lot, but I figured that there would be time enough for that later, when there were other people around. An empty house was a rare thing when you're seventeen, and I didn't want to waste our time together with conversation.

I went to class like a dutiful student on Tuesday, and made it all the way until lunch time. That was when Wiley sent me a text that said, *Do u know the difference between another screaming orgasm and a ham sandwich? No? Would u like to meet me 4 lunch, oh, say 1 ish?*

I left school like I was a recidivist truant, used to doing so. I met him at his house, and was again MIA from my life until dinnertime. When I was getting dressed to leave, he grasped my hand and suggested that a clever girl like me could surely think of some way to manage to sneak out on a Tuesday, and if I could indeed figure such a thing out, then I was more than welcome to come back and spend one last night with him.

After dinner, as Jen and I helped Mom clear away the table, I broke Nate and Deneen up mercilessly – they'd had a fierce, wailing argument. I told my mother that it was their first, but it had been a doozy, perhaps a deal-breaker. I told her how poor Deneen had sobbed to me about it on the phone, how she needed me to come over there and comfort her. I didn't want to leave her alone at a moment like this! I'd take a change of clothes, just in case I had to stay there with her through the night, and I'd just go to school from her house in the morning.

Mom considered me for a long minute. Then she said, "I haven't heard you mention Dave in a while, Brendee."

I said, "Who?" before I was smart enough to stop myself. Mom's eyes widened a little bit and I hurried to recover. "I broke up with Dave, Mom. It wasn't working out."

She continued to stare at me. "Wow. You went out with him for a long time. Just like that, huh?"

"Que sera, sera," I said and shrugged. I suddenly became quite interested in a tiny blemish on my shoe.

"Is there someone new?" she asked.

"There's that boy she's tutoring," Jen said, all the shrewdness of her thirteen years uncoiling. How the hell did she know I'd been tutoring someone?

"That's right!" Mom said. "You've been helping your cousin Willie!"

"Wiley," I corrected, again thinking how Mom's jaw was going to hit the linoleum when she laid peepers on her old school chum's little boy, now so fabulously grown up.

"What about him? Are you gonna replace Dave with your cousin?"

Just keep saying cousin, *Mom,* I thought, *when you know as well as I do, that we're not cousins at all. That's why you're so curious about him. Thank you, Jen.*

"She's been spending every day with him," the little tattletale reported. How *did* she know so much about my business? Perhaps Jen was a more observant fly on the wall, a more watchful kid underfoot than I'd given her credit for.

"He's kinda dumb when it comes to math," I confided in my mom. She lifted her chin, like she understood, and ceased to look so curiously at me. Her daughter would never be interested in a boy that was dumb, she reckoned. Dave had obtained a scholarship, had been accepted at San Diego State; he hadn't hung around too much, but my mom knew that much about him. She knew Dave wasn't dumb. Dave was going to be a successful, contributing member of society someday. He was going to live in a big house, drive an expensive car. All the things that I would no doubt also do. It was what was expected of me, what I expected of myself.

But Dave would be doing it with someone else now, and for that I was grateful.

And Wiley . . . I could tell that Wiley was as smart as a whip, just from what little conversation we'd had so far. I wondered distantly if it would matter to me if Wiley *was* dumb. I conceded that it might matter in the long run, but it surely didn't matter right now. Someday, if I discovered that Wiley was as shallow and one-dimensional as Deneen, let's say, maybe I'd get bored with him then. One cannot spend one's entire life in bed, after all, like we'd more or less spent the last couple of days. One had to talk and listen, too. We hadn't done a lot of that yet, and I didn't speculate about Wiley's intellect too much at the moment, either.

Wanting to be with Wiley had led me to exercise my own intellect, in the area of problem solving. It had led me to a streak of deviousness in myself that I never would've guessed was there. I'd made up that ridiculous story of depression and helplessness for Dave as easily as falling down the steps, and here I was, concocting tall tales about Deneen and Nate, lying like a rug to my mother and sister. I'd never lied to my mother before. But Wiley . . . Wiley was turning me into quite the inventive little tale spinner.

But it really wasn't Wiley who was compelling me to lie, I reflected. Wiley had only suggested that I might be clever enough to sneak out and see him again, *if I wanted to.* He hadn't said, in so many words, that *he* wanted me to. He'd left it entirely up to me;

although I was quite sure that he knew I'd be there. I was sure that Wiley wasted not one second wondering whether or not I'd show up. If not tonight, then the next available moment. Wiley knew what I wanted.

So here I was, telling Mom outrageous lies about how I had to go and comfort Deneen, in the throes of a possible breakup. And I was making Wiley out to be dumb, just to deflect my mother's on-the-mark suspicions.

Just you wait, Mom, I thought. *Wiley's not in the least bit dumb, except for math. And when you see him, I bet that how smart he might or might not be won't be the first think you think about.* Any more than it was what I was concerned with right now. I wasn't hell-bent on seeing Wiley tonight because I wanted to *talk to him . . .*

The dishes secured in the dishwasher, I kissed my mom on the cheek. I said, "Text me later. I'll tell you how Deneen's holding up."

Jen stuck her tongue out at me from behind Mom's back. Maybe she wasn't as much of a little girl as I thought she was.

****

I sat in my car and texted Deneen. *I'm sorry u broke up w Nate.*
WHAT??
☺ *I'm coming over right now 2 comfort u.*
WHAT R U TALKING ABOUT??
I'm just kidding. I needed an excuse 2 get out of the house. I told Mom u guys had an argument. U need me.
Fuck, Brendee, that's not even funny.
Did u break up w Nate?
No. We're solid.

I waited for more info on that score, but Deneen was obviously pissed and didn't want to talk to me. *Then there's nothing 2 worry about. I'm sorry, Deneen. I needed an excuse 2 get out.*
Where u goin?
2 c Wiley.
Again?
☺
He's changing u, Brend. This isn't like u.
I'll text u 2morrow.

Oops, I thought. I hadn't meant to upset Deneen. Well, it didn't matter now; Wiley's parents would be home tomorrow, so I wouldn't need Deneen for an excuse anymore.

I thought about what she'd said, that Wiley was changing me. It was ridiculous. Missing a day and a half of school hadn't hurt me – school was almost over, and if anything, I'd been able to concentrate and pay attention a little better for the half a day that I'd been there, because I wasn't consumed with all the *what ifs* about Wiley. The *what ifs* had been put to rest. I'd still thought about him during class, but it was with satisfaction – the burning distraction of not knowing and wanting to find out so badly, was gone.

I hadn't changed. I smiled to myself. It wasn't as if I was suddenly addicted to Wiley. That had happened the moment I'd seen him. At least by being with him, the cravings were under control.

****

I might've yawned in class a few times on Wednesday, as Wiley had made our last night alone together spectacular. I thought that he *was* like a drug to me – I just wanted to keep doing him until I passed out from exhaustion. I smiled at my own cleverness.

But all seemed as it should've been when his parents got home from the airport on Wednesday evening. All traces of marathon sex had been removed, sheets freshly laundered and replaced, skylight opened, room aired out. We were sitting at the dining room table, studying, like good Christian children, when they walked into the house.

Wiley leapt up and hugged them, then with a flourish, he snatched a piece of paper off of the table and handed it to his mom. It was an Algebra test he'd taken on Friday. "I got a B, Mom, can you believe that?" he said, like a proud school boy.

Instead of the incredible ravening beast that I know him to be, I thought, and looked down at the table, grinning to myself.

"Thanks so much for helping him, Brendee," Mrs. Royce said. "He couldn't have done it without you, I'm sure."

I looked up and said, "It was my pleasure." I made a point not to look at Wiley. Just how much of my pleasure it had been might've showed on my face.

"I sincerely doubt that," his dad said, and attempted to smack his son playfully on the head. Wiley ducked, but smiled. "But you do have our thanks."

"There's something else," Wiley came back and grabbed my hand. "I'm gonna ask Brendee to be my girlfriend."

Mrs. Royce's mouth dropped open in surprise. Mr. Royce smiled blankly at me, and I saw where Wiley got it: it was the same friendly, open smile that revealed not a single thing that he might be thinking. He nudged his wife, and she also smiled.

Wiley grinned. He was the picture of the innocent school boy, the same one that had so gleefully said, "I got a B, Mom!" He was just a shy, solitary high school senior, who'd never had a date that anybody had ever heard about. Least of all his parents, it appeared.

It was an utter fiction. *He must've had a date sometime,* I thought, and more than one. I heartily thanked her, or them, for all the incredible stuff he'd learned.

This was all so childish, so childlike, Wiley telling his mom and dad that he was going to ask me to be his girlfriend, like we were Jen's age, as if we hadn't spent nearly every waking moment that they'd been out of town going at each other like animals . . . Wiley had asked me to do a lot of things, and I had eagerly, willingly agreed. But to *be his girlfriend* had not been one of them.

It was so sweet, and so sweetly offered, the further answer to my most secret wishes. Because, how would I ever live with this addiction I had to him, if I wasn't his girlfriend?

I blinked speechlessly at him. He took my other hand and looked guilelessly at me, his eyes just as blue as a summer's day. It was all an act; there was absolutely nothing innocent, nothing guileless about Wiley Royce. I suddenly recalled, with a start – as I hadn't thought about it once, just like I hadn't thought about being *his girlfriend* – exactly how he'd summoned me to him. How had he known I'd been watching him? How had he known to hold up that sign that said, *I know what you want?*

Why didn't it matter to me in the least?

"What d'ya say, Brendee?" he was asking me. "Do you wanna be my girlfriend?"

I know what you want.

Still speechless, I nodded.

"Well!" Mr. Royce clapped his hands together, making me jump, just like Nate had done, a million years ago, the moment he'd introduced me to Wiley. "Come on, son, help me get the luggage out of the cab." They went outside.

"Would you like to stay for dinner, Brendee?" Mrs. Royce asked.

Since I was no longer caught in Wiley's eyes, my composure immediately returned. "Yes, I would, Mrs. Royce. That's very nice

138

of you." She hugged me, as if Wiley had just announced that we were getting married, instead of making this rather juvenile pronouncement. "Can I help you with anything?" I asked, just for something to say.

"No, no, it's okay," she said and smiled at me. The relief was plain on her face. Whatever girl or girls it had been that had taken her sham-shy son in hand, *whenever* it had been, Mrs. Royce hadn't known anything about it. Just like everybody else, as far as she knew, I was the first girl that had ever given him the time of day. "You just sit right there." I sat. She went out into the kitchen, then called back to me, "How's your mom? I've been meaning to have lunch with her again."

You'll want to discuss all this news, I thought. *How your babies are now* going together.

"She's fine. She was just talking about having a dinner party and inviting you."

Oh, yeah, that would definitely be on the horizon now, I thought.

Mrs. Royce came back into the dining room, gave my shoulder a little squeeze. "That sounds like fun!" she said. When Wiley and his dad came back into the house, laden with some of the ugliest luggage I'd ever seen, she said, "I don't feel like cooking, tonight, Alex. Let's go to *Paul's.*"

Paul's was the most expensive restaurant in town, practically a Riverside institution. Mr. Royce set the hideous suitcases down, took out his wallet, and pretended to look doubtfully into it.

"I got it, Dad," Wiley said, "if you're short. It's drop-your-phone-in-the-pool season."

"Can you fix a wet cellphone, Wiley?" Mr. Royce asked with a grin.

"I can fix damn near anything," Wiley said. "Anything electronic, that is. Wet or otherwise," he added under his breath, and didn't look at me.

I was just starting to consider Wiley and his Sharpie-d signs again, when I realized that I should probably tell Mom I wasn't gonna be home for dinner. I watched Wiley and his parents make their luggage disappear, and not quickly enough, and texted my mom.

Unusually suspicious, she wrote back, *Where r u?*

I'm at Aunt Amy's house.

Mom didn't reply, and a few seconds later, I heard Mrs. Royce exclaim, "Oh, hi, Darlene! We were just taking Brendee out to celebrate, to thank her! Wiley got a B on his math test!"

****

Wiley continued to bat his baby-blues innocently at me throughout dinner, except when he was sure his parents weren't looking. Then he'd smirk fondly at me, and one corner of his mouth – his glorious mouth, that had kissed me so many times, in so many places – would quirk up a little bit on one side.

"Now that it looks like you're going to graduate, you should be applying to UCR," Mr. Royce said at one point. "I know you were worried about it."

"Where are you going to school, Brendee?" Mrs. Royce asked.

There was really no choice, was there? "I've been thinking about UCR, myself," I said. Where else would I go, except where my drug, my addiction, *my boyfriend* was going?

Mrs. Royce asked what I planned to major in and I told her, "Maybe law. And computers." Wiley grinned at that.

"Maybe you guys'll be in the same classes!" Mrs. Royce said in delight.

When we got back to their house, the proud parents thanked me again for helping their boy pass *the math,* said they'd be sure they'd be seeing me again soon, and went into the house. Wiley silently walked me to the car.

Now he favored me with that smoky, sexy smile, all pretense of boyish purity vanished. I couldn't help but smile back at him. "You're nuts," I said.

His eyebrows rose slightly. "Better men than you have said so."

"You don't even know me," I said.

His eyebrows went up the rest of the way. "Sure I do, Brendee. You're my girlfriend."

I know what you want.

I thought I might cry then, because it *was* what I wanted, and the best part about it was that he knew it, and was more than happy to give it to me. He sensed my incipient tears, and kissed me tenderly. "Same time tomorrow? One B will not a passing grade make."

I nodded, and got into my car, still speechless.

****

I used my two back-to-back Thursday afternoon study halls to actually study, for the very first time ever. I caught up on any material that I might've missed while I'd been skipping school and engaging in delicious, extra-curricular activities with my *new boyfriend.* I reflected that my *ex-boyfriend* had made not one single attempt at reconciliation; Dave hadn't called, had not texted. Again I marveled at how easy it'd been to get rid of him.

Satisfied that I was on top of things as far as school was concerned, I drove over to Wiley's to wait for him to get home, hoping I might get a chance to be *on top of him* for a little while before his parents got home from work. I again smiled at my own cleverness.

Wiley was surprised to see me, sitting on his front porch. "I have study hall on Thursday afternoons," I explained.

He unlocked the front door, and as soon as we were inside, I threw myself at him. "When do my aunt and uncle get home?" I asked, kissing him on that delicious hollow where his neck joined his collarbone.

"About forty minutes or so." I grabbed his hand and tried to pull him toward the stairs, but he wouldn't let himself be dragged. "There's not enough time, Brendee," he said and grinned curiously at me, almost as if we were still strangers. "I hate to be rushed."

"Haven't you ever heard of a quickie, Wiley?"

"I have not." His grin widened. "I'm shy, remember?"

"Come on, then, I'll show you." And I again tried to tug him toward the door.

But Wiley wouldn't budge. "There's not enough time," he repeated. "Besides, I have a surprise for you. For your birthday. On Saturday."

"My birthday's on Sunday, Wiley." On May first, the Year of Our Lord 2033, I'd turn eighteen. Supposedly, my first step into adulthood. Only Wiley, and maybe Dave – at least a little bit – knew how much of an adult I already was.

"I know," he enfolded me in his arms, and kissed me on the forehead. "But I have a surprise for you on Saturday. You can wait two days, can't you?"

"I supposed I'm going to have to." *I suppose you're going to make me,* I thought.

He kissed me then, just the way he knew I liked it. But as soon as the blood began to thrum in my ears, as soon as I wrapped my arms around his neck and started to get into it, he stopped, and grinned at me. "I've got a test tomorrow, my tutor."

"You're a tease, Wiley," I said, just the tiniest bit put out about it.

He shrugged. "Abstinence makes the heart grow fonder."

"That's *absence.*"

His eyebrows rose in faint surprise and he put his hand on the door knob. "Did you want to go?"

Now I was surprised, at the smug carelessness, the almost-but-not-quite cruelty of his remark. "No, Wiley. I don't want to go."

He grinned and kissed me on the forehead again. "I've gotta study. You can think about my surprise."

"What is it?"

He gave me that condescending look again, like I was too old to be believing in the Tooth Fairy. "Then it wouldn't be a surprise, would it?"

NATE

On Friday after school, I went over to Wiley's house. I hadn't heard from him all week, except when he'd texted me at lunch, saying, *I still have 2 draw u those diagrams.*

I don't wanna c any diagrams, but I will come 4 a visit.

He was sitting on his front porch, barefoot as always, waiting for me. "I think I might've aced my math test today. I still can't believe that they make us learn this incomprehensible shit."

"Have to keep up with everybody else in the world, Wiley. How can you know so much about computers and hate math so much?"

"I like Ovid, but I have no desire to learn Latin." He waved his hand. "There was this problem today – something about, if coral grows so much in a year, then how long will it take for it to grow this much?" He shook his head. "Why would I possibly care?"

"Still –"

"You don't need to know Algebra to program computers, Nate, or fix electronics. You just have to know what you're doing. It's a fucking conspiracy. There's no funding for English Lit, but you have to have your math and your football."

"You're nuts, Wiley."

"So the lovely Brendee has told me." He grinned. "Are you sure you don't want me to draw you a picture?"

I shook my head. "Maybe some other time."

He clapped me on the shoulder. "In the meantime, let's go celebrate my success, small and worthless as it'll ultimately prove to be. Call your woman and I'll call mine. I have no doubt that they'll come running." He looked at me curiously. "How's all that going? You and the slender Deneen?"

I frowned. "There hasn't been the opportunity yet."

"Ah, you're taking my advice! You're making her wait."

"Not intentionally."

Wiley grinned wickedly. "Then you have my deepest sympathies, my son. Our parents want us to have responsibility, we're all practically of age, yet they treat us like children. They give us no privacy, no room to *explore* the exciting world around us."

I grinned at him. "But what they don't know won't hurt them, and the rumor is that *Deneen's parents* are taking her little sister to see the new kiddie movie tomorrow afternoon."

"Don't do anything I wouldn't do."

"Not a chance."

"I look forward to the diagrams." Wiley took his phone out of his pocket. "Let's take our ladies out to celebrate tonight. You guys can pick whatever chemical-laced, fast-food, sheep trough you want. My treat. *Baaa,*" he bleated.

It was decided that we'd go out for pizza, as that was the least offensive to Wiley. The backseat of his car was still piled with shit, so I waited for him to find some shoes, then we started walking back to my house to get my car.

Halfway down the block, I saw a sign that said *Free Kittens.* An idea struck me, and I told Wiley to hold on a minute, and called Denny. "Would your parents let Delia have a kitten?"

"I want a kitten!"

"I've got something else for you," I told her. Wiley grinned at me.

"That's what you keep saying," she said and giggled.

"Tomorrow," I told her.

"She can wait 'til tomorrow, right?" Wiley said.

I glared at him. Denny said she'd go ask her mom and call me right back.

"How domestic you've become, Nate!" Wiley marveled. "How thoughtful and kind and *husbandly.*"

"Shut the fuck up, Wiley, you fucking hypocrite. I didn't ask Denny to be my girlfriend in front of my mom and dad."

Wiley shrugged. "What difference does it make? It legitimizes everything, right? It makes my parents happy, it makes Brendee happy. I always try to give Brendee what she wants." He grinned evilly at me.

"But it doesn't mean anything to you?"

"Does it mean something to you?"

"I didn't say it like you did, in front of my parents. But, yeah . . . it means something to me. I really like Denny."

"Thank Christ," Wiley said. "I thought you were never going to give up on this ridiculous obsession with Brendee. You were pitiful, my son. Why would you yearn and pine for one girl, as if there weren't so many other girls –"

"Is Brendee just another girl to you, Wiley?"

Wiley shrugged. "Brendee's the only girl for me, Nate. I told you, I only need one at a time. But things happen, people change, life goes on . . ."

"I might have to kick your ass, Wiley, if you hurt Brendee."

"Ah, some longing remains!"

"You're an asshole, Wiley," I said. "No *longing remains*. She's my friend, like she's always been, and I won't stand by and watch you hurt her. I had to put up with the way she looks at you – doesn't that mean anything to you?"

"There's that word again: *meaning*. Everybody's always trying to assign *meaning* to everything! What if there *is no meaning?*"

"I don't know what you're talking about, Wiley. There's love and family and the future –"

"I'm not even nineteen yet, Nate. Life's a great big bowl of the sweetest cherries. I'm not concerned with the future."

"But, Brendee –" I was gonna say, *Brendee loves you, Wiley!* She'd loved him from the day she'd met him. I could tell by the look on her face. But he cut me off.

"Like I said, Nate. Brendee's the only girl for me. I'm not considering anyone else. I don't even *see* anyone else. Just like you said, there's no bigger turn on than the way she looks at me." He sighed. "But there may come a day when she doesn't look at me like that anymore, when she just says, 'Oh, it's only you, Wiley, what the fuck do you want?' And then what?"

"Why do you waste your time thinking about shit like that?" I asked, exasperated.

He shrugged. "I told you before, Nate. I believe I could stand anything, except being bored; or seeing that she's bored with me." He grinned. "So, it's my life's ambition to make sure she's not bored, and I'm confident that it's not gonna end any time soon. I have a surprise planned for tomorrow night –"

My phone rang. Denny told me that her mom thought it was the cutest thing ever, that I would want to give Delia a kitten. "Just be sure to get a girl," she said. "Mom said she doesn't want any tomcats."

"Unlike her daughter," Wiley said, and I tried to slap him.

"Who's that?" Denny asked.

"Nobody," I told her. "I'll make sure to get a girl."

"You're so sweet, Nate," she told me.

"Like an all-day sucker," Wiley yelled.

"Is that Wiley?" Denny asked with more than a little distaste.

"No," I told her. "Wiley's dead. I'll see you in a little bit."

We knocked on the door, and a nice elderly woman showed us five adorable orange tiger-striped kittens. Wiley said something about the choice being already made for us, since they all looked alike. "Pick one," he said. "I'm hungry."

I asked the lady if she knew which ones were girls and which ones were boys, and she shook her head. "I can never tell until the boys get their little . . . *puff balls.* " She grinned at us.

Wiley picked up one of the kittens and gently lifted its tail. "They're not born with . . . *puff balls?* "

She smiled and shook her head. "They don't come in 'til later."

"Then how do you know . . . I promised my girlfriend I'd get them a girl."

She looked at me like I was dim-witted. "There is the internet, sonny."

"Indeed there is!" Wiley cried, and took out his phone. "Let's see . . . *Kitten sex . . .* "

The little old lady grinned at Wiley and shook her head again. "I wouldn't try that one."

Wiley looked at the search results on his phone, and his eyes widened a little bit. "And you would be right. How about . . . *Sex of kittens?* "

She shook her head a third time. "How about something specific to the problem, son? How about, *determining the gender of kittens?* "

Wiley found a site with pictures and diagrams. Even with all that, it was still difficult to tell, but after a few minutes of looking at his phone and lifting up tails, the three of us came to a consensus – we were pretty sure that there were three girls and two boys.

Wiley looked at the girls' little furry faces, one by one. "This is the smartest one," he decided. Since they all looked the same to me, I went with his choice, and we thanked the nice old lady.

As we were leaving, she said, "I hope you boys don't have similar problems in the future. Like with human girls. If you do, just try that first search condition again." She giggled, and shut the door.

"I bet *she's* never bored," Wiley said.

BRENDEE

Wiley called on Saturday morning and said he'd have my surprise all ready for me later that evening. He was going shopping with his parents and said that he'd be gone all day, but I should show up at his house at six o'clock, he told me, and I should tell my parents that I wouldn't be home 'til late. "What is it?" I insisted, and shivered. But he refused to tell me.

I kicked around the house all day, distracted, wondering what kind of a surprise Wiley could have for me. What kind of a new and wonderful trick was he gonna show me now? I tried to imagine, but failed. Still I anticipated. Whatever he'd thought up, I was sure that it was gonna be incredible.

It was noon, then it was two, then it was four, and my anticipation kept creeping higher, like red mercury on an August day. Not too much longer now . . . Then at five o'clock, Deneen called, wailing.

"Oh, Brendee! I think we've broken up! Just like you told your mom the other day! You jinxed me, Brendee!" She sobbed uncontrollably.

"What are you talking about? What –"

"My parents are gone, and he came over. We were going to, but then he couldn't, and I laughed at him –"

"You laughed at him?"

"I know, right? I shouldn't't've laughed! But I couldn't help it! He tried, but – it was so funny! How ridiculous they are! It's such a simple thing, but when it doesn't work . . . I couldn't help it. I laughed. Oh, Brendee! He got so mad, and he stormed out, and now he won't answer the phone, he won't answer my texts! What I am going to do?" She wailed again. "Brendee, can you please come over here? Maybe you can call him for me?"

"Me? I don't think that's such a good idea, Deneen." I was sure that my talking to Nate wouldn't help at all. He'd only get more pissed off, if he knew that Deneen had told me about his unfortunate failure under pressure. I was embarrassed for him. He didn't need to find out that I knew. "I'm supposed to go see Wiley –"

"Wiley? All you ever talk about is fat-mouthed Wiley! OMG, Brendee! Nate's left me and you don't care about me, either!" Again she sobbed.

Shit! I thought. *Looks like no birthday surprise for me tonight.* And least not until I calmed my friend down. "Try to stop crying, Deneen. I'll be right there."

I texted Wiley. *I might be a little late.*

It's ok. We just got home & Mom asked me if I'd go 2 the store & pick up onions & cucumbers. She makes this salad; it's great. I'll text u when I get back.

I told him okay, took a deep breath, and drove over to Deneen's.

Her family still wasn't home, and I thanked God for small favors. Her obnoxious, nosy little sister was like my shadow, every time I went over there. She wanted to show me her dollies and her drawings, and I always thought that they all needed to teach the child a little *discipline*, a little *sense of boundaries*, that she shouldn't have the run of the house and be allowed to pester her big sister's friends. My little brother and sister knew better. Gary and I were barely a year apart, so we were simpatico – we respected each other's privacy.

When Deneen opened the door, she was clutching a little orange cat.

"Aw, isn't he cute?" I said. "Where did you get him?"

"It's a girl. Nate brought him over for Delia, and, oh! What have I done, Brendee?" She practically threw the cat at me and covered her face with her hands, boo-hooing afresh.

The little cat, tired of being clutched and thrown, took off like a shot and hid under a chair. I put my arm around Deneen and sat her down on the couch, and let her cry into her hands. After a few minutes, I said, "What do you want me to do?"

"Let me call him on your phone. If he thinks it's you, he'll answer."

I took my phone out of my purse and handed it to her. I certainly didn't want to talk to him. It was a touchy enough situation just between the two of them, without bringing me into it. But Deneen was right. Nate would answer if he thought it was me calling him. He didn't stare at me longingly anymore, not since he'd started going with her, but we'd been friends since grade school. He'd answer the phone for me.

"It's me, Nate," Deneen said. "Don't hang up!" She got up and started pacing back and forth. "I know you don't, Nate!" I was thankful that I couldn't hear his side of the conversation from across the room. "Do you want to talk to Brendee?" I shook my head. "Please, talk to me, Nate! I'm so sorry!" Nate said something, and I

148

watched the second hand creep around the clock on the wall beside their television. It was now five-fifty.

"Deneen, I really need to –"

"Don't say that, Nate!" Deneen wailed. "I don't want to break up! Please, just talk to me!"

I saw Deneen's phone on the coffee table. If she wouldn't give me mine back, I would just use hers and text Wiley again. If he was trying to get through to me, I was sure that Deneen was ignoring the beeps. I scrolled through her contacts: *Tammy, Terri, Tom, Zack.* No *Wiley.*

"You don't have Wiley's number?"

"What? Hold on, Nate. Please don't hang up!"

"You don't have Wiley's number?" I repeated.

"Look at the beginning," Deneen said, then went back to begging Nate not to hang up.

I scrolled to the top of her contact list. *Andrea, Anthony, Ariel. Asshole Wiley.* I looked up to frown at her, but she'd wandered off. I heard another wail from her room.

I texted Wiley. *Hi! It's Brendee. I'm using Deneen's phone.*

How do I kno it's u?

Ur buying cucumbers 4 ur mom.

Brendee could've told u that.

U have a 6 inch scar on ur left thigh. Has Deneen seen u w/out ur pants on?

There was a pause, like he was thinking about it. Then he texted, *Hi, Brendee! Y r u on Deneen's phone?*

We r having drama. She's talking 2 Nate on my phone.

?

I don't want 2 go in 2 it now. I didn't want u 2 think that I wasn't coming.

Already? ☺

☺ I'll b there as soon as I can.

I'm still at the store. Once I got here, Mom texted a list. Finish w/the drama and go back home. I'll call u, say 6:30 ish?

I looked at the clock. It was already 6:15. *Ok.*

C u then. And Brendee?

?

Keep thinkin about it.

You are a tease, Wiley Royce, I thought, and grinned to myself. I erased the conversation from Deneen's phone and took a deep breath. The sound of sobbing had ceased; I sincerely hoped that

Deneen and Nate had made up, and that he'd let her call him on her own phone, because I really had to go home now. Wiley was gonna call me in fifteen minutes. I shivered in anticipation of his surprise.

I walked into Deneen's room. She said, "Okay, I'll tell her. Bye." We traded phones. "Your mom wants you to come home right away. She says she can't find Jen's blue leotard. She thinks you might know where it is."

If one more person made one more demand on me that kept me away from Wiley for one more minute, I was going to scream. Why the hell did she think I would know where Jen's leotard was?

"She wants you to come straight home," Deneen reiterated.

Whatever. I had to wait for Wiley to call, anyway. It wasn't like I could go over there and sit in front of his house until he got home from the store. He'd laughed at my eagerness before, and after turning me down, he'd asked me if I wanted to leave with an almost mean smugness. I'd told myself that I'd try to put a leash on the obviousness of my desire after that; I'd try playing hard to get. As if that was actually possible: if Wiley wanted me, to deny him would be as likely as trying to deny that I had to breathe.

I looked at Deneen, no longer crying. "Are you okay?"

"Oh, yeah!" she said brightly. "Everything's fine now. Nate's not mad anymore." She blinked serenely at me. "Thanks for coming over, Brendee. I don't think he would've answered the phone for me."

I blinked back at her in annoyance, trying to think up something nice to say. I wasn't feeling very nice at the moment. The world was conspiring to waste my time, to keep me away from Wiley and his surprise. "Anytime, Deneen," I said at last. "But I gotta go now."

"Okay, see ya later!"

I stalked through the house, picked up my purse from the coffee table, and slammed the door on my way out.

I drove home, still fuming at Deneen and her stupidity – why would she *laugh* at him? No wonder he was pissed! And I aimed to give my mother and my sister a piece of my mind, too, about keeping track of their own damned clothes. I squealed to a stop in front of the house, slammed the car door. I stomped up the steps and threw open the front door.

And that's when everybody yelled, "Surprise!"

****

150

Everyone was there: Mom and Dad and Jen and Hal and Gary, and probably eight or nine kids from my school. There was a birthday cake, and presents. I was definitely surprised, and I hugged everybody. I heard a car door slam, and went to look out the door. It had to be Wiley. He had to be in on this. No wonder the description of his errand to the store had been so detailed!

But it wasn't Wiley, it was Deneen and Nate, arm in arm. There hadn't been any argument. From the way they looked at each other, I guessed that there hadn't been any problems earlier in the day, either. It was all a sham. Deneen came in and hugged me, and apologized for the deception. Mom said, "You have to thank Deneen for this, Brendee. It was all her idea!"

"You don't turn eighteen every day," Deneen said and hugged me again. After Mom wandered off to put the candles on the cake, she said, "I couldn't believe they weren't going to do anything for you!"

"Oh, there was supposed to be a cake," I said.

"But no party?"

I shrugged. "We're not really a big birthday party family, I guess."

"I'm going to have a party."

"Shush! As far as my mom knows, you already had one." I heard another car door slam, and walked to the door again. But it was only a couple of Gary's friends. "Where's Wiley?" I asked Deneen.

"I didn't talk to Wiley," Deneen said with a little frown. She didn't care for him too much.

I looked around for Nate; he was talking to my dad, and I had to wait for a break in their conversation. "Where's Wiley?"

Nate shrugged. "It's not my day to watch him, Brendee, but he said he'd be here."

I heard another car door slam, and once again went to the door. He'd parked across the street, and he paused while a car drove by, then looked up at the house. He was wearing black jeans and a dark blue t-shirt; all that was missing was the leather jacket and the snake skin boots, and of course, the black guitar. I'd forgotten about what I used to do all by myself on Friday nights, but now the telegraph operator in my head started to tap out W-E-S, W-E-S, W-E-S, again, just like it had on the first day I'd met him. But of course, it wasn't Wes. It was my *boyfriend.*

"Mom," I called. "Come meet your nephew."

151

Mom started to say, "How nice that Deneen invited your –" but she never got the word *cousin* out, because her mouth dropped open and she stared at him as he ambled up the walk. He saw us standing in the doorway, and smiled. My mother turned and looked at me; she opened and closed her mouth once, like a dying fish. I looked back blankly, absolutely no help whatsoever; I'd only seen the video to *My Disgrace* once for all she knew, and I hadn't liked it; he didn't look *just like* anyone to me. She blinked several times, took a few deep breaths, until her composure returned.

"Are you okay?" I asked her.

"A goose just ran over my grave," she said and took another deep breath.

Something ran over something, I thought.

Mom smiled and extended her hand as he came up on the porch. "So nice to see you again, Willie!"

"Wiley," we said in unison, and he shook her hand.

"So nice to see you again, Wiley," Mom corrected herself. She stared at him for another heartbeat, then said, "You look just like your dad."

"So I've been told." Wiley smiled at her, and I watched my mom blink in amazement again. "So nice to see you again, too, Aunt Darlene." She stood stock still while he gave her a big friendly hug, and I imagined her picturing Wes Thomerville and all the excitement of her unrequited groupie days.

That's what you get, Mom, I thought, watching her continue to look at her *nephew* in wonderment. *That's what you get for showing your daughter dangerous videos from another era. I might never have noticed my* cousin, *shy (but not so shy)* Willie, *if you hadn't shown me Wes Thomerville. I might've just gone on along, lived my boring life. Now we're caught – you and me both.*

My dad came up and shook Wiley's hand. He said, "Long time no see, son. You were just a little guy last time I saw you. Now I hear you're my daughter's new boyfriend." My mother blinked as if slapped; her mouth fell open again. Dad regarded her mildly and said, "I just *overheard,* actually."

He nodded over his shoulder at Deneen and Nate. I looked in that direction: Jen was talking to them, just like she was an equal. When she saw me looking at her, she stuck her tongue out at me. *You're never gonna find that blue leotard,* I thought.

"If that's all right with you, sir," Wiley said, the picture of politeness.

152

Dad clapped him on the back and said, "She's eighteen tomorrow, son, and my authority ends. Besides, you're family already." He grinned at my mom. "You sure look a lot like your dad."

"So I've been told, Mr. Comstock."

"Call me, Bo, Willie."

"It's *Wiley,* Dad," I said.

"I'll bet," my dad said, and led my new boyfriend into the living room.

****

Mom and Dad transferred two hundred dollars into my savings account; Nate got me a gift card, redeemable at any store at the mall. Deneen gave me a new cover for my phone, all sparkly and bedazzled with rhinestones, just the way she liked them. Wiley smiled sheepishly and said he'd forgotten my present at his house.

"What is it?" I asked again, even though I was pretty sure that he wasn't going to say in front of Deneen and Nate and my little sister's big ears, hovering nearby.

"It's a surprise," he said, just like I knew he would.

The party broke up early: my school friends had better things to do on a Saturday night than hang around at a chaperoned, alcohol-free birthday party. In twos and threes they wished me happy birthday and left to chase more grown-up adventures, finally leaving Wiley and me, and Deneen and Nate, sitting in deck chairs in the back yard.

"So you were in on this all along?" I asked Wiley.

"Pretty much. It was my idea to have Deneen tell you that they'd had a real argument, just like the one you made up before. Nothing like a little nervous impotence to make a person stop thinking about themselves and pity their friends."

"You never stop thinking of yourself, and you don't pity anyone," Nate said.

"If it was true, I'd pity you," Wiley replied. "And our lovely Deneen."

Our lovely Deneen scared up a blush and squeezed Nate's hand. "Save your pity, Wiley. It's unnecessary."

"Take pity on me," I said to him. "Tell me about this surprise."

"It's something that I bet you've never seen before, maybe never even heard of." He grinned at me and Nate rolled his eyes. "Better demonstrated than described."

I consulted an imaginary watch on my wrist. "Mercy! Look at the time!"

Nate stood up. "I'm thinking that that's our cue, Denny. Time to blow this Popsicle stand."

Deneen smiled at Nate and Wiley grinned wickedly at her. "Time to blow something."

Deneen blushed furiously now, and Nate smacked Wiley on the side of the head. "You kids have fun," he told us. They wished me happy birthday again, and left by the back gate, hand in hand.

Wiley sat up straighter in the deck chair and slapped himself on the knees. "So, Birthday Girl! You wanna go over to my house and watch a movie? Or something?"

****

When we entered Wiley's house, his parents were still up, but the television wasn't on. I looked at the dark square in surprise – it occurred to me that I couldn't remember ever seeing a television on in Wiley's house. His mom was curled up on the couch, staring intently at her laptop; she was obviously reading something, because all I could see was text. His dad was sitting in the recliner with his tablet. He was wearing black half-spectacles, and occasionally consulted a notebook on the little table next to him. I thought as I had before that he was a pleasant-enough looking older man, but as far as that legendary resemblance was concerned – I couldn't see it. He did have the same blue eyes as Wes; the same August-sky blue that he'd passed on to Wiley. But the inky, curly black hair had long departed.

"We're gonna watch that new science-fiction flick," Wiley told them. "The one where the moon explodes and sends the world into chaos and all. What's it called?" He looked at me and I shrugged. I had no idea what he was talking about. Science-fiction wasn't really my thing.

"The Last Tide," Mr. Royce supplied. He considered Wiley over his spectacles. "I'm not even gonna ask you where you got a copy of that already."

"That's probably for the best, Dad."

Mr. Royce waved his hand and went back to his tablet. Mrs. Royce didn't even look up, and I marveled at how much they trusted that their devious boy and his first girlfriend were going to be doing nothing but watching the latest pirated movie all alone in his dark bedroom. But then they didn't know him like I did. Their good little boy was just as bad as he wanted to be. As bad as I wanted him to be, as bad as I was myself, only worse. And much, much better. I grinned like a sailor on shore leave as I followed him up the stairs.

Wiley locked the door behind us. He smiled at me and I took him by the hand and led him over to the bed. I started to sit down, but he held onto my hand, preventing me from doing so. He shook his head. "The floor creaks." He kicked off his shoes and rocked back and forth on his toes: the floor squeaked loudly.

"Then how are we gonna –"

Wiley held up his finger, then pushed the wheeled chair up against the desk – I imagined Mr. and Mrs. Royce looking up at the ceiling at the noise *that* made. He picked up the remote and turned on the television; then he pointed it at the laptop and the first notes to the surf-crashing opening sequence to *The Last Tide* reverberated through the room.

"That's going to cover up the squeaky floor?" I asked uncertainly.

Wiley shook his head. "That's kind of a structural thing."

"Then how are we gonna –"

"You don't wanna watch *The Last Tide?*" He glanced over his shoulder at the TV. "It's getting great reviews."

"This is my surprise?" I asked, unable to disguise my disappointment.

"I said it was something you've never seen before. Have you seen the moon explode before, Brendee?"

"But it's just a movie, Wiley!" I pouted. "I thought . . . I thought you meant . . ."

Wiley grinned at my disappointment, then crossed the room and switched off the lights. The room was suffused with the blue glow from the ocean scene playing on the television, and it bounced off the peaked green walls, so it seemed as though we'd been plunged underwater.

Wiley walked back into the center of the room, reached up and pulled on the thin rope above his head. The trapeze dropped immediately this time, and he ducked quickly, so it wouldn't hit him.

"Let me show you something the clowns taught me, that time I ran away from home and joined the circus." Wiley pulled the dark-blue t-shirt off over his head, and I just had time to admire the smooth perfection of his chest before he unbuttoned his pants and dropped them to the floor. He kicked them out of the way, and naked (Wiley never wore underwear), he grabbed the ropes and vaulted up onto the trapeze. He sat on the black bar, and said, "You're gonna have to *dribble off those Bobby Brooks,* Brendee, like the old song says. *Let me do what I please.*" I had no idea what he was talking about. He grinned and said, "This won't work if you've got your pants on."

I quickly slipped my jeans off, and after a moment's hesitation I took off the rest of my clothes.

Wiley slid lightly off the bar, and with his feet once again firmly on the floor, he pulled me to him and kissed me hungrily. The floor creaked. "Oops," he said.

He released me abruptly and brought the stepladder over from where it leaned against the wall. It had four wide rungs, and I figured he must stand on it in order to tie the trapeze back up against the ceiling. He grabbed the black bar and steadied it, then slid the step ladder underneath it. The top rung was probably a foot beneath the bar.

"I want you to climb up on the ladder." He held my hand and I walked up the rungs until I was standing on the top, feeling as clumsy as a naked dancing bear. The floor creaked again. "Put your hands on the ropes, about even with your shoulders." He held the middle of the bar so it wouldn't move. "Now step onto it. Put your feet all the way to the sides, against the ropes." I did as he instructed.

Wiley looked up at me and smiled, then bit me lightly on the calf. "Comfy?"

"Not at all." He moved the stepladder out behind the bar, and I looked over my shoulder at him. "I can't reach it now. How am I gonna get down?"

"Oh, you're gonna get down. You're gonna *get off.* Trust me." He walked around the trapeze until he was facing me; he grabbed the ropes and vaulted onto the bar again, so that he was sitting between my legs. He wrapped his arms around the ropes so they hit him on the inside of his elbows, then lightly caressed the back of my leg. He stretched his own legs out in front of him and put his toes on the step ladder: one foot near the end of each side of the top rung. He gripped it with his toes and bent his knees a little bit. The trapeze moved.

Wiley grinned up at me. "Now slide your hands down the ropes a little and bend your knees. Just sit down, Brendee."

When I was halfway into a sitting position, Wiley put his hands on my waist. "Okay. I've got you. Lift your feet off the bar." I did as he told me, and he slowly lowered me down onto his lap.

I was sure that my yelp of pleasure was audible, even over the roar of *The Last Tide.*

"Just hold onto me," he whispered. "I've got you." I crossed my ankles behind his back and wrapped my arms around his neck. Still holding onto my waist, Wiley bent his knees and pushed off of the step ladder. The trapeze swung back and then over it, and I bit him on the neck to keep from crying out at the unexpected, unfamiliar, incredible movement.

Wiley rocked the trapeze back and forth, back and forth, and it *was* something I'd never seen before, something of which I'd never even *dreamt,* all gliding momentum, and when the moon exploded on the television, I again buried my face in his neck and positively whimpered in ecstasy.

I clung to him until the trapeze slowed its arc, then eventually stopped. Wiley took his hands from my hips and put them above his head on the ropes. "Squeeze me, Brendee," he said. "I'm gonna stand up."

I wrapped my arms and legs tighter around him and he pulled himself up until he was standing on the bar. Then he slid his hands down the ropes and hugged the small of my back. "Okay, I've got you. Put your feet down."

"I don't wanna let go, Wiley."

He laughed softly in my ear. "We must compose ourselves, Brendee. This stupid movie is half over. Put your feet down," he commanded gently.

Wiley was concerned with maintaining the fiction of our innocence to his parents, it occurred to me. Apparently, from the lack of noise we'd made, he was sure that they believed that we were innocent indeed. We must've been sitting stock still while watching *The Last Tide.* The ceiling didn't creak.

I unwrapped my legs and clumsily found the bar with my toes, then the balls of my feet.

"Now grab the ropes." I took one arm from around his neck and groped blindly for the rope, then did the same with the other. Wiley slid down quickly until he was again sitting on the bar. He bit me on the leg again, and I shuddered. He hopped lightly from the trapeze and placed the stepladder under the bar again. I stepped off the bar and he again reached up for my hand and helped me down.

157

Once back on the floor again, I collapsed against him, my arms around his neck. His body felt like steel covered in damp velvet against my naked skin; he'd barely broken a sweat. "I think I love you, Wiley," I sighed, because I couldn't think of one other thing to say, and because it was true.

"That's just what the clowns said." When I looked up at him, he whispered, "I love you, too, Brendee!" and hugged me gently, so the floor wouldn't squeak. Then he released me.

"But seriously. We need to get dressed. Run a brush through our hair." He pushed my hair back off my forehead, out of my eyes. "Nobody's gonna believe blowing up the moon was this exciting. We look like we've been fucking on a trapeze."

Happy birthday to me.

****

The rest of the school year passed uneventfully. Nate and Deneen didn't break up, as had been pretended twice, and Wiley passed math with a C. He actually made a B for the last quarter, but all those Ds from the rest of the year brought his final grade down. All he cared about was that he'd passed.

As the last few weeks of high school flew by, I discovered that Wiley wasn't only a tease – he was a *consummate* tease. He'd text me or whisper suggestions in my ear at times when it was impossible to act on them, which never failed to distract me completely until they could be fulfilled, sometimes not until days later, when we could be alone, when he wouldn't *feel rushed,* when he was assured that no one would catch us, when he knew I couldn't wait another minute. Wiley never initiated anything, never said, "Hey, Brendee, ya wanna?" unless he sensed that I wanted him to be the instigator, which once again made it my idea. Wiley was a mirror: he only reflected my own desires back to me. But he never allowed me to glut myself; he never failed to leave me wanting more. It was deliciously maddening.

Since I knew him and loved him so utterly physically, it was only slowly that I began to gauge the rest of his personality. It amazed me that all the worn-out clichés were so true: you can't judge a book by its cover, you shouldn't make assumptions about people, still waters run deep, and all that claptrap. I had been so wrong in my assessment of Wiley Royce. He was not a boy and he

158

was not at all shy, and not just about sex. Wiley wasn't shy about anything. Shy and Wiley had not even been introduced.

Whenever Nate or Deneen or I would make a comment, Wiley would put in his two cents, and sometimes none-too-gently point out the details that he considered to be mistakes in our way of thinking. But he wasn't an attention-seeking blowhard; he didn't pour his opinions out to everyone; just us.

Wiley was indeed smart as a whip; he was well-read and had a firm grasp of history, something I'd learned about in school and had then just more or less forgotten, as it didn't seem of any value to me. The same for politics, which I was sure concerned me not in the least. Wiley laughed at my ignorance, called it self-induced.

When I protested that I intended to be a good citizen and vote in the next election, now that I was eighteen, despite being uninformed, he again laughed at me.

"Who are you gonna vote for?" he asked. "Have you even read the issues?"

"Well . . . I'll just vote for the woman," I replied firmly. "We need more women in power. As for the issues . . . I'll just make an educated guess."

"If you don't understand the issues, why bother voting? If you don't know what your woman stands for, then voting for her is just as bad as voting for the other guy. Why even bother?"

"Because it's important to vote," I insisted.

"But if you don't know what you're voting *for* –"

"I'll just vote like you do then," I said, because I couldn't think of a better defense.

"Baa," he bleated at me. "That's why things are the way they are. No one looks up from Facebook long enough to see that they're being led by the nose." He nodded at my phone. "There's the ring right there, and you put it in yourself."

"Do you think you can save the world, Wiley?" Nate asked.

"Not me, *my brother and only friend,* and I'm not even bitter about it. Our brave new world is entertaining enough, don't you think?"

Nate seemed to get this reference and rolled his eyes.

Wiley continued. "I'm just unfortunately aware. I can see the slaughterhouse at the end of the chute."

"That's gross, Wiley," Deneen said.

"Let me buy you a burger, Deneen. You're looking a little thinner than usual."

"You really think so?" she said, brightening. "Thanks, Wiley!"

Wiley loved his mom and dad and Nate, and maybe me. He was fond of and amused by Deneen. He tolerated the rest of mankind, those he didn't actively deride.

We read about these Japanese soldiers that chose to live in the bush in the Philippines after WWII; they either wouldn't or couldn't accept that they'd lost the war. Wiley was like that a little bit. Man is a social animal, and nothing delighted Wiley more than hanging out with the people he loved. But other than that, he was like those Japanese soldiers, peeping out of the jungle at civilization – he preferred his own company to any of that.

Perhaps because he was an only child, Wiley was perfectly happy with his own company. If his three best friends weren't around to distract him, he wasn't going to go out and wallow with the unwashed masses. He wasn't particular proud or contemptuous, although he surely could be. He didn't brag on himself without merit, and certainly not to the rabble. He wouldn't cast his pearls before swine – he couldn't possible care what they thought, so why try to impress them? It was just how he was. Impressing the three of us was enough for him. He might be lonely without us, but probably not. Regardless, he could do without everybody else.

He and Nate loved each other like brothers, even though the insults flew constantly between them. Wiley would tell Nate that he was dumb, and Nate would tell him that his arrogance was going to get his ass handed to him someday, and that he was gonna stand by and laugh when it did. But it was obvious to me that Wiley didn't really think that Nate was dumb – just uneducated about what he considered the finer things in life: art and history, poetry, literature, old movies and music. He felt the same way about me, although he never came right out and told me I was dumb.

Nate loved Wiley because he never ceased to be amazed by the next thing that came out of his mouth, even if it pissed him off. I felt the same way. Wiley loved Nate because Nate refused to let it show that he was awestruck by his smart-mouthed friend, even though Wiley knew that he was. We all were. He was awesomely intelligent, sometimes hilariously funny.

But Wiley sincerely believed that Deneen was stupid. Dumb as a bag of wet hammers; unteachable, unreachable. He talked to her like he would to her little sister Delia: when she would mention something she'd seen or heard or thought, Wiley would smile benevolently and say, *"You did?"* as if she were a baby showing off

160

her latest childish accomplishment. But since she was Nate's girl, he started to be more polite to her. He made a conscious effort not to demean her shallowness, and after a while, even she reluctantly joined the Wiley Royce fan club, once she became assured that he wouldn't turn that fierce wit against her anymore.

He often quoted cryptic poetry, old song lyrics and lines from movies that none of us had ever heard of. He'd pause for us to get the reference, and when we most often didn't, he seldom explained, unless one of us asked.

Wiley was like that. He offered little explanation. He never talked about the girl that had made him the man he was today, the man whose incredible, undeniable ability to always know exactly what I wanted had enslaved me. I found out from Deneen that he'd told Nate that it'd been his physical therapist, when he was seventeen. I also found out that she now lived in another country, for which I was devoutly grateful. But Wiley never mentioned her, and I didn't think it would benefit me in the least to bring her up. I didn't want him thinking about her, this mysterious world-traveler, who, according to Nate, had been just as interested in the odd bits of history and literature and computers and old songs and old movies as he was. She'd also obviously been just as interested in having sex with him as *I* was, and since he never mentioned her, I hoped he never thought about her, either. But I didn't hate her. I mentally sent her a little blessing of thanks now and then for all the things she'd taught him, along with a fervent wish that she stayed wherever she was.

I believed that Wiley and I were in love, and I was mostly confident about our relationship. I never heard him express anything but amused disdain for any other girl; I knew that he didn't so much as look at anyone else. They held no mystery for him, so I knew that he'd never cheat on me. Where would Wiley ever find an adoration such as mine, anyway, one that had been created by the harmonic convergence of old bad videos and coincidental genetics? Sex between us was transcendental. I was confident that I was the only girl for Wiley, because he told me so.

****

My graduation ceremony was the day before my three best friends'. They sat in the auditorium with my family, and Wiley didn't whistle or whoop when they called my name, even though

161

he'd threatened that he would. It was a small, dignified event, befitting the amount of money it had cost all our parents to bring it to fruition.

Poly High School's Commencement Ceremony for the Class of '33 was a horse of a different color, however. It took place on the field at Riverside Community College, and the bleachers were crammed with all the happy friends and relatives of the three hundred or so graduates. Each faction cheered and stomped when their kid's name was called. I sat with my Aunt Amy and my Uncle Alex and did likewise when they called Nate's name, and Deneen's, and Wiley's, when they finally got around to the R's.

Deneen's parents were allowing her to throw a combination birthday party/graduation bash. Her birthday wasn't actually until the middle of July, but by then, Deneen figured that all her lifelong chums would've dispersed to the four winds, now that high school was over, so she'd made sure to invite every single person she knew, graduating seniors and underclassmen alike.

Her mom and dad were taking her annoying little sister out for the evening. They warned Deneen that they would be home at eleven o'clock sharp. They told her not to wreck the house, not to make so much noise that the neighbors called the cops, told her to do her best to keep the party in the backyard. She told me that her dad had winked at her and told her to make sure all the empty beer bottles were in the recycle bin and out of her mother's sight when they arrived home at eleven. I told her that I'd help her get rid of them.

Commencement had ended at five, and the party wasn't supposed to start until eight. Deneen was very excited about hosting this unchaperoned shindig, and I was excited for her, but she said she couldn't bear to putter around at home, waiting for her parents to take her little sister and *just go*, so the three of us went over to Wiley's to watch a movie and kill the time until the festivities were supposed to begin.

The movie ended at seventy-thirty, allowing us just the right amount of time to have a leisurely drive to Deneen's house and start welcoming guests. Wiley was designated driver. It had taken more than a little convincing to get him to agree to attend – he was above all these people, after all – and he certainly wasn't going to drink with them.

But as we were walking out his front door, his phone beeped. He paused, read the text. His face grew a little pale. He softly said, "Fuck!" I asked him what was wrong, and when he looked up at me,

162

his expression held more gravity than I'd ever seen on his face before. He frowned. Wiley never frowned. At last he said, "Look, Brendee, something's come up. I can't go to the party right now."

"But you're driving, Wiley!" Deneen wailed. "How are we gonna get to my house?"

Wiley handed his phone to Nate. Nate read the mysterious text. His eyebrows went up, but he didn't seem as upset as Wiley was. But he didn't smile either.

"You wanna come with me?" Wiley said gravely to him. "I'd sincerely appreciate it."

Nate nodded and handed his phone back.

"Brendee can drive you, Deneen," Wiley said. "Nate and I have to take care of something. We'll be there in a little while."

"But –"

"We'll be there in a little while, Denny," Nate said, his seriousness now matching Wiley's. "Go on, now." He gave her a little hug and kissed her on the forehead.

But the whole thing seemed a little too pat to me. The perfectly timed text, the solemn faces. I thought that Wiley was making a play to get out of going to Deneen's party. I thought that he didn't care that it would hurt her feelings, that because he thought he was smarter than her, it meant that her feelings didn't matter. And he was giving Nate an excuse to get out of it, too. All of it made me furious.

It was just a stupid little party, and it meant so much to Deneen that we all be there. There was going to be drinking and hilarity and fun. Her first unchaperoned party. Memories would be made, the last memories of high school. Who the hell did Wiley think he was, that he could just so cavalierly bail on her, and take Nate with him? It was the first time I'd ever been angry with both of them, but I was completely so. "Just what the fuck are you trying to pull, Wiley?"

He blinked in surprise at my anger, but his worried expression didn't change. "We'll be there as soon as we can, Brendee. Something's come up. I have to deal with it."

"This is bullshit, Wiley. Let me see what's so important." I reached for his phone.

I knew Wiley could be cruel. I'd heard stories from Deneen about the outrageously filthy things he'd said to girls at school; I'd heard him make cuttingly unkind remarks about, and occasionally *to,* complete strangers, if he was annoyed at what he perceived as their ineptitude or ignorance. I'd heard him tell his best friend how stupid he was, right to his face. But he'd never turned this dark talent on me, past a rare smug reference to my lust for him. And that was all right. He was allowed to me smug about that.

But now he jerked his hand back and gritted his teeth. "I said, *we'll be there as soon as we can.* How can I miss you if you won't go away?"

It wasn't so much *what* he said, as it was his tone, which spoke volumes. Whatever had come up was more important than Deneen's party, and it was far too important for him to explain it to me. It was none of my business, and if I didn't shut up and go on my way, the next thing out of his mouth was going to be a lot more insulting than the last. He didn't care if I was annoyed or upset; if I said another word, he was going to make sure that I was hurt and offended, in addition to being annoyed and upset.

Deneen blanched to the roots of her hair. She'd never heard Wiley offer even such a mild insult to me – because he never had – and she'd never, ever heard him use such a tone. He'd never done that, either. She was afraid of what he might say next to me, or even worse, to her. It was obvious that Nate was staying with his friend, so he was no help. "Let's go, Brendee," she said, and actually tugged at my hand. "Let's just go get your car."

Wiley didn't even wait for me to leave, but nodded at Nate. They turned and went back into the house.

NATE

The text said, *Hi, Wiley. My name's Chas. Bradley needs a favor. Meet me where u first met him in 15 minutes.*

Wiley paused in the living room, answered the text. Then he looked out the window and waited until Brendee and Deneen turned the corner. Satisfied that they were gone, he said, "Let's go."

We got into the car. It didn't occur to me to refuse to go until I found out what I was getting into. Wiley was in a hurry, and I didn't really want him to cut me dead, like he had Brendee. This was apparently one of those rare opportunities when he needed my help with something, and I didn't want to get in an argument with him by asking too many questions. Even if I didn't trust Bradley, I did trust Wiley; I knew he wouldn't get me into anything he couldn't get me out of. I hoped.

"What's up, Wiley?" I asked conversationally.

He sighed as he quickly negotiated the traffic. I knew where he was going. "There's only one favor Bradley could want from me. I've been keeping some money for him." He grinned humorlessly at me. "I just hope it's enough."

A thin, dark-haired guy was standing in front of *Radio Shack,* smoking a cigarette. He scanned the parking lot, and as we pulled up, he glanced mildly at Wiley and nodded. "This must be Chas," Wiley said, mostly to himself. We got out of the car and walked over to him.

Wiley eyed the guy darkly. They didn't shake hands. "This is kind of a dumb place to meet, Chas." He nodded at the store front, then over his shoulder at the parking lot. "We're on about forty cameras."

"I recognize you and your bitchin' car from Bradley's description, Wiley," Chas replied, just as unfriendly. "Who's this asshole?"

"Don't worry about him," Wiley said. "What the fuck is going on?"

"I won't worry about him, and you don't worry about the cameras. We're not doing anything illegal."

Chas grinned at me, and I was amazed at his more than passing resemblance to Wiley. He was the same height, more or less the same build. He had the same blue eyes, the same black, curly hair. Insanely, I thought, *Maybe Bradley's a Wes Thomerville fan, too.*

But how many of the old guy's knock-offs did he know? When this one smiled, I noticed that he was missing a few teeth on the right side; he wore a ratty, yellowed tank-top and his arms were covered with bad ink. He had a teardrop tattooed under one eye. He looked shifty, unhealthy. He was a little older than Wiley, and had obviously had a rougher life, but the resemblance remained.

I thought suddenly that this is the way Wiley might've turned out, if Bradley would've let him go ahead and buy those stolen components from that undercover cop. I looked at Wiley and saw that he was thinking the same thing.

"Bradley's in a little bit of a jam. He got picked up on some little possession beef. I told him that he should never make deliveries, but he never listens to me." Chas shrugged. "Now he needs to get bailed out, before they get around to a warrant to search his house. Then it'll be a big possession beef." Chas grinned again, dropped his cigarette and stepped on it. "He needs that money. And quick."

"Ok," Wiley said. "Follow us."

"I'm kinda walking," Chas said.

"All right. Let's go."

We drove back to Wiley's house in silence. I thought that two little happy high school girls, just graduated today, were supposed to be in the back seat of Wiley's car. Not some creepy, grinning, possibly diseased ex-con. But what they didn't know wouldn't hurt them. And Wiley had made sure they didn't know, insulting Brendee and pissing her off so that she wouldn't call him, wouldn't text him, wouldn't bother him. Maybe she wouldn't even talk to him at all for a minute.

I'd been surprised at the venom of his words: Wiley had dismissed his girlfriend as if she'd been some overeager whore that he was through with. *How can I miss you if you won't go away?* Wow. I knew that he was confident in his ability to get her to forgive him, but still, it'd been a mean thing to say. But Wiley would soothe her, I was sure, if we got through this.

I glanced over my shoulder at Chas. He was right; we weren't doing anything illegal. But who knew if the cops weren't after him, too? Words like *accomplice* and *accessory* kept flying through my mind.

We pulled up in front of his house and Wiley told Chas to wait in the car.

"What's a'matter, Wiley? You don't want me to meet your parents?"

Wiley looked at him calmly in the rearview mirror. "You can wait in the car, like I told you. Or you can tell Bradley I said he can suck my dick and come get his money himself.

"'He wouldn't give it to me, Bradley,' you can tell him, and when he asks why not, you can say that it was because I didn't like his bitch's smart mouth."

Chas sat back in the seat.

"And don't touch anything."

Thankfully, Wiley's mom and dad weren't home, so we didn't have to waste time making small talk with them. I followed him upstairs and watched him take everything out of the large bottom drawer of the desk beside his bed: wires and circuit boards, a soldering gun with a broken cord, the keyboard half to a laptop. Then he wiggled his eyebrows at me, and took the false bottom out of the drawer, and showed me more cash then I'd ever seen before, in neatly rubber-banded stacks.

"Fuck, Wiley," I said in awe. "How much is there?"

Wiley sighed. "Five thousand bucks." He took the pillowcase off of his pillow and stuffed the money into it. When the drawer was empty, he looked into the pillowcase and said, "Trick or treat."

I followed him outside. "Now you can get out." Chas complied, and Wiley shoved the bulging pillowcase at him. "Get the fuck off my block, Chas. Give Bradley my best."

Chas looked into the pillowcase. "How much is here?"

"The whole five."

Chas looked up at Wiley. "His bail is ten, Wiley. He said you'd have it."

Wiley sighed. "If I didn't know you'd drop that money in the street, I punch you right in the mouth, Chas. Where do you think a kid like me would get five thousand bucks?"

"Bradley said you'd have it, Wiley. He told me to ask you for it."

"Then why did you wait 'til just now? Why didn't you say something before?"

"I thought you'd know how much it'd be."

Wiley took the sack from him, glanced down the street in annoyance. "Get back in the fucking car, Chas. And still don't touch anything."

This time Willy lifted the case off of the ancient desktop monitor on his desk. He didn't even have to unscrew anything. The CRT was flat on the back, fake. The case was full of money, also in neatly rubber-banded stacks.

"I thought you told Brendee this worked."

Wiley shrugged. "I lied."

"How do you know this asshole isn't playing you, Wiley? Like you said, why didn't he ask you for all the money up front?"

"He's not smart enough to play me, Nate. He probably just forgot. He talks big, but I'll bet he's just another hanger-on at Bradley's. Probably not much more on the ball than Casey. I don't think he's a junkie, but what do I know? Either way, he's not the brightest crayon in the box."

"But how can you trust –"

"I trust Bradley, Nate." He looked at the money, and sighed, then started stuffing it into the pillowcase.

"Why are you doing this, Wiley? You could've told him you didn't have any money. I mean, this is yours, right? There's no way Bradley could know that you still have it."

"Yeah, it's mine. This represents a lot of busted cellphones. A lot of viruses cured. Some of this is even the money Bradley paid me to put in his cameras. There's no way he could know I didn't spend it."

"Then why, Wiley?"

"It's bail, Nate. I'm supposed to get it back." He winced a little at the unlikelihood of that. "Besides, it's only money. There's a world of broken electronics out there, my son. I'll make it back. Bradley saved me from going to prison once. It's the least I can do to do the same for him."

Chas got out of the car when he saw us coming down the walk.

"It's all there." He handed the sack to the skinny ex-con, who started to open the bag. "Don't, Chas. I just told you, it's all there. Tell Bradley the bank of Wiley is now officially closed."

"You know you're not getting this back, right? Bradley's gonna skip. They're too close, he said. He said they were just waiting for him to drive out of the neighborhood, like they knew he was riding dirty."

I thought, *Does anybody still say* riding dirty?

"Bradley says he thinks there might be a snitch," Chas added darkly.

168

Wiley didn't comment. "Get the fuck off my block, Chas. And don't come back."

"Thanks, Wiley," Chas said, with all the sincerity he had. "Bradley thanks you."

"Get the fuck off my block, Chas," Wiley repeated.

We watched Chas lope off down the street. After a second, Wiley shook his head, ran both hands through his hair, looked at his feet. "Fuck, Nate."

"Fuck, Wiley," I said. "You used to be a good friend to have, and I didn't even know it. Now you're broke."

"Ah, college is coming. I'll make it back in no time."

"Can we go to this event now?"

Wiley ran his hand though his hair again and opened the car door. "I might even have a beer. Fuck, Nate. I was looking at this little place. No attic, but still . . . The things I don't do for my friends."

"You're a good man, Wiley," I said, still reeling a little bit from just how good a man he was. It would've been so easy for him to tell Chas to eat shit and howl at the moon, to leave Bradley to his completely deserved fate. He looked down the street for another long moment.

"You're thinking of moving out?" I asked, to change the subject.

He looked over and grinned ruefully at me. "Not anymore. Not for a while."

"Shit, Wiley, then you'd have to get a job, to make the payments." I cocked my hand to my ear. "I think I hear *Radio Shack* and minimum wage calling. Or maybe the *ATT Store.*"

Wiley's grin widened. "And then you woke up, Chumley."

"Brendee will make it all better."

Wiley rolled his eyes. "Oh, yeah. And then there's that. I was hoping to entice her away from this bacchanal early. Mom and Dad went out to congratulate themselves on what a brilliant boy they've raised. But now I'm not so sure."

"You must be slipping, Wiley," I said in surprise. "Is the honeymoon over already? I would've thought all you'd have to do is ask her."

Wiley grinned wickedly. "Are you kidding? Where's the fun in that? Like I told you, if you ask them, it gives them the opportunity to say no."

I remembered the time he'd said, "Brendee's already more than halfway there, on her own. All I'd have to do is touch her . . ." I remembered how he'd told me that they want to be *conquered*, to give themselves over to the action of a more dominant will. Brendee had wanted Wiley to take action since the moment she'd seen him. If he always made her wait until she wanted him – hell, she wanted him every time she looked at him. And if he still made her wait . . . I marveled at the idea of the control he must have over her. *The control she gave to him.*

But I'd always agreed more with the other thing he'd said once, that he and Kitana had been equals – that they'd wanted each other equally. I'd never been so sure about his *making 'em wait* theory, that all these involved games were really necessary. I believed that Denny and I were equals, and that was how it should be, not some master/slave kind of deal.

I considered again how much Brendee had always so obviously wanted Wiley, and how he'd studied girls and their motivations like lab rats. Just like he said, he knew what they wanted. I wondered distantly if Brendee meant anything more to him than just more gravy to his towering ego. I shook my head. It wasn't any of my business.

"Shall we do this thing?"

Wiley squinted at me. *"Lay on, Macduff, and damn'd be him that first cries, 'Hold, enough!'"*

BRENDEE

The party was in full swing. There were probably forty people there, grouped in threes and fours, drinking beers bought for them by older siblings and indulgent parents. Empties stood in rows beneath the umbrella on the table by the pool, solemn dead soldiers, their cheer gone, destined for nothing but a quick, furtively applied dump into the recycle bin. I sighed. Such a thought was proof of my bad mood. I was not feeling very festive.

I didn't know anyone at the party except Deneen. The kids from my school were probably drinking somewhere also – even brainy kids wanted to alter their consciousness in celebration – what else was there for us to do on this once in a lifetime Friday night but get drunk? But apparently Deneen either hadn't bothered to invite them or hadn't been able to get them to attend.

So I just stood there talking to her. We bitched to each other about Wiley and Nate ditching us, and my anger only grew. It was a fucked up thing for them to do, I stated. I was beginning to almost enjoy my anger: Who in the hell did Wiley think he was, anyway, that he could so disappoint my best friend this way? His arrogance was insufferable, and for what? What could he possibly have to take care of that was more important than Deneen's party? He didn't know anybody but the three of us. It was all a sham, and I knew it, and I made up my mind to have further words with him about it.

And did he really think I was gonna let him get by with talking to me like that? It had hurt, what he said, maybe more than it should have – *How can I miss you if you won't go away?* I'd hide my pain behind anger. I'd tell him that it was a mean, rude thing to say; not just to your girlfriend, whom you were supposed to love – but to anyone. Nobody likes to be dismissed, and so coldly. I'd let him know that I wasn't taking it personally, but I'd tell him that I still didn't appreciate the disrespect. I aimed to knock Wiley Royce down a few pegs, tell him that someone with so few friends ought to be a little nicer to the ones he had. If and when he showed up.

An exceptionally pretty girl walked up and smiled at us. She was wearing a dark blue halter top and tiny black shorts, all the better to show off her bare midriff and the three rhinestones set in her navel. I noted with surprise that she was also wearing a tiara. I'd heard that it was all the fashion, but between it and her scanty clothing, she looked like the Princess of Sluttown. How could anyone go out in public dressed like that?

Like I say, she was very pretty, like Malibu Barbie. But she gave the impression that all it would take would be a nod from Ken or G.I. Joe or anyone else for her to take off her two articles of clothing and do their bidding. She'd only have to pause for a moment to untie her gladiator-style shoes, whose golden straps snaked around her calves all the way up to the knee, and then she'd be ready to party. Or maybe she'd just leave 'em on.

"Where's your boyfriend?" this school boy's fantasy asked Deneen.

"Bev, this is my friend, Brendee," Deneen said, not answering her question. "Brendee, this is Bev. She's a year behind us."

Bev looked me up and down like I was for sale – *just like you are,* I thought. She blinked at me in distaste, as if she found the fact that I was fully clothed to be objectionable. She continued to frown when she asked, "Aren't you going with Wiley Royce?"

I wondered how a complete stranger could know who I was going with, and moreover, why she would care. But she was Deneen's friend, and they all went to school together, and I realized that Deneen, God love her, had probably been putting my business out on the table for this tramp's consideration all year. She'd probably first talked about me and Dave, and then talked about me and Wiley. It was easy enough to discuss people that you knew when they were sitting across the room, nonetheless people who weren't even there. God, how I would not miss high school!

"He and Nate are probably getting in a quickie, huh, Deneen?" she said and grinned nastily at my friend. "We all know Nate went queer once he quit the team, and Wiley? Wiley's a fag through and through. What's that like, Brenda? To have to wait your turn? To have to wait until your boyfriend gets finished with *his* boyfriend? Sloppy seconds, eh, Deneen?"

Who are you? I thought incredulously. I looked at Deneen in amazement. *And why did you invite this filthy bitch to your party?*

"They'll be here," Deneen said lamely.

"R-i-i-i-ght," Bev crooned. "Or maybe they're just afraid my brother'll kick their asses again." Bev nodded across the pool, and I looked at three big jocks, each wearing Poly team jerseys, as if anyone cared that they used to play high school ball. *That's all over now, boys,* I thought. *Time to start applying for those ditch-digger jobs.* One of them was standing up, and the other two were sitting in deck chairs, not too far away from him.

"That's not how I heard it," Deneen said brightly.

Bev's frown deepened. "Whatever," she said. "Catch you bitches later. Oh, hi, Jerry!" she wiggled her fingers at another football player, who nudged his buddy and grinned back at her. Bev sashayed away.

"Seriously, Deneen?" I said.

"She's just kidding, Brend. She actually likes Nate." She looked around at all her guests and frowned. "It's only Wiley that she doesn't like. I'm going to start not liking him again, too, if he makes Nate miss my party." She stamped her foot. "Fucking Wiley! Goddamn him! He ruins everything! If he isn't making some comment that makes no sense, he's monopolizing Nate's time, and keeping him from coming to my party!" She looked around again, then looked back at me accusingly, as if it was my fault that Wiley had absconded with Nate. "I'll never understand what you see in him, Brendee. I don't care how good he is, he's still an asshole!" She stamped her foot again.

Deneen's completely unexpected attack made my anger at Wiley lessen a bit, and redirect itself at her. How could she care so much about the opinions of that . . . that oversexed princess? I looked around at the group, getting louder and drunker as the party progressed. How could Deneen care about any of them? They were just a bunch of ridiculous children, trying so hard to be grown-up. I began to see why Wiley looked down on them.

Deneen turned away from me and went over to talk to Bev again, who was now lightly caressing the sleeve of Jerry's football jersey. As I watched, she leaned in and whispered something in his ear, and quite unbidden, I imagined her legs in the air in the backset of some car, the beam from some streetlight glancing off of the gold straps of her gladiator shoes. I shuddered in disgust. *Oh, the hell with this*, I thought, wondering how soon I could sneak away.

Then I saw Wiley and Nate step out of the house. Deneen ran over to them and threw herself into Nate's arms, all her anger forgotten. She ignored Wiley. Nate was here, and that was all that mattered. She gave him a big kiss, just to demonstrate to the assemblage that he was, indeed, a heterosexual.

Wiley raised his eyebrows hopefully and smiled innocently at me. *The hell with you, too, Wiley,* I thought, and turned my back on him. I wasn't going to forget his words or his tone that easily. He'd been nearly as insolent to me as had that slut Bev. Who did he think he was, talking to me like that?

But after a second, I peeked over my shoulder to see his reaction to my snub, and was surprised that he was threading his way through the crowd toward me. My anger softened by another degree. I'd expected him to ignore me, just like I was ignoring him. That was how he was. Wiley always waited for me to come to him, and I figured it would be the same after this, our first disagreement. It hadn't been that much, after all – it wasn't like I wasn't going to forgive him, and he knew it.

So I'd expected him to wait until the flow of the crowd of milling graduates brought us together. He'd apologize then, and I'd accept his apology. Maybe he would even tell me what had come up, but probably not. He was here now, so everything was going to be okay. I'd expected him to wait me out, as he was never the petitioner. I thought suddenly that Wiley didn't care about me as much as I cared about him – his carelessly tossed off insult had shown that. And if I didn't accept his apology – hell, if I told him I didn't want to be with him any more – I realized that it wouldn't matter too much to him. It was a humbling thought.

Yet here he was, trying to make his way over to me, just like a normal, dutiful boyfriend might. But still I didn't turn and look at him. Let him come. I had some pride. Maybe it was time for me to play hard to get, even though I anticipated his smile and his voice, like I would the coming of a cool breeze in this desert of high school banality. I'd listen to his apology, and later I'd enjoy it all the more when he showed me just how sorry he was.

I peeked over my shoulder again. He was halfway through the crowd. As he passed the three jocks that Bev had nodded at earlier, the biggest one, the one who was standing up, shouted, "Going after your bitch, Wiley? What kind of a dog would fuck the likes of you, anyway?"

A titter ran through the crowd, and the big guy turned to accept the appreciative guffaws of his seated friends. Then he turned back to Wiley and swung on him, just for fun, just because it was the kind of thing big guys did when they didn't like somebody. Add a little injury to the insult.

But Wiley saw it coming. He grinned and ducked, at the same time grabbing one of the empties from the table. As quickly as a jungle cat, he bent his knees and swept his foot behind the big guy, laying him out flat. I heard a tink as he lightly tapped the bottom of

174

the beer bottle on the concrete beside the pool. Before anybody had the chance to *even flinch,* Wiley had his knee of the big guy's chest, and was holding the jagged glass against his throat.

Mikkelea wailed one long last note from a speaker somewhere and then silence reigned. The crowd was frozen, *like a painted ship upon a painted ocean.* I'd just heard that one in English last week. Insanely, I wondered if Wiley knew the poem.

"You picked the wrong day to fuck with me, Neal," Wiley said, his voice carrying clearly over the stricken crowd. "After the day I've had . . . but it's time someone taught you some manners, anyway, and I'm just in the mood to oblige." Neal tried to move, but Wiley shook his head. "I wouldn't do that. This glass is sharp and my hand might slip if you should feel froggy and decide to jump. And quickness isn't really your forte, now is it?

"If I cut your throat and push you in the pool, you'll drown, before any force in the universe can save you. Your blood will leak out and mix with the chlorine; your lungs'll fill up." Wiley glanced at the hushed crowd. "And no one here will say that it wasn't anything but self-defense. You're gonna die, Fat Boy, and I'll go scot free." Wiley caressed Neal's neck with the edge of the broken beer bottle. "Now, I'm not really discourteous enough to soil my friend's pool with your blood. Shit, they'd have to drain it to get it clean. They've got a little girl, and God only knows what diseases a puke like you might've picked up. I wouldn't want her to catch something. So maybe I'll just cut your throat and let you bleed out here on the concrete. But first, your lesson."

One of Neal's friends jumped up, but Nate, who had materialized as if out of thin air, shoved him back down onto the chair. "Wait your turn, Ed," he said. Neal's other friend remained seated.

Wiley grabbed Neal's face with his left hand and squeezed it viciously, still holding the bottle to his throat with the other hand. He turned Neal's head so that he could see Bev. "There's your sister, Neal. That's what a dog looks like, a bitch, a whore. She's fucked every guy here, except me and Nate and you. And I'm not so sure about you." Wiley turned Neal's face a little farther until he was looking at me. I thought I heard his neck creak, but I might've imagined it. "That's Brendee, Neal. That's what a lady looks like. A beautiful, intelligent lady, who's gonna go far in this world. Maybe she'll let you park her car someday.

"Now, perhaps it's your bad eyesight that's allowed you to mistake a dog like your sister for a lady like my girlfriend. I'm sure you don't have to have 20/20 to toss a football between your legs. But I've shown you your error. Apologize to Brendee, Neal." When Neal didn't speak quickly enough, Wiley pushed the broken bottle harder against his neck. A tiny drop of blood appeared.

"I'm sorry," Neal immediately croaked.

"That's a good boy," Wiley said. He released his face and patted him heavily on the cheek. Without looking over at me, he continued. "Neal's sorry, Brendee. Do you accept his apology?"

All eyes turned to me. "Y-Yes," I said quickly. All eyes turned back to Neal and Wiley again, like fans at a tennis match.

"What a shame," Wiley said. "You're so much more forgiving than I am. But I guess it means that I'm gonna have to allow you to live, Neal. But I'm just letting you know. I'm sick of your shit. If you ever even speak to my girlfriend again, if you so much as look sideways at her, I'm gonna kill you." He glanced up at Nate, closed one eye and squinted. "And bury you in the backyard." He looked back down at Neal and again whispered the broken bottle across his neck. "Are we clear?"

Neal nodded slowly, aware of the sharp glass at his throat.

In one fluid motion, Wiley leapt up. He took a step back and tossed the beer bottle into a nearby trash can. He glanced at the crowd, still staring at him. "My apologies," he said, and waved his hand carelessly at them. "As you were."

Then he again looked down at Neal, who was now sitting up and rubbing his neck. His two friends hovered over him, like anxious parents. *Mama Bear and Papa Bear*, I thought. "Neal?" Wiley nodded at the shards of broken glass on the concrete. "You think you could find a broom and dustpan and clean that mess up?"

"Fuck you, Wiley," Papa Bear said.

"Try me, Ed," Wiley said. "Ask Neal if he thinks I'm in the mood. Come on, all by yourself, once. You'll never fuck anybody again."

Ed glanced at the crowd, and finding no help there, remained silent. "That's what I thought," Wiley said. He looked over and winked at me, then started back toward the house. The crowd parted to let him pass.

Nate followed him. He slapped his friend on the back and said, "Hot damn, Wiley!" in admiration. Wiley grinned at him and they disappeared into the house.

The crowd began to murmur and move around again. *Nothing more to see here, folks,* I thought. Someone started Mikkelea's track over again. Neal's buddies continued to hover around him, and his sister came up and tried to touch his neck in concern, but he slapped her hand away. "Get me a beer for fuck's sake, will ya, Bev?" Bev scuttled off to comply.

Deneen gaped at me. Before I could think of a single thing to say to her, my phone beeped. I took it out of my purse. *I think I've worn out my welcome,* Wiley texted. My phone beeped again. *Have u had enough excitement 4 one night? Or do u want 2 come home w me?*

I'll b right there, I texted back.

I eat the air, promise-crammed.

Whatever that meant. *I'll b right there,* I texted again, and put my phone back in my purse. I looked up at Deneen, whose expression of shock still hadn't changed. "I'll call you tomorrow." When she still didn't speak, I added, "I'll send Nate back," and quickly threaded my way through the crowd. Just like they had for Wiley, they parted to let me by.

I found Wiley and Nate leaning against my car in front of Deneen's house, sharing a beer. Wiley grinned at me. "I guess chivalry isn't dead," I said, because it was obvious that they expected me to say something.

Wiley's grin widened and he bowed. "My lady," he said, and opened the car door for me. I got in the car without further comment, and he closed the door. He said to Nate, "Are you gonna be all right?"

Nate took his phone out of his pocket and looked at it. "Her parents are gonna be home in an hour. This shit's gonna break up long before then, if I have anything to say about it. I'll be okay."

Wiley handed his car keys to Nate. "Call me if you need me."

"That was awesome, Wiley."

"A little public humiliation goes a long way. *School's out for summer! School's out forever!*"

Nate didn't recognize the song any more than I did, but they slapped each other on the back, and again I was struck with the strength of their friendship. Whatever Wiley would be doing with me later, I knew he'd drop it in a heartbeat if Nate needed him.

We drove in silence for a few minutes, then Wiley said, "Sorry about all that, Brendee." He gestured vaguely, to indicate the violence, the earlier insult, everything. "I've had a bad day." He grinned, but offered no further explanation. Try as I might, I couldn't help but notice that he didn't apologize specifically for the mean thing he'd said. "Do you still love me?"

"You know I do, Wiley," I said, and squeezed his hand. *But does it really matter to you, one way or another?* I thought. *Would you really miss me if I did go away?*

We walked into his dark house, and Wiley said, "Are you hungry, Brendee? I think there's leftover veggie tacos."

I put my arms around his neck and hugged him to me for a moment. *Ah, Wiley, you irresistible tomcat!* I thought. *You know what I'm hungry for, and it isn't veggie tacos. We can eat something later, after your parents get home.* But as always, he was gonna make me ask for it. So I just took his hand and led him up the stairs.

Afterwards, I gazed at him, thinking that there were unknown parts to him that I hadn't guessed at, a depth to him that I hadn't even begun to sound. I hadn't even had the thought to try yet. I'd enjoyed his body and his skill too much to think a lot about what kind of a person he really was. He was an ideal lover, and he knew that he had to but crook his finger at me . . . hell, he didn't have to even do that. He just waited for me to ask. Never had I known someone as confident as Wiley Royce.

He was also a lippy, self-satisfied son of a bitch outside of the bedroom, and after this performance tonight, I realized for the first time that he wasn't all talk. He was more than able to back up his smart mouth. He was fearless. Someone like him could surely get by without someone like me.

I looked at him for so long that he finally said, "What?"

"Do you really love me, Wiley?" I asked, before I had the chance to think better of it and stop myself.

"To the height and depth and breadth my soul can reach," he said, without hesitation. He looked at me curiously. "Do you doubt me, Brendee?"

I put my face on his chest and hugged him, to hide my doubt. I wondered if it was possible for me to love Wiley more than he loved himself; it was certainly doubtful that he could love anyone *as much* as he loved himself. I'd have to be content with believing that maybe he loved me as much as he could, that the height and depth and breadth of his soul was wide enough to encompass someone, something, besides just his own ego.

NATE

We celebrated Wiley's nineteenth birthday the next weekend at Brendee's house. The whole family was there: her mom and dad and her little brother and sister; only Gary was absent. I couldn't really blame him, as I knew he didn't care too much for Wiley and his sometimes cruel observations.

Wiley's mom and dad came along, too, and it was just like a big ol' family reunion. Brendee's dad wore a tattered red apron that said *Kiss the Cook* and manned the barbeque, and also mixed mint juleps for the whole tribe. What difference did it make if the whole family, minors and adults alike, got shit-faced? Everybody but Deneen lived within walking distance. I even watched Brendee's sister sneak a sip of her mom's julep, when she thought no one was looking.

The parents sat at one picnic table, and Wiley and Brendee and Deneen and I sat at the other. Jen and Hal didn't want to be bothered with either group, and sat in the deck chairs and looked at their phones. It was just a fun all-American Saturday afternoon in Riverside.

At one point, Brendee's dad called over to us from the other table, "Have you ever wanted to learn how to play the guitar, Wiley?" Brendee choked on her drink, and Denny pounded her on the back.

"Not really, Mr. Comstock. Why do you ask?"

"Oh, no reason. If you ever want lessons, just let me know. I'm sure your Aunt Darlene would love to watch you play."

Wiley's Aunt Darlene had her hand over her face and was blushing like a school girl. Wiley's mom giggled and then all of them burst out laughing. I was certain that the conversation had come around to the good old days – Brendee wasn't the only one who'd noticed Wiley's resemblance to Wes Thomerville – and Aunt Darlene's friends and her own husband were making fun of her about it.

Wiley looked at his girlfriend, now recovered from her brief coughing fit. "What's that all about?" he asked her innocently.

"I'm sure I don't know," Brendee replied, just as innocently. "They're drunk."

Wiley shrugged, like it was all a mystery to him, then his eye fell upon Deneen, sitting next to Brendee, across the picnic table from us. "You haven't said a word to me all day, Denny," he said, using my pet name for her. "Are you still mad about last week?"

Deneen leaned back a little bit and positively cowered behind Brendee. "No, Wiley," she said and looked down at the back of Brendee's shirt. "I'm not mad."

Wiley looked curiously at her. "Can I get you something? Another drink, maybe?"

"Sure, Wiley." She didn't look up.

Wiley stood up and took Denny's red plastic cup from the table in front of her. Still she didn't look at him. He went over to the parents' table, where the pitcher of juleps sat. They all greeted him cheerfully. "Sit down here next to your Aunt Darlene, Wiley!" Mr. Comstock said gleefully. Brendee was right. They were drunk.

"What's wrong with you, Deneen?" Brendee asked. "Why won't you talk to Wiley?"

"She's afraid of him," I told Brendee with a grin.

"What?"

"She's never known a real broken-beer-bottle-wielding bad-ass before."

"Fuck you, Nate," Denny said softly, still looking down.

Brendee looked at me, then back at Deneen again in amazement. "You can't be serious, Deneen."

"I told her, he's just the same old asshole Wiley, but –" I looked over at the other table, as did Brendee. Her dad was showing Wiley something on his phone; Wes Thomerville's plaintive voice was clearly audible across the yard. "I know your dad's a musician, Brendee," I said to her. "But what *is* that?"

BRENDEE

I ignored Nate, and got up and crossed the yard. My mom had her face in her hands in embarrassment again, but then she looked up at me and smiled. But I wasn't concerned about that. How had she gotten Wes's video on her phone? Surely she hadn't gone in my room, looked at my laptop? No. Not a chance. She'd never do anything like that. It was an unspeakable breach of privacy. Still, how was *My Disgrace* on her phone?

Wiley looked up from watching Wes and shook his head. "I don't see it. Show Brendee. Do you think I look like this guy, Brendee?"

My dad hit a button and the video started over again. He handed the phone to me, and with a flood of relief, I saw that Wes's ancient video was on *You-Tube*. He must have at least one other fan, somewhere, that had posted it there. Maybe one of those other groupies, friends of my mother's, that she'd mentioned. Or maybe his wife.

Ah, Wes! I looked down at the phone, and ran my finger across the screen before I quite realized I was doing it. I hadn't watched Wes again since that first time I'd watched Wiley, and now I discovered that I'd missed him a little bit. He was just as sexy as he'd always been, as he would always be, frozen in time for three minutes and thirty-five seconds. That little yelp in his voice still went right through me.

But when Wiley said my name again, I looked up immediately. Here was reality, sweeter than my dreams of Wes could ever be. "Do you think I look like this guy?" he said again.

I looked down at the phone again, as if to make the comparison. *Yes, Wiley,* I thought, *you look* just like him, *and if it wasn't for him, and what he and his little song used to do to me, I never would've noticed you. And the things that you do to me . . .* there really was no comparison. Real life was so much better than anything I'd ever imagined about Wes.

The song ended and I looked up, shrugged. "I dunno. Maybe a little bit." I was so cool that ice cubes wouldn't melt in my pockets. I handed the phone back to my dad. It wasn't even Mom's phone; it was his. As far as they could tell, I was just as uninterested as I wanted to be in Wiley's proposed resemblance to some old singer from yesteryear.

I went back to Nate and Deneen.

She was whispering furiously at him and she stopped when I sat down next to her again.

"What was that all about?" Nate asked me curiously.

I shrugged. "Who cares? They all think Wiley looks like some old singer." Deneen glanced nervously over at him, then back at Nate.

"Deneen wants me to tell you that she's not really afraid of Wiley," Nate said and grinned at her.

Some other ancient tune started emanating from Dad's phone – no more Rolling Blackout, *thank Christ* – and to my amazement, my parents and Wiley's parents arose and began to dance. Wiley grinned at me.

I looked at Deneen again. "Why are you suddenly afraid of Wiley? It's not like he's gonna bite you."

Deneen looked at me, frowning, fearful. "How do you know? He was . . . he was *ferocious."*

Nate grinned gleefully at me. "Do you think Wiley's ferocious, Brendee?"

NATE

Brendee grinned slyly at me. "Most definitely," she said, and winked at Deneen. "But I'm not afraid of him."

The man himself was back. He said, "I believe our ancestors are in their cups."

We watched them dancing for a minute, and then I asked Wiley what they'd been talking to him about. His eyebrows went up and he grinned. "They're kidding Aunt Darlene. They think I look like some singer she used to like. I guess they thought Dad looked like him, too, once upon a time. Is this the guy who you were talking about, Brendee? When you said your mom was gonna lose her hillbilly mind when she met me?"

"I wanna see it!" Denny leapt up, but Brendee caught her by the hand.

"Oh, for the love of God, Deneen! Don't make them play it again!"

"You don't like it, Brendee?" I asked, remembering Wiley's clip of her, singing along, her pupils big and black in ecstasy. I doubted that she'd ever liked anything more in her life, except for Wiley himself.

"I only saw it once," she lied. Then to change the subject, she said to Deneen, "Tell Wiley why you're afraid of him. Tell him how you think he's ferocious." She kissed him quickly. *"Rawr."*

Again Wiley's eyebrows went up in surprise. "I'm sorry, Denny. I promise I'll never attempt to murder anybody in front of you again." He offered her his hand. "Come on. Dance with me."

Deneen looked up at Wiley, then at his hand, then over at me, then back at him again. "You've got to be kidding."

Brendee said, "You know how to dance?" The *too* hung in the air, unsaid. She took the hand he'd offered to Deneen and put it on her waist, put her own hands lightly on his shoulders. "Show me."

Wiley kissed her quickly and then stepped out of her arms. Wouldn't do to be too chummy in front of the *ancestors*. He sat down next to Deneen. "My mom always said that a man that knows how to dance surely knows how to . . . but then she'd trail off. I never did find out what dancing men were supposed to be able to do, so it's a skill I never picked up." He glanced over at their parents, then back at me again. "But I'm sure I could fake it."

"Maybe you should ask Brendee's mom," I suggested.

Brendee barked laughter. When we all looked at her in surprise, she looked over at their parents and shook her head. "Jesus." She sat down next to Wiley.

"I dunno, Brendee. I think you're too hard on them. They look like they're having fun. I think we should –"

"No, Wiley," she said. "You're out of your mind. I'm not dancing with my parents. It's bad enough that I'm drinking with them."

BRENDEE

I looked over at Deneen again; she was watching Wiley as if he was a giant spider, a poisonous one that might indeed suddenly show his fangs again and bite *her* this time. Her expression held none of the admiration that Nate's did. Deneen was genuinely scared of Wiley. It wasn't a playful fear, one that was actually a secret longing, like one might harbor for a sexy bad boy. It was an honest terror, like one might feel for a violent criminal, whom you'd witnessed holding a jagged piece of glass to someone's throat, and over what? A meaningless insult to his girlfriend?

That's why Nate thought it was so funny: it was real fear, and we hate what we fear. Deneen wasn't going to suddenly jump up and dance with Wiley, not suddenly find him as attractive as I – and apparently my mother, ha ha, ho, ho, hee, hee – did. It was going to take months of kind words and gentleness on Wiley's part to get Deneen to be comfortable around him again. He was *ferocious* to her, like a rabid dog, and she looked at him as if he was just as dangerous.

We hate what we fear. Loathe as I was to admit it, Wiley's little smart-assed remark still stung me. It still played over and over in my mind – *how can I miss you if you won't go away?* – as if he'd actually told me to go away. As if he'd told me to go away, and I'd begged him to stay. As if he'd allowed me to stay, at least for the moment. Sometimes I feared the idea that Wiley *would* tell me to go away some day.

But the thought was ridiculous. He'd never before nor since given me a reason to doubt him. I sipped my mint julep, and squeezed his hand. I loved Wiley, and he loved me. He'd never tell me to go away, and I'd never have to hate him.

****

The summer flew by, much more quickly than I remembered it passing when I was a little kid.

Wiley and I enrolled at UCR for the fall; I had a scholarship, and Wiley's parents were more than happy to pay his tuition. Nate and Deneen planned to go to community college, where the tuition was not nearly as steep. Their parents were more than happy to help them out with theirs, too, so all that was covered. Happy parents, happy graduates, happy siblings – we were four families of contented success-stories-in-the-making.

And Nate and Deneen and Wiley and I could've gone on as we had in high school, furtively sneaking grown-up afternoons when our families were elsewhere.

It was an eccentricity of Wiley's, that he would never kiss me or hug me or even hold my hand in front of his parents. It was the most immature thing that he did, but he just wouldn't let them see any physical affection between us. We were all of the age of consent, now; we were *allowed,* finally, for Christ's sake. But he acted like it was 1933 instead of 2033, as if we were high school freshmen instead of about to be college freshmen.

I couldn't believe that his parents didn't know what was going on, anyway. My mother certainly knew – I could tell by her little wistful smile when she'd ask me, "How's Wiley doin'?"

"Wiley's great, Mom," I'd reply neutrally, with absolutely no double meaning to my words. *He's just like you'd imagine someone who looks so much like Wes would be,* I'd think smugly.

But regardless if they knew or not, or if they cared of not, Wiley didn't want his parents to see that we were past the hand-holding stage. *Way past.* We didn't discuss this oddity – it was just something I noticed about him. I don't even know if he did it consciously, but he always behaved as if I was his sister in front of his parents, and my parents, too, for that matter. And there was absolutely no hanky-panky to be had, if he thought that there was even a whiff of a chance that they might catch us.

But Nate and Deneen where through with all that childish shit. They were in love. Deneen got a job at Starbucks, and Nate went back to hanging drywall – at least for the summer. They got themselves a tiny, studio, efficiency, postage stamp-sized downtown apartment and moved into it together. They were unsure how much money they'd be able to earn once school started, going full-time and also working. They weren't sure that they'd be able to keep it all together then. But plenty of people did it, and if it didn't work out, they could always go back and live at their parents' houses. They could become children again, like Wiley and I still were.

But they were in love, and they wanted to be together. For now, they would live like adults. It was the most romantic thing I'd ever witnessed.

****

Nate and Wiley and I were sitting in their living room one evening, about a week before school was scheduled to start. We were waiting for Deneen to get off of work. The Starbucks was just down the street; she was able to walk to her job, so that was one more expense that was saved. Wiley was supposed to take us out to dinner – Wiley always took us out to dinner. I didn't mind that he always paid, and he seemed to have an understanding with Nate, so Nate didn't mind either.

"I make bank fixing people's electronics, Brendee," he'd explained to me one time. "They're my friends. It's the least I can do for them. It's only money."

"When are you gonna get your own little place, Wiley?" Nate asked on this particular evening, as we sat in his living room, which was really also his bedroom. If you took out the little counter separating them, it was also his kitchen. The only other room was a tiny bathroom. There was a closet, but it was also tiny.

"Grow up a little bit?" Nate continued smugly. "Make an honest woman out of Brendee?"

"Wiley'll never leave his parents' attic, Nate," I joked. "That's where his trapeze is."

Wiley tilted his head curiously, but he didn't smile at my little dig. He said, "Take a little ride with me, Brendee. We'll be back in a few minutes, Nate. Give Deneen some time to relax after working all day."

"All right, Wiley," Nate replied in surprise. "You just got here. I thought you wanted to get something to eat."

"We'll be right back," Wiley assured him.

I followed Wiley silently to the car, and when he still didn't say anything after a few minutes, I wondered if I'd pissed him off with my little insult about never leaving home. Well, we were even now. He'd surely pissed me off by telling me he couldn't miss me if I wouldn't go away. I still remembered that, although I was sure that he'd forgotten it. *Right after he'd said it,* he'd forgotten it, apparently, because he'd never apologized for it.

"Where are we going, Wiley?" I asked at last.

He pulled the car over and stopped in front of a tiny house, set far back off the street on a thin, long lot. There was a realtor's sign in the front yard with a *Sold* sticker splashed across it. He looked up at it for a moment, then softly said, "Damn." He started the car and pulled away from the curb.

"What?" I asked.

"Nothing." He shrugged. "I was looking at that place for us."

"To buy?" I asked in astonishment. "Where would you get the money for . . ." *For us?* Had he really just said, *for us?*

Wiley shrugged again. "I had a little money saved up, but . . . it's gone now." He shook his head. "Nate was right, though. I'd have to get a job to make the payments. Too much trouble to work some chickenshit job and go to school at the same time, like they do." There was that Wiley superiority that I was so familiar with. "It'll be cheaper to stay at home 'til I finish school. Save my money. Wait 'til I've got a real job."

I didn't know where Wiley thought he was going to get the down payment for a house. But even if he'd managed to put some by . . . What had he said? *It's gone now.* He was right. It was so much more financially sound for him to stay at home until he finished college. Nate and Deneen had gotten chickenshit jobs; they were tired, they struggled – because they wanted to be together. Wiley was happy with whatever stolen moments we could share when our respective parents weren't around, just like we were still in high school. *Abstinence makes the heart grow fonder.*

For us had just flown out the window with the realities of economics. Wiley could wait.

Besides, I was only eighteen years old. College was ahead, just next week; that whole great big unknown oyster. Did I really want to move in with Wiley, worry about house payments? I'd have to get a job, too; some low-paying slave enterprise, just like Deneen. And Deneen was always exhausted anymore. Exhausted but happy.

There was so much on the horizon right now. I always felt like a grown woman when I was with Wiley. But when I was alone, sometimes thinking about all the things I still had to accomplish . . . Thinking about the big wide world still made me feel like a little girl. Would I really want to take on all the extra responsibilities that would come from a house, from moving in with Wiley?

In a heartbeat. As my dad used to say, in *a Detroit minute.*

How wonderful it would be to curl up next to Wiley every night, to sleep beside him. I'd only been permitted to sleep with Wiley once, to experience his hot body draped around me, arms and legs still graceful in repose; to feel his soft, sleeping breath on my neck. We'd fallen asleep together just once, one afternoon when his parents had gone to the beach. I awakened when I heard the downstairs door slam, but Wiley dozed on. We would've been busted before I could wake him up, if Mrs. Royce had been in the habit of coming up the stairs instead of just standing at the bottom and calling up to him.

How wonderful it would be to sleep with him, to wake up next to him, to finally be freed from the worn-out parent/child paradigm. They all knew what we were doing, I was sure of it, no matter how much Wiley didn't want to admit that they did. But it still wouldn't do to get caught, like thoughtless, randy teens, doing it in their house. I could tell that the very idea absolutely mortified Wiley.

But if we had our own place, our own privacy . . . how glorious that would be. *A place for us.*

I looked over at Wiley, and decided that he was just teasing me again. He was showing me a little house where we could be together, where we could finally, publicly be the adults that we'd privately been for so long. But then he showed me the *Sold* sign, and started talking about staying home with Mom and Dad for another four years. Another four years of sneaking around like naughty children. He was teasing me. *I know how much you want this, Brendee, and I'll surely give it to you . . . someday.*

Wiley Royce was intentionally fucking with me, and I realized again what a humbling experience it was to be in love with him. He didn't care about moving in with me, or if he did care, he surely didn't mind waiting for another four years.

He was a loner. Since he'd been doing it all his life, no one could amuse himself, all by himself, better than Wiley could. He enjoyed the time we spent together, whatever we were doing; but if life intervened and he couldn't see me, he was more than content alone.

This idea of playing house together – he was just having me on. I wondered if he'd ever seek out my company any more than he was just as happy with his solitude. Wiley liked being with me because I liked being with him – he loved me *because I loved him.* But I was always left with the impression that there was more to it on my side – that if I failed to call him, or in the unlikely event that I *stopped* calling him, he wouldn't be on the phone begging me to come back. I was by no means a necessity in his life, just a diversion. If I was gone, he's just go back to being by himself, like he'd been when I met him. Like he'd always been. He loved me and it was great that I was around, but just like he'd said – *how could he miss me if I didn't go away?*

In the perversity of ego, every girl likes to think that her boyfriend would be devastated if she would leave him, even if, like myself, she has no intention of leaving him. It gave one a feeling of being in control. I knew beyond a shadow of a doubt that it wouldn't be so with Wiley. He wouldn't be devastated; he wouldn't even be distressed. It was humbling.

And now, once again, he was just teasing me. *Sure, we'll be together . . . someday. Can you wait that long, Brendee?*

"Do you ever get lonely, Wiley?" I asked him.

Do you ever miss me when I'm not there with you? Do you ever hug your pillow in your narrow little-boy's bed in the middle of the night and wish it was me? Do you really want to wait another four years? Do you think it's funny, that you've planted this suggestion in my mind, let me see it and think about it, when you have no intention of acting on it?

"There's no such thing as lonely anymore, Brendee," he replied. "It's a twenty-four hour news day. All you gotta do is turn on the TV and pretend that they're talking directly to you. Just talk back if it makes you feel better." He grinned. "But I've never been lonely. I've always had the world at my fingertips. If I'm bored, I just find something to read; I can delve into the glorious past, or the sometimes disappointing but no less distracting present, or the wondrous future. If you're not here, I can always send you a text. Or Nate."

And that was all good enough for him.

He looked over at me curiously. "Do you get lonely, Brendee?"

"Yes, I get lonely sometimes. I'd like to live with you, Wiley." *Now that you've brought it up.* I nodded over my shoulder. "It wouldn't have to be a house. It could be a little apartment. Like Nate and Deneen. That would be great."

Now the smug smile bloomed, and I realized that I'd played right into his hands. Just like I'd suspected, it'd all been a come-on, but a tentative one. He wasn't sure if I'd snap at the bait this time, like I usually did. But it had been so tasty and inviting, I'd just taken it in my mouth and run with it, not feeling that hook at all.

But there it was, the sharp metal of our inequality: that big ol' toothy Wiley grin. The person that cares the least controls the relationship – that was Wiley. He delighted in stringing me along. There was always a big payoff in the end – Wiley was never a tease to no purpose. But sometimes my patience wasn't up to the wait. Sometimes I wanted what he'd promised *right now*. Sometimes I didn't appreciate the delay.

And this was just another test of my patience. He wasn't happy that I liked his idea of moving in together, as much as he was happy that I'd expressed an interest in just one more tease he'd carelessly tossed out. Wiley didn't care if we ever moved in together. But now that he knew that I was down for it, it amused the hell out of him.

It was at times like this that I doubted my love for Wiley; it was at such times that I chafed a little bit at his enslavement of me. I sometimes thought that I might've been better off with Dave – I was the master in that relationship. Maybe I would've been better off with Dave as reality, and when that was boring, I could've always revisited my little ancient video and my fantasies of Wes Thomerville. Dave and Wes. I'd been happy enough with them, right?

Until I saw Wiley. Just *seeing* Wiley had driven out all thoughts of Dave *and* Wes. Wiley was incredible, Wiley was . . . Wiley was an arrogant son of a bitch. Maybe I would've been better off if I hadn't answered his vampiric call: *I know what you want. Come get me.*

I'd never asked him how he'd known I was watching him that night, had never brought it up. Not once. He'd never mentioned his program again, never again discussed watching people, so I didn't say anything either. It was one of those mysteries that I felt it best not to investigate. To the romantic in me, there was a kind of magic in it, and I didn't want to break the spell. Sometimes, I'd wake up in the middle of the night, always alone, and a little snatch of a thought would reverberate out of my dreams – maybe he knew I was watching him *because he'd been watching me.* He'd written the program, after all; he had to be watching somebody with it.

But I'd just met Wiley, then. Why would he want to watch me? He didn't even know me, and once we'd been introduced, and before that fateful night, he'd never so much as looked at me twice. Why would he want to watch me? After I met him, there wouldn't have been a whole lot for him to see. I'd not spent a lot of time sitting in front of my computer, after I'd met Wiley.

Before that night when he'd called me to him, I'd tried to spy on him a couple times, but the connection had only gone through once before. So I'd only seen him once, besides watching him every second when we were together, while he ignored me or just smiled blankly at me. How had he'd known I was watching him that second time? How had he known to hold up those signs? *I know what you want. Come get me.*

191

What difference did it make how he knew? It was probably some kind of security trace on his computer; it probably showed him my IP, somehow. Apps like that had never been my thing, and besides, I really didn't want to think about it too hard, anyway; I didn't want to vivisect the mystery.

It didn't matter how he knew. It would never matter how he knew. All that would ever matter was that he was right. *He knew what I wanted.*

But maybe I would've been better off if I'd just kept watching Wiley, instead of answering the minute he called. Brendee had indeed felt froggy that night, and look what I'd jumped into: when I'm alone, I'm thinking about him. When we're out with Nate and Deneen, I'm thinking about being alone with him. When I'm alone with him, he never fails to make it awesome.

But sometimes, there was this nagging doubt. *Nagging* and *doubt,* the two things that irritated me most in life. Why did they have to align themselves in my mind sometimes – not all the time, but certainly sometimes – about Wiley and how I stood with him?

The doubt would disappear if I just quit right now and went back to only dreaming of him. Could I really wait around for four more years, to see if the suggestion that he'd put in my mind tonight would ever materialize? Would I ever get to have Wiley as my one and only, as an adult, as Deneen got to have Nate?

I'd never felt this kind of painful doubt about Wes, because Wes wasn't real. I could love him, and pretend that he'd love me, if it was possible for him to step out of that video. I had an entire personality made up for Wes. In my imagination, he was of course an awesome lover, just like Wiley, but he certainly wasn't an arrogant smart-ass like Wiley. It was all just girlish insanity, but still, Wes and my dreams of him were perfect. He would never, ever let me down, frozen as he was for those three minutes, always the same. A part of me would always love Wes.

I loved Wiley, too, and he was real. The two of us together, that was also real. For now. Could I ever go back to just the fantasy of him, even if just the fantasy of him wouldn't hurt me like this doubt did sometimes? Our sex life was ethereal, heavenly, supreme, Yin-Yang bliss – just like I'd always dreamt it would be. Could I just go back to a fantasy of it? But on the other hand, did I want to mar its glory with the resentment of worrying about whether or not it was all just one big tease? But a fantasy was really just one big tease, too.

I had Wiley now, but on that day when he finally stepped out the door of his parents' house into his own life, was I going to be a part of it? Or was he just gonna say, *Later days and better lays, Brendee*, and laugh at me?

I felt tears well up in my eyes. Indecision gripped me. Maybe I should just keep Wiley as a fantasy, and let him go as a reality. Maybe I should look for someone who I was sure loved me as much as I loved him. Or someone who loved me *more* than I loved him. Then I could be in complete control again.

"I'll see what I can do, Brendee." Wiley was saying. "Are you ready for all that? I'd never want to think that you were lonely."

I wiped the tears away before they could fall. "I'm ready, Wiley. I love you."

"This whole thing – still sneaking around like kids – it's making you a little bit crazy, isn't it?"

You have no idea, I thought, and quickly wiped my eyes again.

"I'm sorry, Brendee, but I just can't let my parents see that we're . . . Then they'd think we were doing it every time we went up to my room."

"Because we are doing it, every time we go up to your room?"

"Not when they're home," he said. "And even when they're not home, it's not *every* time." He grinned at me.

No, not every time, you fucking tease. Why should I have to yearn so much for something that Nate and Deneen had achieved so effortlessly? *I thought you were smarter than everybody else, Wiley? Can't you see that I may just have to kill you and bury you in the backyard if this is just another one of your elaborate games?*

He looked over at me and squeezed my hand. "I love you, too, Brendee. If you think you can stand to live with me, then we'll do it."

Stand to live with him. I couldn't stand to live *without* him, and the idea that he'd be there all the time, that I could have him any time I wanted, that we'd never have to worry about parental interruptions, that he'd never make me wait because he didn't want to *feel rushed* was incredible.

But I knew he'd still tease me. *OMG, Wiley! There's nothing sexier than a man who knows he can make you beg for it.*

Wiley was in control, as always. And really, that was okay. He'd said we'd do it, and I'd see to it that we started looking into it immediately, like maybe right after dinner. I'd say something to Nate and Deneen – we'd just pulled up in front of their apartment – and then he'd have to go through with it, or my good friend Nate would never let him live it down.

Wiley was going to be mine full time. And it wasn't like he actually did make me beg for it. At least not much, at least not out loud. And it wasn't as if I didn't like it.

****

My Disgrace

(Lyrics by Wes Thomerville, 2010)

Met you in a parking lot
It would become our garden
You caused my sin and my disgrace
And I still beg your pardon

Watch out for that railing, baby
There's not one thing to see
The drop makes people look like ants
Too far down for me

You corrupted what I've been
But I can't forget your touch
I'm not sure but if this is love
I must thank you very much

Don't go out on the deck right now
It's not a place to dance
One slip and you'd be gone for good
Not one single chance

You're the witch that stole my will
Always miss my will the most
I have become your spineless slave
Your private transparent ghost

Sorry these old stairs are so dark
The bulb blew out today
Just go on down ahead of me
You can lead the way

194

My sky's always black like night
Yet you remain my sun
Your light is the demonic kind
You are my only one

The jumpers really like this bridge
Once here they seldom fail
Only one step into the air
Past this fateful rail

Hope they catch you when you fall
It will be from my shove
How can I endure all this pain
And believe that you're my love?

****

Also by LM Foster

A Passing Resemblance
Contrariwise – A Tale of Twins
Corvino
Crypsis
Duck Feet
Peter's Sisters

Two Green Keys:
Two Green Keys
Adapted for the Screen

One Wilde Ride Trilogy:
Part One: It Might Have Been
Part Two: An Exceptional Boy
Part Three: What Should Never Be

Stars and Guitars:
Talk To a Movie Star
Where The Guitars Play

Tom and Wiley:
This Carnival of Strange
Wiley Royce
Generally Recognized as Safe
Wiley Royce Versus The Martians

www.ingramcontent.com/pod-product-compliance
Lightning Source LLC
Chambersburg PA
CBHW071714140626
46557CB00011B/180